OUT OF THE FRYING PAN
INTO OBLIVION

A single motorcycle popped up from the side road, racing its way across the empty asphalt.

Cinderblock revved the motor of her own cycle, as Alexander waited anxiously in the accompanying sidecar.

"*NO!*" the robot yelled, throwing itself in front of them. Alexander felt his heart go dead—*It's going to stop us. It's how it's programmed. It's after me!*

At the same moment, the approaching enemy on the motorcycle drew a small laser and aimed for Alexander.

My God, Alexander thought, *we're trapped!*

Then Cinderblock pushed off. For one second it looked as if she were snatching up the chance offered her by the intervening robot to escape down the hill. But she swerved, shooting forward so fast it took a moment for Alexander to register the truth.

"Hold on!" yelled Cinderblock over the roar of the motor.

And then they were flying off the cliff. . . .

CINDERBLOCK

CINDERBLOCK

Janine Ellen Young

A ROC BOOK

ROC
Published by the Penguin Group
Penguin Books USA Inc., 375 Hudson Street,
New York, New York 10014, U.S.A.
Penguin Books Ltd, 27 Wrights Lane, London W8 5TZ, England
Penguin Books Australia Ltd, Ringwood, Victoria, Australia
Penguin Books Canada Ltd, 10 Alcorn Avenue,
Toronto, Ontario, Canada M4V 3B2
Penguin Books (N.Z.) Ltd, 182–190 Wairau Road,
Auckland 10, New Zealand

Penguin Books Ltd, Registered Offices:
Harmondsworth, Middlesex, England

First published by Roc, an imprint of Dutton Signet,
a division of Penguin Books USA Inc.

First Printing, April, 1997
10 9 8 7 6 5 4 3 2 1

Acknowledgments

Thanks to Lorne Lanning and Keith Goldfarb of Rhythm and Hues and Eric Enderton of Industrial Light and Magic for their information on Virtual Reality and artificial intelligence. Thanks to Professor Louis Narens of UC Irvine for his information on holographic universes and Tibetan mythology.

And special thanks to John Turley for keeping pet rabbits and giving them unusual names.

Chapter 1

The companion was dead.

Alexander stared out the window at the distant lights of Actor's Carnival, at the hypnotic neon glow of the Ferris wheel's rotation, and contemplated this existential fact.

The companion, his eighth to date, was dead. Apt, that, since eight was a number that folded in upon itself, two and two and two and two, sets that faced each other as in a square dance, forever crossing to the other side, circling around and crossing back. That was eight. And that had been this last companion.

He pulled his favorite summer quilt higher around his shoulders, even though he was not cold. *Ought to get another,* he thought. *This one's threadbare.*

But it had belonged to Christine, and so he wouldn't. That's what came of caring; you clung to old blankets as if they were warm human bodies. Christine had been his fourth companion: his best and truest. Christine, Christine, sweet Christine. A spicy, lemony fragrance clung to the threads of the blanket, a perfume reminiscent of her, one that always reminded him a little of fresh gingersnaps.

Companion number eight had smelled cloyingly of honey and orchids, even in death.

"Send another!" he'd shouted to the hidden microphones upon finding her stiff and waxen body. Within minutes, a set of King players, robotically armored and just as mechanically silent, had rolled out of the elevator and removed the body. And the woman's sticky fragrance, oddly enough, had vanished along with the corpse.

Which, Alexander reflected, was reason enough to be thankful for her death. There were other positives as well: he wouldn't have to endure his former nursemaid's muzzy voice as she came from below to ask him, dully, halfheartedly, why he was screaming in his sleep. Nor would he have to watch her go through her morning ritual of getting high on Blues. And he wouldn't have to endure her quaint, yet terrifying fantasies: no more strobe-light images of pills or of bright, clean needles interfering with his research, clouding his crystal-clear mind.

So why did he feel so sick and afraid? Why did his mind keep turning and crossing back again to the other side?

"Bitch!"

Alex jumped. No, that wasn't in his head. It was coming from below.

"Bitch!" A man's distant screams seeping in through the aluminium window slats he had never closed.

"Bitch!!" the man echoed hoarsely. *"I . . . love . . . you, Biiitttcccch!!"*

Alexander limped closer to the window. Beyond the crosshatched shadow of the warehouse fences flowed a Milky Way of campfires: bright hot flowers blossoming up and down the streets and highways. Above loomed erratically lit skyscrapers with their punch-hole windows and puppet-show shadows.

The outside world.

Los Angeles, sun-kissed, starstruck, was the one myth Alexander dared to believe in. For the whole of his eighteen young years, he'd learned all there was to know about it; he knew about the Daevas of the forgotten rail lines, the valkyries who rode on motorcyles, the muses who inhabited Actor's Carnival. Most especially, he knew about the city's celestial deities. They were called Virtuals; they were the ones who kept the water flowing, the power generating, and the movies showing in the broken-down theaters. They controlled the highest technology, what little of it remained. And from their glass towers, they controlled the city.

And, he suspected, that they controlled him. Why he wasn't altogether certain, although he had his suppositions.

Once his dreams had been light and frothy, childhood wishes for sunshine and sweets. Now his dreams were foul and alien. Some he recognized as flashbacks, like the one about needles, a sour remnant of the drug-addicted nursemaid.

But most were foreign dreams, dreams that belonged to strangers. And those dreams, he was certain, accounted for his imprisonment. That had to be the case, the truth. If it was not . . . then someone was tampering with his reality.

Dreadful, shattering, tragic fear, that.

At least the city was still there. Still with him. He looked out on it as an anchor whenever he felt himself slipping away.

But this time the lights of the city offered no comfort, and he wondered, what if it were all gone come morning? What if it disappeared now? It could. It could all be an illusion: microwave transmissions and superconductors playing off dendrites and nerve fibers, conspiring to create the buildings, the sounds, even

the myriad smells. Alexander could never really
know—not unless, someday, they let him out.

He fretted over that possibility constantly. It was
unendurable, unthinkable, that it might all be just another dream.

A fresh companion, the ninth, would arrive some-
time today. A terrifying number, nine: the triangle of
the cave locked within the triangle of the mountain,
beginning and end, completion, the number of the
circumference.

Alexander watched the bright neon Ferris wheel,
the benchmark of his life, circle around again.

The companions were real. Weren't they?

Alone in his dark loft, the city too much like a
picture, it was easy to fear and worry and fear.

Chapter 2

The Rodney King Hockey Players brought Urban topside, fifty-eight stories at least, to the height of wealth and opulence. The office was Executive class, no mistaking.

Rats and alligators, was it ever!

There was a view of the city, a fantastic panorama of bright towers and blue sky. He could even see the distant Ferris wheel of Actor's Carnival. There was a thick oriental carpet and an armchair, deep and old with padded leather. And there was piano music, dropping note by note from the walls, sounding like a child determinedly going over his lessons. And, of course, there were monitors, dozens of them, flat screens distinguished by thin black threads of space.

But richest of all, there was a desk and two chairs made of wood—*cherry wood*!—so rare, warm red, and delicate, that Urban was afraid to look at them. But look he did, and the longing he felt was agonizing. He loved real wood, polished and gleaming; to him, it was unfailingly, sweetly erotic. This was due, he was well aware, to the fact that he'd been introduced to sex upon the hard pine floors of a Marin County wood-land home. To clench the fixation, his first true love had been a carpenter, a strapping, raven-haired won-der woman, fifteen years his senior with callused hands divinely skilled.

"Is this the offender?" a voice cut through the per-sistent rise and fall of the music, and Urban reluctantly turned his gaze to the Virtual.

Dressed in a suit of fine gray tweed and shoes of real saddle brown leather, the Virtual was a lean, tall, and brittle-looking man. *Bones all hollow,* Urban might have said. His features were sharp and deathly pale in contrast to his black hair.

And he was standing still, still as a Fanny on deep down, still as a waiting buzzard, staring steadily at Urban with that black, shining Virtual stare. Lenses darker than pitch and fitted tight to the retinas gave the eyes that notorious, cavernous appearance. At the man's right temple, Urban caught the faint gleam of a cricket.

How could they do it? Urban wondered with a shiver. All the power in the world could not have induced him to plug himself into a computer.

Behind him, Urban felt rather than saw one of the King boys answer the Virtual's query with an affirma-tive lift of the hand.

The smallest quirk of a smile on the Virt's narrow lips, a single, bony finger rising to touch upon those lips as if to apologize for it. On the wall behind, the Virtual's image moved on the monitors, perfectly in sync; it was difficult to tell which was talking, the man or the image.

"Your name," he went on, "is Urban Myth. You are twenty-three years of age. Male, Caucasian and Indo-European mix, one meter eighty-four in height, eyes gray, hair"—a cock of that oblong head—"brown."

Urban shifted. He wondered if the Virt were really looking at him or at an image of him drawn from satellite data streams, reassembled and projected directly into the eyes. It was disconcerting to be both there and yet not there.

"Born"—the man moved heebie-jeebie slow to a tinted window and stared blindly out at a scenic view that the grounded castes, so far below, would have killed for—"you do not know where or to whom for that matter. Nor are you allied to any tribe. You are a wanderer, a *Sierra*." The voice was both somber and amused. The King soldiers, following some invisible signal, moved in to brace their prisoner tighter between them. A gleam of light rippled over the black grids of their faceplates. Their hockey sticks rose.

Now, Urban decided, *is a good time to sweat.* He could almost see the trickle seeping down from his hairline. *Damned as an unseen hitchhiker,* he thought, because the only reaction he could think of—to fight back—was impossible. If he struck out against the Kings, a dozen more would swarm out of nowhere and take turns beating him to death. He wished they hadn't confiscated his gym bag; pathetic as it was, he might have used it for a shield.

What in God's name had he done?

"D-base is my *nom de guerre* among those of your ilk." The cadence rose and fell like the piano music that continued to play all around them. Belladonna eyes flickered his way. "Not that such has any bearing whatsoever on these proceedings." Another birdlike tilt of the head and this time Urban got an eyeful of the tiny, bejeweled cricket chip, no larger than a zipper tab, sparkling at the man's left temple.

And his heart plummeted. Not a *Per My*—a "by half"—this Virtual. Of that the Sierra was sure. His kidnapper was *Per Tout,* a "whole." Of all Virtuals, only a *Per Tout* could legally wear a diamond cricket.

Why, Urban wondered, insides shivering all jelly, *would a Tout Virt of Executive status drag a dirt-poor Sierra up to his bird's nest?*

"Your case has been assigned to me. Have you any objection?"

Fuck. Urban had a lot of objections, but he dared not voice a one. Virtuals ran Los Angeles; any tribe objecting to that could find itself cut off from the water supply; any individual doubting it could find themselves nailed by a Virt agent armed to the teeth with high-tech weaponry. Fact was, whatever this Exec said was law, was law.

"No?" The black retinas went back to watching the walls or whatever else the com-sats were sending. "Then, I will pass sentence."

"Like hell you will!" Urban snapped, even though he knew he'd be sorry. The blunt, weighted ends of the hockey shafts slammed into him, driving the wind right out. He doubled over, seeing, with eye-popping helplessness, the sweat fly off his face.

Breath gone, he held his belly, and waited for the inevitable bash to the head.

It did not come, but Urban remained bent in half until the King to his right grabbed him by the vest and jerked him upright.

"I hear you tried to evade arrest," D-base blithely continued. "Even managed to escape." There was admiration in the tone. "And sent three Kings to the emergency center."

"You mean they survived?" Urban asked, and flinched as the guards brought up their sticks.

D-base halted them with a lift of his narrow hand. "Have you taken note of the music, Urban?" he asked suddenly, disturbingly. "It's Debussy. Do you like it?"

Urban swallowed. He nodded even though he didn't like it, not in the least. Too slow and dreary.

God, did it really matter what music he liked?

"Debussy is syncopative. That is why I listen to him. His music mirrors the tripping qualities of human thought patterns just before they slip into madness. That is one of my special projects: insanity. Particularly, paranoid schizophrenia. How does the mind do that? Suddenly, switch over, like a step out of time, like a beat gone wrong, into imagination complete, inescapable?"

The lean man set a finger beside his beak of a nose, seeming to concentrate on that thought, which frightened Urban the more.

"Look, mister, please," the Sierra ventured. He hated to beg, but it was his only option. "I didn't—I haven't—"

"I'm afraid you have," the *Tout Virt* interrupted, forefinger tapping at his cheek. "Have you ever wondered if there will be another plague of hate, Urban?"

"I—"

"I fret over the possibility perpetually. You see, that is what comes of humanity's failure to appreciate its cognizant state. Sentence," he added, "has been passed." He smiled a rigor mortis grin. A row of perfectly square, grayish teeth gleamed for a second.

Blues in the java, Urban thought frantically, there must have been blues in that dead diner coffee. Ah, Jesus, he'd rather have spiders in his head than this nightmare!

Why him!?

"What have I been sentenced to?"

"Death."

Urban felt his stomach lurch.

"Given the . . . extenuating circumstances, however, I am inclined to leniency."

"Thanks," Urban managed to croak. *Bastard!*

Again that quick, symmetrical smile. "Your sentence is hereby transmuted to six years servitude."

So that was it! The man wanted a servant. Urban resisted an urge to wipe away the sweat.

No, that couldn't be right. If that was all, why not just grab him and put him to work?

Could he have really broken a law?

"Ah," D-base said, gaze tilting up as if to examine the ceiling; his image on the monitor also looked. "There it is," he went on, speaking to someone only he or his image could see.

Abruptly, a white row of lettering appeared on half a dozen of the black screens, breaking up the image of D-base like a checkerboard.

Numbers, words, moving almost in step to the odd flow of the music. Urban mentally shook his head. He really had to learn to read. Providing he lived long enough and kept the parts necessary for reading. Was that what D-base meant by servitude? A sudden, strangling fear: he was young, healthy. An operating table and some surgeon removing his eyes, liver, kidney, pineal gland—anything a Virtual might need?

Rats and alligators!

"Wall Street exchanges," D-base suddenly remarked.

"Wha'?"

A vague feathering of fingers toward the letters marching across and down the multiple screens. "These symbols once mesmerized the wise and powerful. There is, supposedly, a code in them, a formula that, spoken aloud, brings instant wealth."

"That so?" Urban licked dry lips.

"You will think it futile, but I am attempting to decode the nature of greed. I find it a nuisance—and mysticism, too."

"Mysticism?"

"The farthest point from the center of common sense is mysticism." The man's forefinger waved like a wand. Urban thought if he watched it carefully, it would teach him where he had gone wrong.

"Mysticism and common sense run parallel, like lines to infinity."

"Uh, yeah—I mean, yes sir. Sir?" Urban glanced nervously at the King guards; their black masks seemed to be laughing. "If I might ask—" Polite. Real polite and upscale. "What do you mean by servitude?"

He was ready for the blow this time. His hand shot out, clamping onto the stick before he even saw it coming; his arm held strong and steady. The King player stiffened with shock as his swing reverberated back up.

"Don't even think it," he warned the other King player, who turned, prepared to fight. His heart was racing. *They were not going to get his organs!* He'd crash out the window first!

"Servitude," D-base said, as smoothly as if nothing had happened, "means that for the next six years, you will be acting as companion and helpmate to a very unique individual."

Urban relaxed a very little. Had he heard what he hoped in those last words?

He kept a tight, careful hold on the hockey stick and an eye on both the King players as he asked, "who might that be, sir?"

"His name," D-base answered softly, "is Alexander."

Chapter 3

A life-size statue of Plato dominated the Red Line amusement complex—a statue once white, now cracked and covered with graffiti, standing dead center against the blue and pink bar.

A constant stream of lazy smoke coiled past that statue, making its way up through the thick, hazy air, past the tulip lanterns, to push up against the high ceiling. There it hovered, like some gray-plumed monster, fed by the sweet wreaths of burning marijuana and the misty fumes of bubbling opiates.

Noel, his pseudonym whenever he visited this place, stopped operating on the Mainframer and peered through the mesh of his épée mask at the gamblers in the corner. His eyes wandered to the man behind the bar snapping on rubber gloves and from there to the Fanny, little more than a girl, who watched the man anxiously.

He shook his head. "Eighty percent of the human population decimated, and still we put no value on ourselves!" he judged, and went back to searching for the computer chip buried in the Mainframer's thigh.

"Thought I left that Virtual claptrap back at the Orange Kingdom, along with the damn chip." The Mainframer tapped his temple. A bandage covered the wound where a cricket had once been. "Thought I was finally free of the Grid."

The Mainframer was a large man with a reddish beard and squinty eyes. He had one bare, hairy leg up on the couch. The other, still in its pant leg, was down and braced. His pale eyes were looking away, obviously squeamish of the operation being performed on his leg.

"You thought wrong." Noel sponged the wound with a coagulant-novocaine mixture. "And you can get down off the high horse, Programmer. Information obsessed. Computer locked. You're no better than the Virts!"

"Virtuals don't interface real time," the Mainframer objected. "We do."

"'Course you do," Noel sneered. "That's how you engender a programmer, and Hawthorne knows it. The net is a novelty to you grinders, a data drug. Those who endure the inconveniences of reality are far more willing to worship at the techno-altar."

That got through. The Mainframer carefully shifted his shoulders, as if stung, and concentrated on the statue of Plato.

The gamblers tossed their dice, and the skeletons on the couches stared up at the misty ceiling. The persistent music from the Ferris wheel of Actor's Carnival swam down the stairs.

Plato just took it all in, eyes wide and blank.

"Do you think they know yet?" the Mainframer asked. There was reconciliation in his voice, a peace offering.

"That you've escaped? Not yet. Otherwise they'd have traced us by now. I estimate about three days before the autopsy reports correct their misapprehensions. Longer if the Kings reexamine your escape route with infrared."

Another moment of silence. "Do you really believe all that rubbish we Mainframers always hear from the higher-ups? Ethics and virtue and restoring civilization?"

Noel cut deeper with the scalpel. "Ethics, virtue, and civilization didn't stop people from staring into a mind-set as they would stare into the abyss. That's why the globe caved in on itself."

"You hold us programmers to blame for that?" the big man asked defiantly.

"If I did, I wouldn't have helped you escape."

"Hm." The Mainframer did not sound satisfied. He moved his shoulders again, clearly uncomfortable. "Damn embarrassing, sitting here with my trousers down! Wasn't there anyplace less public you could have brought me?"

"No. Ah!" Noel triumphantly held up the tweezers. Pinched between them was a chip, round and silver, gleaming wet and faintly red in the candlelight, as if dipped in cherry juice.

"So you were right." The Mainframer was sullenly unimpressed.

"Had to be here." Noel dropped the chip and vengefully cracked it under the heel of his silver running shoe; then he pulled a roll of gauze from the pocket of his green trousers. "A wine taster does not overlook the cork!" He knelt and set to bandaging the wound. "If a holist is going to implant an unconscious Mainframer with a chip for computer access, it'd be stupid not to implant a backup sensor."

"Say it a little louder, why don't you," the Mainframer grumbled.

"No one's listening!" Noel pushed at the mask. He no longer noticed that he was seeing through mesh, nor, most of the time, that he was even wearing it, though the gray cowl at the back got hot and itchy.

He tied off the bandage and got to his feet. The Mainframer hastily struggled into his pants, managing to zip up just as a pair of Brainiacs arrived, right on time.

"Here," Noel hailed, recognizing one of the two as Strawberry. She was petite and freckled, a girlish-looking woman dressed in shorts, leggings, and a sleeveless tee. Pink computer glasses hung from around her neck.

"Wish you'd pick a better place," Strawberry complained, then, "Hey, brother." She smiled happily at the big Mainframer, who nodded back sheepishly. "We're here to take you home. No more running, you're among fellow chip heads now." She pointed proudly to the tiny scar at her temple, where her cricket use to be. "Take him up." A wave to her partner, a dark-skinned man thin and elastic. "I'll be right there."

"Just a minute!" Noel stopped them. "Where's my payment?"

The Mainframer, who'd been pushing up onto his good leg, blushed. He dug into a pocket and brought out a precious bag of saltwater taffy.

Noel accepted it with secret delight. He'd tried taffy from any number of places, but only the Orange Kingdom made it right. For saltwater taffy alone he'd have stolen out Mainframers.

"You're pathetic," Strawberry muttered as her partner assisted the huge Mainframer up the stairs.

Noel shrugged, untwisting waxed paper from a piece of candy. He had to risk pushing the mask up a little to slip the taffy into his mouth. It was worth it. This one was peppermint, a smooth melting mint flavor, not sharp. It quieted his irritation and kept him focused. "You wanted to tell me something?"

"We made maps of the towers."

"Waste of time! They're just window dressing. Candy?" He didn't really want to offer her one, coveting the whole bag for himself. But the Brainiacs, former Mainframers all, were the only ones willing to conspire with him, willing to believe and help him.

"If the towers have nothing to do with Hawthorne's plan, why put them up?" she demanded, accepting a pink-colored candy.

"I didn't say they had nothing to do with his plan. They're just not the important part."

"And what's-his-name is?"

"Alexander? Believe it."

"Not a very subtle name. Sure you don't want us to break him out? We might be able to."

"No. Not yet. Let's free more programmers first."

"You heard the latest? Hawthorne's put out an APB."

Noel grew very still. He hadn't heard. And that meant that this development was probably related to Alexander, Hawthorne's best-kept secret.

"Tell me."

"He's hunting down this Sierra—"

"He's after Sierras?"

"*A* Sierra. Just one. Went out yesterday."

"Really." Noel chewed thoughtfully on another candy. This one was chocolate, his favorite.

"The Sierra's name is Urban Myth."

"Now that *is* interesting!"

"Name's familiar?"

"Maybe." Noel sighed impatiently. He wanted to scratch his nose. "I have to go. You know how to contact me."

"Yeah." Strawberry crossed her arms and looked disgusted. "Does it really have to be here?"

"You know it does."

She took a gander at the ceiling. "Not a comfortable place to wait, Noel."

"It's safe," he said, thinking all the while, *this is where it began.* And it was here, he knew, that it would someday have to end. Justice demanded it.

"You're one fucked-up mother," Strawberry judged.

"Take care of the new one."

"Teach your grandmother to suck eggs, Noel! We all were newbies from the Mickey net once!" And with that offended reminder, she spun on her heel and made for the stairs.

"Not all of us," Noel murmured, pausing for a moment to sit down on the vacated couch, savoring the feeling of being in a strange, physical place. No matter how many times he came here, it always felt that way, strange.

He tasted the foul air and listened to the odd sounds, the feathery giggles of the tripping skeletons on the couches, the moans of the Fanny behind the bar. All muted, subdued sounds that rose and fell like the ghosts of the transit trains that used to speed down these tunnels.

He unwrapped and snuck another piece of chewy candy up under the mask. He'd be dreadfully sorry when the confectionery was gone, but he had never believed in doling out pleasures crumb by crumb. When he reached the bottom of the bag, he'd just have to rescue another Mainframer from the Orange Kingdom, out from that fantasy into this strange reality. That, after all, was his self-appointed task, his reason for being.

Urban Myth, he suddenly thought. *Urban Myth.* Where had he heard that name?

He shook his head, pushed off the couch, and pinched out the candle flame. The smoke surrounded him as he disappeared into the tunnels.

Only the peaceful, stalwart statue of Plato saw him go.

Chapter 4

It was the longest elevator ride of Urban's life. And all the way up, he found himself thinking, *Old.* Not a hundred-story high-rise with state-of-the-art every-thing. No. This building was ancient, and so was the elevator. Ancient. Liable to break.

And if he got stuck, would anyone know or care? Would they come back in six years and find his mum-mified remains glued to the rotten floorboards?

He'd fought the King boys every step to this fortress of puke green warehouses, and gotten a grinding, roller-bladed kick in the belly for his trouble. His stomach was still tender and queasy. Or maybe that was the lurch and rumble of the elevator.

Christ! Would this box ever get to the top?

He thought of the shadow he'd seen, flitting up high behind the crown of windows. He'd caught sight of it as D-base's bully boys dragged him through the rusted gate, the tallest warehouse; its windows were big, wide, the shadow small, furtive.

Alexander.

His gym bag, all he owned inside, slid about in his

sweaty hands. Thoughtful of them to have brought it along. He hefted it into his arms and hugged it. The King boys had tossed him in so hard, he'd bounced off the walls. As his gym bag landed by his ear, he'd rolled to see the burnished doors slam shut. There'd been a creaky lurch, and then the hum. Up went the elevator, leaving what was left of his acidy stomach behind.

D-base had flatly explained to him that the elevator could only be brought down or sent up from below. Still, there had to be a way out of this. He would find it and vanish. Disappear like a drummer for the legendary Dead.

Filthy, broken-brown floors and yellow lights overhead. And how it stank!

A vibrating halt. At last! Three minutes by Urban's count, not that he was any good at telling time.

The doors swept open.

Before him spread a vast, windowless storage area, crates piled everywhere, bulbs dangling from wires in the ceiling. On some of the crates were icons. Supplies, he saw, and delicacies that even Virtuals would have been hard-pressed to get. There was a cot, unmade, and clothing: female.

The last servant, he had been told, *had not proved satisfactory.* The last servant, he had been as good as told, was dead.

His heart was going rapid-fire now. Slowly, he edged his way forward, glancing about in fear of ambush.

The area smelled of old perfume, canned chili, and marijuana smoke. There were picture magazines, a black-market monitor, and priceless vid-disks. He saw a box of junk jewelry and one of cosmetics already caking, both on an antique vanity with a full-moon mirror. On the chair of the vanity was a segmented box open and empty. He glanced over it just to be sure, saw the temperature gauge and knew. The box was to keep Blues from losing their rush.

"She overdosed!" snapped a voice from above, and Urban leapt back, gym bag flying from his arms. Hands up, he crouched, ready, but the shadows were clear, the spots of haloed light empty.

"It is fairly easy to do with years of near solitude ahead and only vid-disks for a change of scenery!"

"Where are you?" Urban shouted.

"There's a staircase to your right. 'Welcome to the prison of my mind.' When you've finished gawking, you can come up and fix me some toast!"

Cocky son of reality. Urban frowned and made his way to the stairs. They turned out to be narrow and steep, cornered right next to the elevator. *Might as well meet the bastard. Draw the lines, stake the territory quick and fast.* He'd learned that in his twenty-three years. Except with Virtuals, you set the boundaries first. Then you engaged in whatever little rituals were demanded of you. And then you demanded your own; and you damn well made sure you left an impression.

The stairs led up through a trapdoor. Urban paused on the top step, squinting at sunlight. Above the storage area was a huge loft; the ceiling reached up twelve feet if an inch, and along one wall was a row of arched windows, wide as church doors; above them, aluminum slats let in fresh air.

As he stepped forward, he saw that the floors were made of wood, blond wood, waxed and polished to a meticulous shine. There was a floor mat and pillows, green plants, and a sleek kitchen from which Urban smelled coffee—fresh beans, not recycled grounds or chicory. He might often be mistaken, but his nose never was. The coffee was real, just like the wood on the floor.

To one side, standing by a computer station the likes of which only myths had known, was a young man. He looked to be about twenty years of age, perhaps younger. The right half of his face was covered with the thin white half-mask of a Web, only the eye visible; the other revealed a pale face, an amber eyebrow, and a thin mouth. Fine, resin-colored hair was fashionably slicked back from a small widow's peak.

"My fourth companion converted me to the Web," the youth announced. He was wearing a velvet smoking jacket of olive paisley, a pearl white shirt with a wide, open collar, and black silk slacks. Urban, connoisseur as he was of vintage clothing, was impressed by the outfit.

The young man, moving with a pronounced limp, crossed over to an old oil drum filled with what looked to be crushed glass and bits of stripped, metallic wire. With a pair of tweezers, he meticulously picked out a tarnished sliver of copper.

"I was young and impressionable. Not devout enough, however, to ruin my face, though I hate it."

He limped over to the window side of the room, where stood a telescope and five easels, each supporting five, large, differently textured pads of paper. One was filled with concentric squares, each one an intricate mosaic of intertwining pictures and symbols. All the squares, Urban saw with amazement, were formed out of tiny slivers of glass, bits of wire, and crushed plastic.

"I'm only half here, you see," Alexander added with a glance back, and the look in his eye, for some reason, brought to mind the sound of a single violin, the bow madly working its way over and over the lowest strings.

The young man contemplated the picture, then, using a small brush, dabbed a drop of glue in the corner and carefully added the copper to the spot.

"My mandala," he explained. "Eight sangsaric regions of the mind leading to the unconscious. I'm thinking of adding a ninth."

"Why?" Urban couldn't help asking.

"Nine circles of hell, nine gates," Alexander suggested with a faint smile. "To exorcise ghosts, shout out nine times: '*Avaunt, ye spectres,* from this house!' I've been told that Virtuals can call up menus like spirits from the air," he added suddenly. "They point to what they want, any information in their legendary supercomputer, theirs anytime they like." His voice was thick with old grudging envy. "And here I am working at a database so antiquated it squeaks!" He wiped his hands on his jacket. "What are you? A pirate?"

Urban glanced down at himself, at his stained white shirt and brown vest. His worn gray pants had black stripes down the sides and fitted snugly into tall, worn boots. He felt suddenly and irately self-conscious. "I'm a Sierra."

The young man shrugged. "Haven't had one of those yet. Bread is in the box." He limped over to a set of heavy shelves lined with row upon row of old bottles. "I baked it fresh this morning. Knives are in the third drawer to the left, and there's butter on the table." He snatched down a tiny, unlabeled, blue bottle, and tapped out some yellow powder onto a square of paper. "It's on the white dish under the white cover in case you've never seen a butter dish before."

In point of fact, Urban never had seen a butter dish, but he wasn't about to admit that. He straightened his back and crossed his arms.

"I think we ought to get something straight—"

The youth spun, turning on the Sierra with a look that made Urban's mouth go dry. "I think you're right," Alexander agreed, setting down powder and limping up. He was a few inches shorter, but he dominated all the same. "You are here to serve me. That is the only reason you are here. And there is nowhere you can go and nothing else you can do. Is that straight enough?"

Urban dropped his arms. "Yes."

"Good." The voice was smug. "Any other questions?"

"Yeah. Just how ugly is your face?"

The young man caught his breath, and Urban smiled. "And who is going to make me serve you?" He took a threatening step forward. "And if I decide to beat you bloody, who is going to stop me?"

The youth took a limp back. He looked shaken for a moment, a strange brilliance in his eyes, but then his composure returned, along with bitter arrogance.

"If you've a death wish, be my guest." He headed for the telescope. "I had one rather sadistic nurse when I was seven. She didn't last the week." Alexander bent to peer into the scope. "Do you think I'm not watched? They've got a camera in every corner, a microphone under every floorboard. Ironic, isn't it. We're all alone and never alone."

Urban shifted. D-base had emphasized that Alexander's welfare was his servant's. Stupid to think the young man wasn't aware of that.

All right. Wrong way to start. Try a new set of boundaries.

"So"—awkwardly, Urban stuffed fingers into his back pockets—"your name is Alexander?"

"Alexander Julunggul Damaxion Kitatimate."

"Make that name up all by yourself?"

"The three surnames, yes. Names are the most basic means of self-definition. You, however, may simply call me, 'Your Majesty.' "

"I think I'll call you Sander instead."

"Sander!? What happened to Alex?"

"You don't look like an Alex, you look like a Sander. My name is Urban, Sander, Urban Myth."

"Wonderful." Alexander shuffled to a freestanding

bookcase near the kitchen. "Now they're sending me fantasies. Dull fantasies. But then, they dare not let me into their Mainframe with the real fantasies, do they, Urban?"

"I wouldn't know about that." Cripes! Like talking to a Node; only heard his side of the conversation.

"Cinnamon is in the third cabinet from the right," Sander said. "Sugar is beside the sink. You do know what cinnamon toast is, don't you?"

"I've heard of it."

"Then make it."

Urban shrugged, annoyed and confused. It took him a moment to find the bread and a knife to cut it. So far, Sander had set all the rules.

"So," he tried again, "is that why you're up here? So you can't get at the Mainframe?"

Sander, a fat book braced across his arm, did not look up. "Why am I here?" He suddenly shut the book, stuffing it under his arm. The hazel eyes looked wet and bright. "Can you smell the streets in summer?"

"What?"

"The smell of streets in summer!" Without warning he dropped the book. It thudded loudly on the floorboards, causing Urban to flinch.

Alexander snatched a new tome off the shelf. "Here." He flipped it open, searched and pointed. "Smokestacks and power lines. All here. Are they still out there? That is what I want to know!"

Urban shrugged. "Power lines are. Smokestacks, too, except they don't produce any smoke."

"Webs like me believe each *place* is a stage set; not a single stage, but dozens—billions of internal sets, elaborate, karmic. Two slices of toast for me; you do know how to work the toaster, I hope."

"I'm sure you'll let me know if I get it wrong," Urban breathed, slipping the slices onto the rack and into the little oven.

"Were I a Sierra like yourself," Sander went on, "I'd say that anywhere you *could* leave, but do *not* leave, is a trap, a false hope. A Node, wired to listen perpetually to whatever form of music they have chosen to obsessively worship, would assert a metaphysical matrix, each of us set like complex numbers in an astral square. Can we be happy like that, I wonder—as part of a magic square and not as the square entire?"

"We're happy or we're not," Urban ventured. "Doesn't matter if we're part or whole of anything."

"Inane and trite, Urban! And very like a Virtual! A Virtual would say that *where* has no meaning at all. Were I a Virtual, here would be everywhere. Were I a Virtual, the smokestacks would produce smoke and the power lines would crackle. The streets would smell of summer!" He started to shake.

The book went flying. Urban jumped out of the way as the sugar bowl was knocked aside and shattered, sending a shower of white crystals across the counter.

"Jesus!"

"Clean that up," Sander commanded, limping back to his computer. He dropped down into the seat, a finger crooked beneath his lower lip.

"Cripes! You nuts?!" Urban was trembling. "What kind of hook have you got on your hand?!"

"A hook on the hand?" Sander looked up, the exposed half of his face as smooth as the masked. His voice was steady again. "What an original expression. No. There is no hook on my hand. A beetle on my head, perhaps. *Khepera.* That is my problem. Egyptian for a soul trapped between death and rebirth. Don't forget to sugar the toast after you butter it, then add the cinnamon."

Urban took a breath. Too much. It was too much. Capture, for no reason. Sentence, for no cause. Locked away for six years with this!! Locked—

He gritted his teeth. Willed back his composure.

"If you wanted sugar on the toast, you shouldn't have smashed the sugar bowl."

"Shelf over the refrigerator—you'll find a bag of it. Yes, a whole bag. Weren't you told? I get whatever material goods I want."

"That explains a lot," Urban muttered, snatching out the hot bread and layering it with butter. The underside steamed against his hand.

"Urban?" Sander was looking at him uncertainly.

"I'm making your damn toast!" he snapped, reaching for the sugar.

There were three bags. *Three!* Urban stared at them, suddenly dizzy. *Three full bags of sugar!*

One was open. Urban brought it down gingerly, looked it over greedily. There was no scoop or spoon inside; he considered searching for one, then, with wicked, wild abandon, dug in and tossed sugar onto the toast with his fingers. The extravagance of fingering and wasting so much coffeehouse wealth gave him a perverse pleasure.

"Urban," Sander repeated. The Sierra turned defiantly only to find himself trapped by eyes in which the light spun like a dancer. "I am glad you've come. I've been here for eighteen years now. I have never been out. And all that I know, I know from those who . . . serve me."

Urban paused, reaching for the cinnamon. The bread weighed heavy with sugar, cracking down one side. He sprinkled it with cinnamon, which went from light to dark as it struck the bread. It smelled sharp and sweet.

He slid the toast off his hand onto the kitchen table.

"Your cinnamon toast."

"Where's the plate?"

"Get it yourself," Urban sneered, "Your Majesty."

Chapter 5

It was a very cold night. At least to Emerson, it was a very cold night. In spite of all those long, chill evenings sitting outside the coffeehouse, staring at the condensation on white tabletops, the great outdoors was still a novelty to him, one he was coming to dislike intensely.

Even worse than the cold was the city itself, especially where they were right now. There was a movie theater from which could be heard filmed foreign voices; there was a freeway upon which campfires burned and a Black Sister wailed her shrieking lament; and there were rows of decaying buildings, each girdled around with its own rusty crosshatch fence.

Somewhere back during the hate wars, managers had closed up, locked the double doors, and pulled fast those cages. No one had ever returned to open them up again. And so there they were, like netted veils hanging down from the hats of grieving widows. They were ugly, and it was cold.

Cinder didn't seem to feel the cold. Nor was she the least bit perturbed by their surroundings. She sat upon the seat of her motorcycle, chatting with Ethelred and polishing her shotgun with a white handkerchief that never seemed to get dirty.

Emerson could make out her face in the flickering of the failing neon theater sign. It was penny brown with wide lips, a longish nose, and sardonic brows over a steady pair of mocha eyes.

Behind her, huddled in the shadows, was a form. What it was could not clearly be made out. But it was large and shaped a little like an antique Volkswagen; "Ladybug-shaped," Cinder liked to say.

That was Ethelred.

"I really don't see how jumping off the building's going to get us inside, Ethelred," Cinder remarked, cracking open the gun and sighting down the empty barrels.

"Gee"—the shadow's voice huffed and wheezed—"you know, now that I think about it, I can't figure it out, either. It seemed a good plan."

"It probably was. Your plans are always good. Original. Wonderfully. Don't you agree, Emerson?"

Emerson nervously pushed his glasses up on his nose. "They're garbage."

Cinder glanced up from the gun, and Emerson grew very still. He'd never encountered a gaze like hers; it never looked quite human. "Use your imagination," she said in that soft, commanding voice of hers, and went on polishing the gun.

"I haven't one," Emerson muttered, shifting and glancing down the street. How cold it was!! Hate wars to blame for that. Stopped everything, including the pollution that was bringing about global warming. *So now we're all doomed to freeze,* Emerson thought. *Can't win for losing.*

"How about"—Ethelred's shadow seemed to perk up—"how about we put nails through our foreheads and sing the 'Queen of the Night' aria from *The Magic Flute*?"

"How about we don't!" Emerson rubbed his upper arms. A fire would have been nice! A fire and a hot cup of coffee. Dark black, searing coffee.

"I rather like the idea of singing arias," Cinder countered. The chin straps of her cap swung loose. The goggles, up on her forehead, flashed. "Music is the voice of the id." She clicked the gun back together and holstered it on the motorcycle, then she set about checking over the sidecar. "Nails through the forehead sounds a bit drastic, though. Don't you think, Emerson?"

"Why ask me?! You never listen to me! And why should you? I'm just a poor Jabberjaw, a coffeehouse hack. Can't even write poetry. What do I know!?"

The eyes fastened on him again. They were bright, but never warm, and they terrified him. "Every human mind's of value, Emerson. Yours included."

"Yes, well, my valuable opinion is that we're going to freeze solid—which, given the probable alternatives of this dreadful place, might not be so bad." He rubbed his arms the harder. "Scientists will dig us up and defrost us in a thousand years, just like the mammoths!"

Cinder looked intrigued by that. "What a creative thought! And wouldn't that be something? To actually be an anthropological study—what do you say, Ethelred?"

"Well, being mythical, I don't think I can be frozen."

Emerson tsked sarcastically, "Too bad!"

"Yes, it is," Cinder agreed, drawing on her short, cracked leather jacket. Emerson had passed it to her enough times to know it was heavy and thick and had a torn, silk lining. "Perhaps if the temperature goes down some more—"

"For God's sake, Cinder! Can we please go somewhere else—preferably before we're stabbed or
mugged?!"

"Ethelred isn't done yet," she insisted, and there
was no arguing with that soft, cruel voice. "And he
can't formulate plans just anywhere. He needs places
that are special."

"What the devil is special about this—this toilet?!"

"It's magical," Ethelred answered, his dark, hidden
shape shifting with enthusiasm. "Just smell the air!"

"It smells like excrement!"

"It's magical!" he insisted.

"Use your imagination, Emerson," Cinder said.

"My imagination tells me that you and . . . and
whatever he is are badly brewed! Can we just get—
What was that?!"

"What?"

Emerson spun. From the other end of the street he
heard the rhythmic scraping of roller blades in
tandem.

King players!

Emerson flatted himself against the freezing stones
of the theater. A patrol of King players appeared,
hockey sticks honed and gleaming, and leisurely made
their way down the street. Foreign voices hummed
through the bricks at Emerson's back.

"Not until Ethelred comes up with a plan," Cinder
said as blithely as if the King soldiers weren't skating
within spitting distance.

"Shhhhhh!" Emerson motioned furtively. "For
God's sake—"

"Hm?" She took a look, saw the Kings. One side
of her mouth dimpled with amusement. "Well now,
how do you like that?"

"Cinder—"

"Ethelred, aren't patrols usually composed of only

five hockey players? Yet there seem to be, let me see, seven, eight—"

"Cinder!" Emerson hissed.

"Twelve." She walked back to the motorcycle, removed a notepad from the sidecar, and scribbled across a page. "What do you make of that, Ethelred?"

"He's going to make nonsense of it! That's all he ever makes of anything!" The King soldiers were gone, and Emerson felt free to snap.

"Nonsense keeps the brain alive and crackling, Emerson."

"What am I doing here?! Why did I ever come along!?"

Cinder eyed him, long lashes brushing her high, fine cheeks. Casually, she put away the notebook, and slid hands into the pockets of her khaki jodhpurs. "You came along," she said, "because you were desperate to escape the couches and the drone, this hiss of the cappuccino machines. You were desperate to leave, and I was leaving."

Emerson took a step back, defensively wrapping his arms around himself. He'd been nearly suicidal when he'd met Cinder. For as long as he could remember, all he'd ever dreamed of doing was writing and sharing poetry, like the Laureates of the Closet. He'd spent his childhood pouring over verse, learning to recite it, analyze it, learning rhyme schemes and meter, metaphor and metonymy. Yet year after year, every one of his submitted poems was regularly rejected. At sixteen, he'd been frankly told that he had no talent for poetry, and he'd been put to work washing dishes and scrubbing floors.

That had been four years ago.

Meanwhile, every one of his peers became a promising poet. And every Monday night, at least one of them was invited to read their verse to the family.

Unable to bear it, Emerson took to spending those nights shivering out on the patio.

That's where he'd been three weeks ago, tracing symbols into the damp tabletop with his finger, when, out from under a street lamp, *she* had appeared, her face accented with shadows, all except for her eyes. They held a light that glowed from deep within, like a fire at the back of a cave. Her stance told him that she was wholly at ease with the world, with herself, like no one he'd ever met before.

"Need a lift?" Those were the first words she'd said to him, as if there were no need for introductions or explanations. He'd felt like a perverse Lady of Shalott then. And like the lady in Tennyson's poem, he'd suddenly realized that he'd spent his entire life weaving to no purpose, watching the world secondhand in a mirror. And now, this strange Lancelot had appeared, offering him an escape from his tower. As in the poem, the mirror, his mirror, cracked then, and his weaving flew apart.

"Thank you, I would," he'd answered, never thinking how crazy it all sounded, how insane it all was. All he knew was that this was his one chance. If he didn't want to spend his life waiting tables and scrubbing floors, he had to leave now.

He'd followed her to her motorcycle and gotten on behind her without hesitation. Only when she revved the motor did he feel afraid. But by then his arms were around her waist and he was bound to her.

Not that her friendship came free. Cinder wanted something from him, he knew that; what she wanted, he was too terrified to ask. But she had to want something. Why else ask him along?

And he, fool enough to go. Because his coffeehouse home was suffocating him. Because no one else had any use for him and he was just in the way. Always in the way.

They told me the tribes would kill me, he wanted to say to Cinder. *They told me if I left I would die. So I couldn't leave on my own. Could I?*

"We invited you along," Cinder observed. "Didn't we, Ethelred?"

The shadow seemed to nod. "That's right. You asked me if we should give him a lift, and I said we should, because I knew, yes sir, I knew right then he was meant to be your squire. Didn't I tell you? I said, 'Cinder, that's your squire.' "

"Yes, you did," Cinder concurred. "And it was only polite to give him a lift."

"Christ!" Emerson cursed. "Forecast it in espresso grounds, and I wouldn't have believed this! Can we leave yet?!"

"If Ethelred has a plan. Do you?"

"Well. Let's get the ears up and . . . Uh, Cinder, my ears won't go up."

"They never do!" Emerson snapped. "Oh, this is ridiculous!"

"Oh, hey!" The shadow on the alley wall rippled. "Wait, wait, an idea is coming. Ah-ha! Got it! And, Cinder—"

"Yes, Ethelred?"

"I'll swear by my back paw on this one. Get another motorcycle."

"Oh, terrific!" Emerson waved sardonically. "Another cycle! And what are we going to do with it? Pour maple syrup over it and ride it over a cliff?"

"Uh, no," Ethelred sounded profoundly bewildered. "Matter of fact, *you're* going to drive it—"

"Me?!" Emerson went rigid. "The hell I will!"

"Another bike," Cinder censored him, just like that. "All right. Anything else?"

"A flashlight. A big one."

"Cinder—" Emerson tried, but it was too late, the shadow was fading to an outline. And then it was gone. He looked over at Cinder. "You're not going to listen to him!?!"

She shrugged. "A squire needs his own horse, Emerson."

"But I—" He was beginning to sweat despite the cold. Behind him he could hear the movie, voices lilting up and down. The streets were so ominously empty, and they smelled so foul. "But I—"

"Yes?"

"Cinder, for mercy's sake, I've only been out in the world a few weeks! I haven't gotten used to the weather, the odors, the very act of moving at high speeds—"

She smiled her distant, eerie smile. "I have every confidence in you, Emerson. Maybe we can find you a pair of goggles and a scarf. Make you look quite dapper. And we will teach you how to squire from horseback." The words were light, but Emerson knew them to be an order. *He would do it,* they said, *or he could leave.*

She made a neat little turn on her heel, strode back to her motorcycle. "Now we can go."

Emerson shivered. Why, oh why had he left?

Screaming woke Urban. He was on his feet and two steps up before he even remembered where he was.

Warehouse storage room. The smell of the air brought it back to him, that lingering perfume and powder fragrance of the previous occupant. The one who'd overdosed.

Moaning from above. He topped the steep stairs and crossed the loft in the next second. The incandescent glow of the city formed long squares across the floor. Framed in one of those was Alexander, clutching a cotton quilt to himself and shivering.

"Sander?" Urban knelt, and set a hand on the

Web's shoulder. The young man jerked away with a start, hissing.

"Hey"—Urban held up his hands—"just me."

Sander caught his breath, eyes huge and pale in the light. It took a moment for Urban to realize the boy was still wearing the mask, the uncovered side of his face being almost as white.

"God! How did you get up here so fast?! I—I just woke a moment ago."

"Sierra reflexes." Urban smiled ruefully. "You all right?"

The young man drew a hand over his hair. "I'd like some water."

"Coming right up." Urban crossed to the kitchen and fetched him a glass. When he got back, Sander, dressed in paisley green silk pajamas, was leaning against the window, one arm up against it.

"Want to talk about it?" Urban handed him the glass.

Sander snorted. "Of course! It's part of the ritual." He gulped down half the water. "Get used to it, Urban. I never sleep the night through."

"You always wake screaming?" he asked, disturbed.

A shake of tousled hair. "The screaming is an added attraction. My way of making the transition from one nursemaid to the next. Once I'm used to you, it'll go away. Mostly." He finished the water, and then, casually, carelessly, threw the glass.

Urban shot out a hand and caught it.

He smiled; then he saw Alexander's face. It was flushed with rage.

"When I throw breakable items, I mean them to break! Understand?!"

Urban blinked, and released the glass. It shattered at his feet causing Sander to flinch—a very satisfying sight.

"Of course, Your Majesty," Urban smiled. *I can*

beat you at your game, he thought. *I can play it your way and still beat you.*

The youth stared back out the window at the Ferris wheel of Actor's Carnival. It seemed to be his favorite landmark.

"Sweep that up."

Urban felt the muscles in his neck tighten. "In the morning."

"Suit yourself." Eyes on the Ferris wheel, on its rocking, spinning gondolas.

Urban waited a minute. Two. "So?" he finally demanded.

"Do you hear the Black Sister out there?" Sander asked.

Urban stepped as close as he dared to the youth, who, chilled and sweating, smelled of cut wood and morning rain. A wailing, faint, barely audible, snaked through the slats.

"Yeah?"

"I dreamed I was a Black Sister. I dreamed that the man in the photograph I worshiped stepped out and made love to me. Then I realized it was all a fantasy, and I screamed."

Urban shrugged. "Weird," he judged.

"Is it?" Sander limped past him, movements suddenly fervent, almost panicked. He seemed to be searching for something.

"Well, yeah," Urban said, watching his charge with concern. Sander was before his precious mandala, chewing on a nail, examining the mixture of metals pasted to the paper. Abruptly, he tore the paper from the pad, ripped the artwork in half, and threw it on the floor. He stared down at the pieces a moment, then spun and strode to the kitchen, throwing open the refrigerator door.

"I don't have any fantasies of my own," he mumbled, picking and searching among the containers.

Ah, hell. More gibberish! Urban sighed. "I don't understand."

Sander slammed the refrigerator door and turned on him. "Don't patronize me! This problem's real, and it's driving me insane! I can't daydream! Is that clear enough?? If my mind wanders even a little, I find myself trapped in someone else's fantasy! During the day I can do something about it, at night—God! If only I didn't need to sleep!"

He was pacing now, one hand at his forehead, rubbing at it. Urban stayed still and quiet. It seemed the best thing to do under the circumstances.

"So now you know what makes me so damn special. That is, if it's real and not just madness. It could be classic schizophrenic visions, I hear you thinking. No, not really thinking. I don't read thoughts. Just fantasies." He stopped and threw Urban a suspicious look. "But not from you. Why not, Urban. I should have had an inkling by now. Don't you fantasize?"

The Sierra shrugged. "No need. Anything I want to do, I do."

Sander's expression, lit in bits and pieces by the city's neon and fluorescence, was unexpectedly serious. "Did, Urban. Past tense."

Urban glanced away.

Sander sat down, quiet now, before his computer. "You know," he said with an almost desperate smile, "that one companion of mine, the sadist, had it right. When you're in pain, all you can think of is the pain. Hard for the mind to wander. I don't suppose," he added, "that you *would* consent to breaking a bone or two?"

There was fear beneath the jocularity, and need. Urban, deeply disturbed, shook his head. "They'd only come and take me away."

The hazel eyes grew distant. "Oh, they'll do that anyway. Sooner or later, they take all my companions away. I am the only certainty in this reality. And sometimes I'm not even sure of that."

For a moment the young man was silent; then he touched on the computer. As the black screen came to life, Urban realized he'd been dismissed.

Wasn't good enough at holding his attention, he thought snidely and marched back to his cot. Not that he was going to get any more sleep this night.

Nor likely for quite a while.

Chapter 6

End of his second day with this lunatic and things hadn't let up, Urban brooded, watching as Sander sketched building after glittering building with a wild, frantic hand. The youth had set up each of the five easels before a different window. Balancing a wineglass precariously on one easel, he drew, moved, sat, wrote, left, grabbed a compass, made a circle on a third, dropped the compass for a triangle, moved to a fourth—

It was rather like watching the quadruple rings of the Web circus, each showcasing a different play or spectacle.

"Numbers, Urban," Sander now said, hurrying back to his original sketch as if afraid it would vanish. He grabbed the wineglass off its perch, gulped down the deep red vintage, and then, snatching up the corner of the paper, tore off the sheet and crumbled it. "In every aspect and mystery of life, numbers!" He dropped the glass, letting it carelessly shatter at his feet.

Urban winced. "You like breaking things, don't

you?" he sighed, getting up from the kitchen table and fetching the dustpan. It was a rhetorical question. So far his charge had smashed a sugar bowl, three plates, two water glasses, a soup tureen, and now a fourth wineglass. Urban found it depressing to think of all the sweeping he was going to do over the next six years.

"Frustration over not being able to break the windows," Sander said with the self-analyzing candor Urban was coming to associate with him. "I remind myself that glass can break. And I sometimes need the sound. I listen to it breaking instead of my mind. A form of sympathetic magic, wouldn't you say?"

"I'd say it's not as if *you* have to clean up the pieces!" Urban knelt and carefully swept the tinkling splinters into the pan. They smelled of fine, old, and very real burgundy. "How many glasses would you break if you had to do the sweeping?"

"Moot point, Urban, since I do not have to do it." With a ruler, Alexander outlined on his paper the tallest building in sight. "Architecture fascinates me."

"It better." Urban dumped the shattered glass in the dustbin. "What else have you to look at?"

"Beavers build dams, birds build nests, termites build their grotesque mounts," Sander went on. "This is what species human builds. And look at what it says! The materials, the geometry, the art, the psychological games!" He limped excitedly from one easel to another. "It is a secret code I want to read, Urban!"

"So who's stopping you?"

"What, not who! And that what is *distance*! Distance and imprisonment! I can't see the back side of buildings with a telescope; I can't swing around to note the punctuation of smaller structures hidden by larger ones! And the night, Urban, the night which is even now coming upon us, robbing me of the light I need! A building artificially lit cannot be correctly delineated, although it can be interpreted, much like our dreams. Numbers, Urban."

"You ever stay on one subject, Sander?"

"I am on one subject! Absolute symbols! Numbers. Perfection incarnate. These are the essentials and basics of architectural structures. Order that can calculate chaos and re-create it as an artifice."

"Um." Urban was getting used to the way his charge went on, like a Halfway at a transit bench. He wasn't like a Node after all. So far as Urban could tell, Alexander *did* listen to others; he just rejected what they said. The Web wasn't a Virtual, either, though his eyes often stared at nothing and his mind moved like a squirrel racing up tree branches. Difference between him and a Virt was that Sander *wanted* to tell you what he was seeing, *wanted* to drag you along with him.

Well, it wasn't as if Urban had anywhere better to go.

"What is that they're building out there?" Alexander was nodding to a distant, four-story tower, woven platinum and iron, sinister but elegant, like a necklace of jet and silver.

Urban shrugged. "Radio towers, so the Virtuals say."

"Interesting architectural choice for audio transmissions. I think they're lying," Sander smirked, moving to another easel. "Don't you?"

"Do Virts ever tell the truth to the grounded?"

"I wouldn't know." Sander added shadows, smudged the pencil tracings carefully. "Virtuals are hypertextual semioticians: they spend their entire lives processing and cross-referencing information for its own sake. Who can say what they hold to be empirically valid." A pause. More smudging. "There has been an architectural pattern to my companions, you know."

"Yeah?"

"Would you like to hear?"

Urban shrugged. "I'm all ears."

"Another curious expression. You're very into body parts, aren't you? But of course you want to hear. Bored already? You don't know the meaning of the word!"

No, thought Urban, *but I'm learning!*

"In brief," the young man went on, "my companions follow a male-female pattern concurrent to my psychological development. Though I cannot trust them, I have memories of a woman, a wet nurse, I would guess, mothering me till age two. The first real companion I remember, however, was male but effeminate, allowing me a gender identification but still maintaining that maternal feel."

Urban's brows went up. "He was a Jimmie?"

Sander smirked. "More likely a Blond Munitions' Moll. He stayed for four years. And, in case you are wondering, it did *not* effect my heterosexual orientation. Whoever sends me companions has proved most enlightened in that respect."

"Maybe 'whoever' just didn't care if you grew up gay."

Sander glanced over at him, a frown scowling the visible half of his face. And then he unexpectedly smiled. It lit his face and, being genuine, shed years off him. "Mr. Myth, you live up to your name. How refreshingly simplistic you are. I wonder that my conspiracy theories can long survive with you here to slay them. Then again, conspiratorially thinking, that might be why you are here. Do you know why conspiracy theories are hard to support?"

" 'Cause they're too complicated?" Urban ventured.

"Not at all!" The youth laughed and moved on to another easel. "We're hardly beyond making our lives and world complicated. The very existence of bureaurcracy negates that faint hope. But you see"—he gestured with his pencil, animated now—"only the most rigidly fascist organizations could effect a true conspiracy because all other organizations will fall into politicking. That is why certain religions and races can-*not* be behind a conspiracy. They are not organized in a rigid enough fashion. There is too much room for dissension, backbiting, and personal peeves, all of which interfere with the focused goal required by a well-organized conspiracy."

"So there haven't been any conspiracies?"

"*Au contraire!* There have. But only in those organizations where there is a rigid, unquestionable, virtually unassailable power structure."

"Or one guy in your case," Urban said unthinkingly.

Sander froze, hazel eyes flashing. He was suddenly both alert and frightened, just as he'd been the night before.

"Do you know something I don't, Urban?" the youth inquired now. "Not in a worldly or facetious sense, but in regards to me and my background?"

Urban fidgeted. Put his foot into it, hadn't he? And D-base had made it clear that his name was not to be mentioned, that his very existence was to remain a secret. "Naw," he said nervously, half to Sander, half, in frantic apology, to the hidden microphones, "I only meant that, well, this kind of setup—"

"You mean kidnapping? False imprisonment? Psychological, emotional, and spiritual deprivation?"

"Yeah, well, it doesn't need more than one Tout Virt to keep it operational. It doesn't need an organization."

"Once more, you cut right to the quick, my faithful comrade in arms. I could begin to find you indispensable."

Now what does that mean? Urban wondered, more than a little alarmed.

"As you say," Sander went on, "there is no need for an organized conspiracy in my case. It would, in fact, complicate matters unnecessarily."

"Uh-huh," Urban readily agreed and, wanting to get off the subject, quickly asked, "So who came after the Moll?"

"Hn? Oh. He was followed by the sadist. As I think I mentioned, she didn't last the week. Rodney King Hockey Players came and dragged her out. I remember watching from the stairwell as they took her screaming away." Sander chewed on his pencil thoughtfully. "That was the first time in my life I'd ever been in the presence of more than one person."

"Who'd they replace the bitch with?"

"Bitch? Yes, I suppose the term is apt. Well, you understand, they could not risk that I might become a misogynist, so they sent another lady. She was the Web. And she stayed long past her time. Seven years. She just refused to leave." His voice softened. "Brilliant woman. Taught me music and math, about the world . . . and death. She was the first of my companions to die on me."

"Sorry," Urban shifted. He wondered if his charge were going to throw or smash something. Sander always seemed to grow particularly violent after growing extremely quiet.

"She was murdered."

Urban locked eyes with the youth. *Wonderful! Just wonderful.* "Sure of that?"

"No. But I have my suspicions. As I say, she overstayed her welcome. After her there was a Son of the One True Mainframe."

"You're kidding!"

"Not at all. I take it that they are rare. Hm. I should have valued him more. We did not get along. He wanted to teach me the proper way to program a com-

puter. Like I needed to be taught that! I taught myself
how to program at age three!

"After him, my companion was a Fanny with Nou'
Art pretensions. I think the powers-that-be wanted me
to lose my virginity. Which I promptly did." The
young man smiled. "She only stayed a year. Then
there was a New Age Nihilist, stayed two years; for a
militant conceptualist his fantasies were shockingly
crude and graphic. Last was the Blue Liner. She spent
her brief time here either dosed on ecstasy or flipping
through old fashion magazines. Which suited both of
us just fine."

"Until she decided to kill herself, you mean."

Sander shrugged. "That may well have suited both
of us, too."

Urban frowned. "What about your parents? I mean,
well, I don't suppose you know—"

Alex threw him an ironic smirk and crossed over to
the computer. With a simultaneous touch of keys, he
brought up a split screen. On one side was a man with
varnish yellow hair and a sheepish grin. On the other
side, a woman with Sander's nose and eyes. Her hair
was hennaed, and her smile was brilliant.

The Web paused, knuckle to lips in thoughtful con-
templation of them, then went back to his sketch pad.

"I remember the man, at least, I think I remember
him. My memory is not photographic, and it's easy
enough to convince yourself of images from when you
were only a year or two old. The woman I don't recall
at all. But when I asked the computer who my parents
were, this is what I got. Truth or constructed image?"

"You are paranoid," Urban muttered.

The eyes flashed up. "Am I? Randomness is ordered in our universe, and nothing is what it seems.
My position is so very strange that I can hardly credit
my own memories. Did I ever have the companions I
think I had? Am I locked away here because I'm in-

sane, and everything I just told you is a mad lie? Are you even real? Is the city outside the windows?" A shrug. "Now is all I know."

Urban shifted. Damned if he was going to put up with six years of this kind of talk! "Were they your parents or not?" he snapped.

A pause, still and prolonged. "It . . . pleases me to believe they were," Alex said softly, and went back to sketching. For a while, the two of them were silent. Outside, the sky darkened to violet. Lights came on in the buildings, and campfires began to appear on the streets.

Urban, staring out at his lost freedom, fell into heavy pondering. How long would it take, he wondered, before young Alexander told him all there was to know, or all Urban cared to learn? How long before flipping through magazines began to look appealing, before he started asking for drugs to speed the passage of time?

"Ah!" Sander's head came up, a strand of resin-colored hair falling before the masked side of his face. "Hear that?"

"What?" Urban asked apprehensively.

"Helicopter."

"So?" Urban shrugged. Helicopters passed overhead all the time.

A smirk. "I forget how new you are. I always know *that* helicopter from the rest. Our supplies have arrived."

"Dropped in by helicopter?!" Urban shook his head. "How are they going to deliver them? Through the window?"

"Hardly!" Sander pointed up. "Twelve feet overhead, within the ceiling, is a sliding door, which should be opening just about—"

There was a crash and a hum, and suddenly a crack appeared in the ceiling, a splinter of starry sky. The *thwup, thwup, thwup* of a 'copter could be heard hovering above, a crate dangling and swinging below it.

"Christ—" Urban grabbed Alexander's arm and jerked him out of the way.

"They won't hit us!" Sander slapped away his hand. "They're experts at setting the box down right there." Even as he spoke, the helicopter lowered the crate directly into the room's center. The wind from its spinning blades whipped about their hair, fluttering the paper on the easels.

The rope tumbled down after the box. *So no one can grab it and escape,* Urban realized sourly.

The deafening monster turned its head and sped away. The ceiling door started to slide shut.

And the electricity cut off. Lights vanished, and the opening in the ceiling froze, still partially open.

"What in—" A spotlight trapped him, dead center.

"Alexander Julunggul Damaxion Kitatimate?" Before he could answer, a ladder tumbled down into the loft. "You'd best hurry on up. Ethelred can only tweak the magnetic field for ten."

Rats and Dobermans! Urban gaped. *A jailbreak!*

The roof reeked of pigeons and mold, but to Urban's nose it was sweet as flowers in spring. He listened to the distant, carnival music and laughter and eyed with delight the neon-lit circle of the Ferris wheel rotating around and around in the distance.

Freedom!

Urban took a deep breath of it, and grinned. *Yes!*

Alexander, arms wrapped around him straightjacket tight, looked about, head moving in little mechanical starts. His eyes, even the one obscured behind the half mask, were round as saucers.

"The tallest warehouse." The woman who'd helped them out seemed to approve. "How apt." She was quickly and efficiently bundling up the ladder. In the light of the flash, Urban saw her stalwart brown face. Her head was covered by what looked to be a swimming cap topped with goggles.

She relatched the ladder and dropped it over the edge of the building so they could climb down.

"How cold it is—" Sander was staring at his breath as it steamed on the air.

"Sander." Urban didn't know why he should care, but he did. "He's in shock," he explained to the woman.

"Dulls the mind," she said with mild disapproval. "Name's Cinder—Cinderblock, just like the bricks making up this warehouse."

"Urban," the Sierra murmured back, "Urban Myth."

"Original," she approved. "Better bustle before the lights and the cameras come back on."

"Or the helicopter gets the word to turn around," Sander said through chattering teeth.

"No worry about that." She smiled. "Let's go," she added, setting a hand on the Web's shoulder.

"Don't touch me!" He suddenly came alive, jerking away.

"Sander!" Urban impatiently took him by the arm and threw him toward the edge.

Alexander balked. "I can't—" he panted.

"Then, we'll be happy to leave you here!"

Sander caught a breath, almost a sob. Getting him up the ladder had taken much pushing and cajoling. It looked like getting him down would take even more.

"I'll go first," Urban said, kneeling on the ledge and reaching back his toes onto the rungs. "Come on, Sander, I'll keep you from falling."

Alexander stared down. For a moment, Urban was sure he would refuse. Then wincingly, the young man knelt on the ledge.

The woman, Cinder, held the light spotted on the

ladder until they were both several rungs down. Then she latched the flash to her belt and swung herself around.

"Keep your eyes ahead, Alexy," she advised. "It's only five stories."

One cool lady, Urban thought, catching sight of her leg, her hip, her round behind appearing in and out of the swinging light. Above him, he could hear Sander panting. At one point, he felt a drop fall on his hand and knew that it was sweat.

And then his feet scraped pavement—blessed tar, dust and sun-seared pavement!—and he was on the asphalt pulling Sander off the ladder.

"Cinder?" someone hissed. "Cinder—" A shadow pressed up against the bricks; a glimmer of light flashed across the round glasses of a thin, black-haired fellow, face white as frothed milk.

"Let's get out of here!"

"Of course," Cinder agreed, heading them toward the gate's entrance. "Emerson, this is Alexander and his friend, Urban. . . Ah! Here we go!"

Barely visible were a glistening pair of motorcycles discreetly parked by the rusted security gate. One was light and small, the other heavy and hitched to a sidecar.

Urban darted for the smaller one, swinging his leg over.

"You take the sidecar, Alexy," Cinder directed, as if assigning seats at dinner.

Going to be out of here faster than a trip on Mickey Mouse Acid, Urban thought, reaching for the key. A white hand clamped on his fingers, stopping him.

"I nearly broke my neck getting this here," the pale-faced man informed him, climbing on behind. "You don't mind, do you?"

"I don't think I'm going in your direction."

"One direction is as good as another," Cinder said,

and Urban heard a chillingly familiar click from her direction. He looked up to see the dull shadow of a shotgun pointed his way. And Cinder, his practiced eye told him, had a steady hand. "Don't you think?"

Out of the locked car and into the killer's arms, Urban observed drolly.

And then the lights came back on.

For a moment they all winced against the brightness flooding down from the warehouse. And then alarms were sounding. Alexander clumsily scrambled into the sidecar, and Urban turned the key on the little motorbike.

It did not take.

Shit! He tried again. From somewhere just outside the fence he could now hear the chillingly distinctive sound of roller blades scraping over pavement.

Cinder, shotgun braced, turned the key on her cycle and released the clutch. With a kick down, she revved the motor so loud Sander's hands flew over his head.

Urban tried his key again. Again it failed.

"Well, don't just sit there!" Emerson yelled as a King player bolted through the open gate.

The motorcycle coughed to life even as a razor-edged stick flashed up, the King's inky faceplate behind it.

Blam!

There was an explosion and smoke, and the decapitated body skated just a little farther before collapsing into a bleeding heap at the bike's front wheel. The head hit a wall and rolled away.

Cinder, gun up and smoking, looked not at her kill but at Alexander, now curled in a fetal position.

"Oh, my God," Emerson whispered in Urban's ear. "Oh, my God, oh, my God, oh, my God."

The woman holstered the gun, pushed the rumbling bike and its sidecar forward and, turning it ungainly, ripped out the gate.

Urban twisted the handlebars, and his bike leapt forward as if of its own will.

With a quick turn he sped after her.

"Oh, my God!" the Jabberjaw was still whining in his ear, loud enough to be heard over the roaring motor and the rushing wind.

"She had to do it!" snapped Urban as they jumped the curb and headed down the street. "It was him or us."

"You don't understand!" Emerson cried. "It wasn't loaded! She never loaded it!"

Chapter 7

With a wish and a sigh of resignation, Hawthorne logged into the Library of Alexandria. To his thinking there was little purpose in going there, but appearances were appearances; he could not expect to maintain his position without making an occasional venture into the soirees, salons, high teas, and *fetes* of the Virtual coterie.

At his command the program snapped into being and a creamy-white, Ludwigan chateau appeared before him, soaring upward, all height and grandeur. Fireworks leapt up from behind, splitting the night sky and showering sparkles over the needle tips of the towers. Below, oblivious to the distant booms of the exploding glory, swans ebony and alabaster drifted over cool reflections of themselves in a glassy pool.

The oak drawbridge came down, swift and sudden even as the iron portcullis flew up; the program, having scanned Hawthorne, was bowing to his cricket; he could enter.

A wind of spinning fairy dust captured him, lifting him off the ground and sucking him headlong into the castle's interior. The song "When You Wish Upon A Star," orchestrated to sound distinctly Wagnerian, swelled and rocketed him forward.

And then Executive Hawthorne, intimidating head of the Ksana family and known, in a whisper among the lowest castes as D-base, abruptly found himself seated in a floating, leather armchair before an enormous hearth of polished mahogany. The fire crackled and warmed him, smelling unerringly of pine. On the slick marble floors could be seen the duality of both his reflection and his inconstant shadow.

Unreality made chillingly, beautifully, almost flawlessly real. A masterpiece.

Hawthorne shut his eyes, distant emotions causing him to take in a brief, mental breath. Credit for the program, from gateway to the incredibly slick, distinctly leather-scented verisimilitude of the armchair was due entirely to his long-deceased niece. Her lost talent for creating VR programs still made Hawthorne, forty years later, feel like an apprentice looking at an old master.

Most annoying, his niece had added her own little touches, cleverly hiding them so that they were only discovered once the artwork was on display. Like that irritating little entrance drama with the castle which Hawthorne, despite years of trying, could neither bypass nor erase. No matter. It wasn't as if such jokes marred the magnificence of the program.

The Library of Alexandria was convention hall, parlor, adytum, and presence chamber for the Virtuals. The digital image had been modeled on Hagia Sophia with an Egyptian twist and a view like Machu Picchu. Dominated by sea-green marble and gold filigree, the structure sported infinite lengths of shelving overflowing with books, scrolls, and pamphlets. Tomes were everywhere, under tables and in nooks between the Tuscan columns. Amid all this "reality," corridors picturing each of the 1,497 currently running programs surrealistically opened and shut like windows. Librarians appeared from and vanished through the openings, followed by colophons, scuttling, spiderlike repair programs hunting down corrigendums and other viruses that could still plague the stacks.

There were no walls. Towering shelves, arches, and a vast dome above, but no walls. That was one of the aesthetic rules of Virtual Reality, that if there was a ceiling, there could be no walls, and if there were walls, there could be no ceiling.

There were glass windows, however, hanging in air, rose-colored and shedding light across fountains and mosaics; vast armchairs floated before the fireplace. There was even a bower enclosed within the frosted glass of eight French doors. But none of those doors led into the bower. Rather, each exited out of the library program into another infinite world.

Overhead, the enormous central dome hanging like the original, as if "suspended . . . from heaven," displayed a continuous, real-time video of the Earth as seen from one of the satellites. Hawthorne gazed up at it now and sighed. A pity his niece had refused to help him build his *Isle of Creation*! He was still adding touches to it that his niece would have instinctively programmed in from the first.

Which reminded him—

He pushed up from the armchair. Instantly, he was among the stacks; other patrons glanced up at him, nodding their deference to his rank before returning to their programs. Hawthorne reached, and the program he wanted leapt into his hand. It fell open, accessing his *Isle of Creation*. There on the pages he saw a woman currently wandering his *Thrill-Seekers Pathway of Fright and Phobias*. He smiled. He'd set this tableau in motion not moments before and was eager to see the results. Envisioning herself as a child with plaited hair, dressed in a plaid dress with a ridiculous bow on her Peter Pan collar, the woman was making her way through a dark, creaky house.

Hawthorne could feel the program running, an old but effective one. The polished floorboards groaned as if in pain, and, distantly, trucks rumbled over a bridge, their lights shining through dirty yellow windows. Good touches those sounds. Hawthorne was proud of them.

"Accessing five other stacks, Executive Hawthorne?"

"Not at all, Madame Sade." Hawthorne shut the book, one forefinger marking the page, and politely smiled at her.

Madame Sade's eyes widened. It was almost outrageously courteous of Hawthorne, an Executive, to put the flow of information on pause merely to address *her,* a mere Controller. Such total attention was wildly flattering, and M. Sade lapped it up. She drifted forward, a preening smirk pushing at the high cheekbones she was wearing.

She was sporting a Native American body: muscular, leggy, and tall, the black hair shiny, fine and streaming down to her hips. A silver-studded belt kept a panther skin locked about her hips, the head yowling out from her crotch. Matching panther-skin boots came up to flag about her knees. She was naked above the waist, as usual and, as usual, the breasts were magnificent.

Not unexpectedly, a lanky blond young man was at her side.

"Do you like my persona?" Madame Sade flashed a pair of long, sharp fangs. Other patrons, noting with envy Executive Hawthorne's eye contact with Sade, pointedly wrinkled their noses at the display. Hawthorne inwardly agreed. For most Virtuals the novelty of being able to wear a VR persona paled upon reaching adulthood. Hawthorne briefly wondered if Madame Sade, going on twenty-eight, would ever grow out of these fantasies; it might be interesting, he mused, to experiment and see what, if anything, could knock her free of them.

"I created this persona after visiting the *Erotic Ashram* on your *Isle of Creation*. I hear there's been some argument over your little playground, and I just wanted to advise you not to let anyone bully you! It saved my life. Really, it did!"

"I'm overjoyed to hear it. I created the ashram so that patrons could discover and live out desires necessary to the well-being of their psyches. It is my opinion that we Virtuals have, for too long, disavowed our more primitive urges. We use our special reality solely for expanding the mind, and the body, not to mention our creativity, suffers for it."

"Exactly!" Sade nodded proudly. "Do you know what I was able to be thanks to your ashram? A sexual Argus. Nothing but orifices, all of them simultaneously pleasured! Wasn't that creative?!"

D-base surreptitiously glanced to Madame Sade's brow. No matter the persona worn, the VR program always gave the image the same MSC implants as their wearers. Sade's silver cricket gleamed at her temple, naming her a *Per My Virt*, able to access up to three stacks—that is, to simultaneously glean and cross-reference information from three sources. Beside it, as Hawthorne had guessed, was the dark birthmark of a second implant. Madame Sade was sporting a Happy.

He pretended not to notice; it would have been in bad taste to point out that an MSC implant had helped to create her "oh-so-original" fantasy.

All this time, unbeknownst to Madame Sade, Hawthorne had been keeping track of the thrill-seeker girl. Long ago he'd discovered that underlings spoke more freely and deeply if they thought they had an Executive's total regard. Unfortunately, like any *Per Tout Virtual,* Hawthorne liked to access several texts simultaneously. So, he had come up with a way to crack open the book just wide enough to give the illusion that he had paused it.

The girl was now finding her way around dark scary corners, her polished Mary Jane shoes, the soles new and slippery, toeing their way forward. She came to the bathroom and reached out her hand to the door.

This time, Hawthorne pressed closed the pages, tight around his finger, really pausing the girl in her program—by not listening to Madame Sade, he could attend to both easily, but he was experiencing, at that moment, a rare feeling of suspense, and he wanted to analyze it.

"Have you met Moon-knife here?" Madame Sade had the young man's arm around her shoulders, one hand planted over her breast. Pipe-cleaner thin with blue eyes, the boy was wearing the persona of an elf, ears pointed, hair long and held back with a leather headband. He looked painfully embarrassed by what his companion was doing to him.

"An-an honor, sir," the youth said, trying to pull his hand from Madame Sade's nipple. "I've heard all about you. I've been thinking of applying for a trip to your *Isle of Creation,* but my father—not to offend, but he does not approve of it."

"Is that right?" D-base smiled politely. "Craig S., aren't you? Max's son?"

"Yes, sir, that's right. Thorstein family." The boy looked pleased, too pleased. A quick glance to Craig's right temple told all. There was the spot of an implant by his silver cricket. A Bashful, Hawthorne guessed. He wondered how raucous and rebellious the boy had been before his father implanted the MSC.

"Come on, Moon-knife." Madame Sade was looking annoyed. She hated being on the outside of a conversation. "Let's read up on torture chambers. Then, when we return to solid state, we can experiment."

The young man paled, but the Bashful implant made him too polite to refuse. He bowed to Hawthorne even as a door opened behind them, revealing a blur of copper, rust, and cobalt shapes, Virtuals transversing the net. Sade and Craig S. melted into the opening, and the tunnel vanished as completely as it had appeared.

Hawthorne stared at the empty-seeming space, reflecting that Craig's father, Max S., had always been a social climber. It seemed extreme and out of character, however, for the puritanical Max S. to subdue his son in order to sacrifice him to Madame Sade. It hinted at a certain amount of desperation. He would have to check his sources; if Craig were enough of an embarrassment, Max S. might be trying to push him off onto the Breke family. Madame Sade was especially good at getting her way with her family.

But that could wait. Hawthorne eyed his book, the program still paused. "Interesting," he murmured; why should he begin to experience apprehension at her entering a—

Ah! Of course. *The bathroom.* Urges he could no longer fully experience were especially intriguing. This particular biological urge with its compendium of imposed shame and social fears was basic to any child, and yet to him it had become mysterious, even fascinating.

He allowed the book to fall open, curious now as to which branch the program would take in accordance with the girl's sociopsycho makeup.

The old bathroom door cracked open, the white porcelain handle pressing down on its side. A mirror looked back at her, swung open from the cabinet and angled oddly on rusted hinges. Having opened the door, she faced not only herself but a reflection of the hall sinking back into a point singularly.

Drip. Drip. Drip. A leaky faucet. The girl glanced at the stained sink, but it was stone dry, crusts of lime on spigot and handles.

Shoes sliding over chipped, checkered tile; a glance into the half-drawn curtain surrounding the bath.

The body within was waxen, the eyes goggling out at her. From the severed throat blood trickled steadily.

Drip. Drip. Drip.

Adrenaline surge, blood-sugar drop. Was she going to faint?

She wet herself.

Typical.

D-base sighed, and slapped the book shut. He wished she had permitted the program to go in another direction, toward such fears as doors opening while defecating, or fear of filthy toilets.

Those reactions were far more complex and closely related to self-hate.

"Was that Madame Sade I saw you hobnobbing with?" The voice that asked was rich, deep, feminine.

"Singhutha," Hawthorne acknowledged, dropping the book, which vanished even as it fell. "I was merely keeping abreast of the *petite noblesse* ins and outs."

" 'Herself' must be strutting."

"Madame Sade always struts," D-base observed.

"You know she's really short, stocky. Hair's all wiry, and she's got this yellowish skin—"

"I know the real face of each and every Virtual. Including yours."

There was an ironic tilt to Singh's thin lips, an affectation that never seemed far from her face. But though she always seemed on the verge of a smile, her eyes remained still and hard. Though not beautiful, there was a hauteur about Singh that captured the eye. She was stretched out above the stacks, as if upon a divan;

dressed in a sable brocade that flowed and draped over her hip-heavy torso. The ultra-fashionable gown was indicative, especially after Madame Sade's juvenile clumsiness, of taste and brilliance. It was not easy to manipulate the program to replicate such fine delineations of pattern and texture. Her shiny black hair was brushed so that it fell heavily on the left side. A sharp triangle had been shaved into the right side, emphasizing, at the hypotenuse, the flashing diamond of her cricket.

"I gave up programming masks for myself when I was sixteen." Her voice was thick, almost a purr. "I'm afraid I don't understand the Madame Sade contingent."

"Das Ewig-Weibliche zieht uns hinan."

"What? The eternal feminine draws Madame Sade like Novalis's *blaue Blume*? Or is that a general commentary on the Faustian nature of all Virtuals?"

Hawthorne shrugged and strolled down the aisle. "Your question, not mine, Singh. The board preaches intellectual manifest destiny; sounds Faustian to me."

"But the illusory blue flower is on your *Isle of Creation*," another voice said.

D-base paused; a tabletop had appeared, set like a compass with four hovering chairs pointing the way down four separate aisles. The man at the table, Min, smiled a weathered, toothy grin at him. The bleached hair and tan face emphasized his beachfront origins.

"Join me?" Min asked.

Singh drifted to a chair, alighting upon it as delicate as a sparrow. With one finger she swept her hair behind her left ear. Hawthorne remained where he was, eyeing them both. The air was suddenly dangerous.

"Sit down, Hawthorne." It was Getty, of course. Where Min was, there was his Executive. Getty Nagata appeared out of the stacks and pointedly sat down, leaving only the chair opposite him free. Serious Asian eyes glared at Hawthorne out of a copper brown face. "Now, if you please."

With a shrug, Hawthorne seated himself. The chair felt hard and cool. He leaned back and crossed his legs. "Is this an official board meeting? If so, where are the others?"

"*Zeitgeist,* Hawthorne." Singh's voice dripped with irony. "No one else seems to be worried."

"Then, why, might I ask, are you three?"

"Because we know what you're doing, Hawthorne," Getty fairly snarled. "No one else wants to believe it. Or is it that you have them tightly wrapped and securely tucked away in your pockets? If we probe deeply enough, will we find you blackmailed, bought, or bribed them?"

Hawthorne sighed. "You really should learn to specify, Nagata."

A miniature of an island, generically complete with palm trees and sand beaches, to that appeared upon the table—Getty's mocking answer. "My predecessor warned the board against allowing family Ksana to train their agents in the Orange Kingdom. It would give Ksana access to our precious programmers, she pointed out, and begged them to reconsider. No one listened to her. Prophetic as Cassandra. You bribed one of the Children of the Mainframe to create your *Isle* for you, didn't you?"

Hawthorne smiled languidly. "Just one?"

"Did you really think you could get away touting this monster as a harmless fantasy? A long untapped use of our Virtual Reality?" There was a high-strung quality about Getty, like an animal too finely bred. The silken simplicity of his elegant black suit and black shirt only emphasized his fragility.

"Isn't that what it is?"

"Inducing Children of the Mainframe to engineer

programs for any purpose other than the geometric expansion of our database is heretical, Hawthorne!"

"I wrote the program myself."

"And that program is stealing memory away from our net!"

"We've nine million, twenty-five thousand, nine hundred and twenty-five terrabytes worth. I rather think there's some left over in the warehouses for me and my little fantasy."

"Not that you ever asked the families if you could borrow any," Singh remarked.

"And it's seducing our collegians away from the Library!" Getty hammered; the miniature island disappeared, white numbers replacing it. Hawthorne was disturbed to find the statistics almost accurate. So Getty really did know whereof he spoke.

"Stats say upwards of sixty percent of our adolescents are immersed in the mental filth of your *Isle*. That's at this very moment, Hawthorne. And forty-three of those will go gallivanting out among the Grinders afterward, no research, cross-referencing or work."

Hawthorne shrugged. "Simple, innocent play. All children need it."

A faint, icy smile. The numbers melted into a face, thin and shy with black hair. "Then, you ought to be willing to take responsibility for what happened to Dresden."

"*Humani nil a me alienum puto,*" Hawthorne pointed out with a sigh; how like Getty to be so dramatic. He flicked his hand, and the young man's face disappeared. "What Dresden did may seem alien to you, but it was merely human."

"He was on his way to being a *Tout* before he joined your Weeklies!" Getty leaned in; despite the utter blackness of his eyes, they seemed to be blazing. "Against his Executive's orders, he deserted his family, his studies, to play in Solid State, to get high wired in the Red Line tunnels while making love to five similarly drugged Grinders!"

"A trinity of disgrace," Singhutha drawled, "disobedience to an Executive, destruction of the mind, and indulgence in unprotected, lower-caste sex. And then, to add insult to injury, he ended up dying down there." She tsked mockingly. "Faust was tempted, and hell was waiting."

"He wasn't a minor. At twenty years of age, he was perfectly capable of making a choice."

"Please, Hawthorne, don't play Larvae." Min shook his head, good-natured face frowning. "You're a Black-Magic Wizard, and you know full well what you're doing. We know, too. We also know you've been doing some esoteric experiments on your *Isle*. Lucky for you they've been with Grinders or the board would have been all over you by now."

"You make it all sound so sinister. What motive might I have for this Dr. Moreau activity?"

Singh snorted delicately. "You have the wrong director, Executive. You're not Erle C. Keaton; try Eisentein."

"Using the most important of all arts to bring equality, fraternity, etcetera, to the masses? I see. You think I want to hand power over to the workers? How very naive of me."

"Not exactly." Getty's words came out tersely, through the teeth. "You don't want to be Lenin, you just want to publish a *Social Contract*."

"I'm not sure I understand your focus behind *that* reference," Hawthorne said softly. A lie and they all knew it, but he wanted the accusation out in the open.

"You want the general will to rule; the caste system can stay so long as everyone gets a vote—and a chance to move up in the world. Don't you know such revolutions are passé?"

"That may well be, but the very existence of the Virtuals as a class creates its own dialectical antithesis. So long as we have sovereign rule, we're easy targets for mob violence."

"What? You think *our* mindless mob has the same pitchforks and flintlocks as we do?" This time Getty sneered outright. His fine, arrogant hands twitched across the table. "Wake up, Hawthorne! We have helicopters, lasers, satellites, laboratory viruses—They have a couple of revolvers. You tell me who's going to win."

"You forget the Brainiacs."

They laughed at him; all three.

"The Brainiacs couldn't fit together a revolution if every American named Franklin and Nikola Tesla himself were to brainstorm with them," Getty snidely informed him. "But you're evading the issue. The question is why do you want to share the shit instead of the wealth? Our kids are going *to them*, and your *Isle* is *their* filth, not *our* wealth. Our wealth is *here*."

"Let's say I see it as a vital élan, the Dylan Thomas force that will sizzle its way through the green fuse to our hypothetical *blaue Blume*. Evolution."

"And so we circle right back to Goethe." Singh sighed and got to her feet. "How tiresome."

"What are the towers for, Hawthorne?" Min asked softly. And suddenly, there they were, floating above the table, graphic representations, exact down to the number of girders.

D-base stared at the structure—*null lines,* as he thought of them, silvery black—caught by surprise, for once in a very rare while. This changed the configuration. These three were sharper than he had supposed, and far more deadly.

"You and family Lise," Getty picked up, "have been thick as gravy. What are these towers you've been having them build? They're not transmitters, we know that."

"They're for tracking," Hawthorne confessed, a half truth. "Crowd control."

"The fuck they are." Getty rose out of his chair like an offended ghost. He swept an arm across the table, breaking the tower apart. "Let's try some straight talk, Executive. Your little playground is anything but. It stinks, and I'm following every whiff of it that comes my way. You better believe if anything, *anything at all*, happens to a minor that even remotely resembles what happened to Dresden, I'll have you up on charges: gross negligence and reckless endangerment are only the tip of the iceberg.

"And I would start to think about whether or not you'd care to take us a little further into your confidence—that is, if there *is* anything innocent or positive about what you're doing. If not, then think about what you'll do robbed of family Sikorsky's air transportation or how you'll ever be able to run your little experiments without Holists from family Nagata."

"Now, which of us is involved in blackmail? And on record yet, Executive Getty!" Hawthorne's tone dripped with mock outrage. "You cannot remove my privileges without a two-third's vote of the board. When it looks like you might get it, come speak to me again. I might be more willing to be intimidated. Good day to you all."

Getty glared at him. The doorway that opened behind the Asian-eyed Executive was very dark; and Getty, in a manner that was both arrogant and defiant, dropped through it, as if daring Hawthorne to "fall" after him. Min, shaking his head at the sorry state of it all, followed after his Executive. Singhutha remained for a moment, ironic smile playing at her thin lips.

"I'd watch that hubris, Hawthorne," she said, twirling weightlessly up from the chair. Her dress swung and swished with a realism that was as beautiful as an aria perfectly sung. "*Sturm und Drang,*" she added, rising ever upward into an opening that gleamed like gold and smelled of violets. "Desiring the primitive over the civilized is an adolescent sentiment; it runs out of energy as the teenagers run out of youth— unless, of course, you're Madame Sade."

Hawthorne watched her go, saw the gleam of a toe ring as the bottoms of her clean, bare feet vanished and the door shut. Aimlessly, he rubbed his fingertips over the tabletop. It felt as cool and as smooth as Solid State. Singhutha was correct in one thing, he was going to have to watch his hubris. It would be danger- ous to get too confident. Those three might very well try to kill him.

And wouldn't that be interesting.

Chapter 8

"She's right, you know."

Hawthorne looked up. It was Filo; he was floating cross-legged above the table, a brandy-colored young man with spiked hair. His costume, like his hair, was staggeringly unfashionable, consisting of flannel shorts and a plaid, hooded shirt with blue-striped sleeves. But then Filo was one of the noblesse d'épée, owner of a diamond cricket and so could eat with whatever fork he liked—or none if he preferred.

"Is she?" Hawthorne asked.

Filo smirked. "About Madame Sade."

"Ah."

"Put you through the ringer, did they?" Filo settled onto the tabletop. It melted and twisted into a wide mattress with shiny sheets. The pearl-colored material shimmered, and yielded up plump cushions of blood velvet and sapphire damask.

"In a manner of speaking," Hawthorne agreed. "To summarize, they accused me of viewing the Virtuals as Faustian and tyrannical, of Socratically corrupting the youth by making them want the base physical reality of Solid State instead of the lofty intellectualism of VR, and of plotting some sort of equalizing revolution."

"Ah, so that's what you're doing." Filo smiled and snuggled in among the pillows. "Does that mean you'll be joining us this weekend?"

"Filo—"

"We're running a crosstown marathon."

"I see no point in leaving the comfort and safety of my home for the dangers of the streets, no matter how stimulating threats to my life might be."

"Reality, Hawthorne." Filo grinned. "Gravity, mass, limits, up and down." He pointed out each direction. "You don't taste it once in a while, you forget it."

"That," Hawthorne said with emphasis, "is the idea."

"You're a hypocrite."

"Not at all. The old always send the young to war. By the by, do you know the young gentleman Madame Sade is currently torturing? Craig S.?"

"Is that why you're here today? To scope him out?" He shook his rag-doll head. "Too late. Daddy made him a Boy Scout."

"Yes, I saw. Do you think you can get him to a Holist and have the Bashful removed?"

"Without his father knowing? That's a tall order."

"Do it anyway."

"And after he's chip free?"

"If he's rebellious and smart, recruit him. If he's just obnoxious, have the Bashful reimplanted."

"As my Executive commands. Anything else your CM can do?"

"I want you to sound out the Nagata family. Chat with some of their staff about—" He stopped, freezing in movement as well as word. Before him, floating where only he could see, was the triangular pager of his secretary.

Filo scowled. "An emergency?"

"It's Blake," he said, which was answer enough, and
stood. "Log off," he said, and the library broke apart,
colors and books seeming to fly away from him. For
a second he was surrounded by the program's exit:
psychedelic lettering spelling out "Good-bye" while a
Hendrix-style version of "It's a Small World" sounded
around him. And then he was out and in the gray
static of a dead zone.

Quite a sense of humor his niece had had.

The triangle was still flashing.

"On," he invited, and there was Blake. Blake had
a large, heavy head that wobbled unsteadily upon a
thin neck and round, dark eyes presently locked forward. His equally dark hair was slicked conservatively
back, almost flat upon his head. As always, he was
dressed in a long-sleeved white shirt with a thin black
tie. He was never late, never impolite, and when he
gave his attention, he gave it utterly and completely.
He was the most mechanical man D-base knew.

"Alexander has been taken," Blake said, just like
that. No lead-in, no hesitation, excuses, or apologies,
no sweating, no stuttering. His white face registered a
fraction more pale and his blood pressure one degree
above the usual eighty-five, that was all.

"Alexander! Taken!?"

"Just after supplies were dropped, the power went."

D-base frowned. He had an almost uncontrollable
urge to say that that was impossible, even though the
evidence clearly argued otherwise. "And so the ceiling
stayed open," he surmised, finger tapping at his chin.

"I tried to order the helicopter back, but all I got
was white noise."

"You sent a patrol," Hawthorne said, not a
question.

"Immediately. The patrol leader arrived first—a
shotgun took his head off."

"A shotgun?" *Stranger and stranger!* "And the perpetrators got away."

"On motorcycles." Blake's heavy, round head dropped ever so slightly with shame. "I confess that I did not anticipate either an armed or motorized break out."

"No, you merely assumed that Alex's servant would, at best, take this remarkable opportunity to find a way to get them out onto the roof. Rational, given the circumstances, but incredibly shortsighted of you."

Blake's face went a little gray. His pulse jumped to the remarkable speed of ninety. "I shall have myself eliminated, of course."

"You will do no such thing!" D-base snapped. "I haven't time to replace you. What's happening now?"

"Helicopters are searching the highways, and patrols are on the lookout."

"I want both Alex and his companion, Urban, recovered—unharmed! Get Kelly on this! If anyone can track him down, she can! I'll download the specifics."

"Yes, sir." Blake reached to sign off, then stopped; it was the first time Hawthorne had ever known him to hesitate.

"Yes?" D-base raised a curious brow.

"The error will not be repeated, sir," Blake said. "You have my most abject apologies."

D-base shook his head. "They are *not* accepted. Get to work."

"Yes, sir." Blake vanished.

Alexander escaped! Broken out. Astonishing! D-base thought back over forty years and more of careful, meticulous planning. He must get the boy back before a glitch formed or, worse, before Alexander's experiences erased everything.

His mind flickered, alighting on the program that was looking after 203 virtual dreams simultaneously occurring on the *Isle of Creation,* one of them the woman who had envisioned herself a child in an old house. He noted emotional responses, brain waves, and chemical reactions. The program was working to refine the images, to make them as perfect as Hawthorne's niece had made her Library of Alexandria.

Meanwhile, the computer running that program searched for a satellite, a mythic satellite Hawthorne had only recently discovered was still in the sky.

Without Alex and Urban, finding the satellite would be quite pointless. They had to be recovered, and soon!

Chapter 9

"Are you comfortable?" The woman was speaking to Alexander, shouting at him over the deafening rush of wind and the rumbling drone of the machine.

It was horrible, astonishing, and it was *Real*.

Out through the roof and onto the other side, Alexander thought wildly, heart pounding in his ears. *The twin half of the mask, the microcosm, adrift; personal id to the right, collective unconscious to the left. Bardo.* He blinked furiously against the wind. *Bardo. Tibetan. Dead and wandering between a former life and the next.*

The city flashed by, as if reaching out its gleaming arms.

As what am I being reborn?

Sounds were hitting his ear oddly, washed away before he could hear them or, as with the louder ones, distantly, fearfully repeated. *Echoes,* he realized. *Reverberations,* like smells, layered foul and sweet. He was most sensitive to the smells. Why?

Because, idiot, your air was filtered! he thought, swallowing again and again.

Outside. I'm out. Out. Out. Out.

Cold. So frosty cold, his teeth were chattering. Not like the inside of a refrigerator unit or the cool of the loft in winter. This was piercing. He could barely keep his eyes open, and his ears and nose hurt.

Cold and dark, so incredibly dark! Only the head-light of the motorcycle defined their way.

Was Urban still behind them?

His stomach would not hold still. Somewhere he remembered, as a child, being swung and spun gig-glingly about. But this was different; he clutched, sweaty-handed to the edges. And the bone-rattling vi-bration, the noise of the motorcycle—

"There's a blanket down by your feet, there. Do you see it? Right there beside the thermos." The woman had an odd sense to her; she wasn't a *blank* like Urban, rather she seemed fluid. When she'd touched him, there on the roof, her fantasies had pooled into him and then bled right out. He knew only that she wanted something from him.

And that scared him worse than anything.

"I told Ethelred to fill the thermos with hot choco-late," she continued, briefly glancing up at the sky, "but I don't think he did."

What was she looking at? Sander looked up, then he heard it; it had been in the background for a while, he realized.

A helicopter.

"Scared?"

He caught Cinder's sidelong look, all black goggles and a strange, mocking smile.

"Of what?" he asked back, but his words were ripped away by the wind.

"Hang tight!" They careened around a corner. Al-exander grabbed in a panic for the opposite edge of the car, sure he'd be thrown.

Up ahead loomed a dumpy building. Branded along its side was the neon red warning: "THRIFT."

"End of the line!" Cinder announced, and shot them plunging down a wide black drive toward a pair of double doors.

Alexander nearly wet his pants.

The doors flew open. The cycle and sidecar bounded up, weightless, and then crashed down into—

Track lighting, flashing mirrors, acoustic music crooning like pigeons. There were tables, couches, milling bodies, and shelving to the ceiling along the edges of a huge room ten times the size of his loft.

The motorcycle came to an abrupt halt, almost tossing Alexander into the car's short windshield. The edges slid under his hand, he grappled for purchase, then froze, his heart seizing up as, behind, the second bike roared straight at him.

"Look out!" someone cried. There was a long screech, and the second bike came to a stop nose to tail with the sidecar.

"Beautiful!" Urban crowed, knocking down the bike's center stand. "Smooth as a fifty-dollar Porsche."

"Glad you like it," Cinder said, dismounting from her cycle.

Emerson groaned. "Could have gotten us killed! Not that that matters to you or her! And who really cares if it matters to me—"

"Alex?" Sander watched Urban's boots as they hurriedly approached. He could feel the perspiration seeping out across his brow, as if misting there. His Web mask felt like a sponge.

What was he doing here?

"Sander! Sander?" Curly brown hair, round friendly face, gray eyes.

Alexander nabbed hold of Urban's arm. *Companion.* He thought. *Shouldn't get close, can't get close.*

Companions are not meant to be permanent. Get close, try to keep them, and you kill them.

A wave of old and terrible guilt, the memory of a tall, reedy woman, skin the color of strong, hot tea; a white Web mask. She used a skin cream that smelled of lemons, and she had the softest voice he'd ever heard. Memory of a woman lying cold and silent.

I did not mean to kill you, he was panting now, emotions churning. *Forgive me. Forgive me.*

"Hey, Sander," Urban said, "it's all right—"

Alex started, realizing then that he was clutching Urban's arm. A tremor ran through him.

Does he care? How can he care? Sander wondered, releasing the arm.

"It's not all right, you know." That was Emerson, appearing behind the Sierra. "You're with us now. We shoot unloaded guns, we let our lives be put in danger by absentminded myths, we careen about at high speeds and, most depressing of all, we haven't any coffee."

"Cheery fellow, aren't you?" Urban snorted, gray eyes flickering over the larger motorcycle. "One smooth machine. Your lady's got good travel sense."

"Straight from the Sierra's mouth." The dark-haired man smirked, but he seemed disturbed. He looked back at Cinder, who was checking over the smaller bike. "She's not my lady," he said.

Alexander's mind kicked in, despite all the shocks, and he *finally* took a good look at Cinder. She had a faint, dimpled smile on her face—a pleasant face, nothing to be afraid of. But Emerson was obviously afraid. Or perhaps nervous was a better word. Alex frowned. Cinder's eyes were almost unnaturally bright. She looked . . . she looked . . .

Damn! He shook his muddled head. Too shaken up, couldn't think—

"So," Emerson said directly to Alexander, pushing

his round glasses higher up on the bridge of his nose, "*you're* what all the fuss is about. Can't say I'm impressed."

"Caffeine addicted, orally fixated," Sander heard himself say past still chattering teeth. "What could impress you beyond a well-baked bran muffin?"

Emerson stiffened, and Alexander smiled bitterly. *Never let them undercut you. Never. It's too easy for them to hurt you. Far too easy.*

"Actually," Emerson drawled, "procuring a cup of coffee in this desolate place, would—"

"We don't serve coffee here," announced a petite blonde. She came striding up to them dressed in *Michiko Koshino* combat leggings, shorts, and a *Calvin Klein* sleeveless tee. Three nylon Fanny sacks were belted to her, one at the hip, one at the shoulder, and one under the right breast. This combative attire was unhinged by the fact that her bright hair was in pigtails and her little-girl face was freckled. A pair of pink sunglasses with plastic daisies dangled from around her neck. "You know that, Emerson. I don't know why you'd want to interfere with the blood flow to your brain, anyway."

"No, I don't suppose you would," Emerson quipped.

"Instead of coffee, why not try some of our hallucinogenics? We've a special on hallucinogenics," she explained cheerfully. "And I just made up a fresh batch of mixed jive—Oh, hello, Cinder! How did the motorcycles work out?"

"Wonderfully!" Cinder rose from where she had been crouching, near the smaller bike's wheels. She came around to warmly shake hands. "You know, Strawberry, I don't know anyone who looks quite so fresh and cheerful as you. Those injections under the skin have really done wonders!"

78 *Janine Ellen Young*

The girl dimpled with pleasure. "Do you think? I've been using lightbulb filaments."

"Very creative."

"Would you like some?" Strawberry called loudly over her shoulder, "Hey! Have we any more filaments?"

There was movement, and Alex saw—

People!

People crowded onto Naugahyde couches, people arguing, moving game pieces, scratching out formulas on chalkboards or milling about Formica picnic tables cluttered with glinting piles of silver chips, tiny wires, and Plexiglas frames. There were pyramids of dissected televisions, disk players, and computers. And there were children, a dozen of them, huddled before a screen, eyes locked on the silvery black-and-white images of a silent movie.

Elsewhere, Alex realized, numbly amazed, *I'm somewhere else! Not at home, not anymore, not there.*

So much clutter and chaos. *And so many people!* Never in his life had Alexander been so close to such a crowd. The smell was different: sweat and plastic, and the reek of chemicals cooking. He ought to have been shaking with fear; strangely, he wasn't. Perhaps it was the children, their clean fragrance, the overlarge teeth in their smiles. A gnawing memory, brief, ached at the back of his mind: himself at six, watching children at play on laser disc. And later, climbing on a chair, trying to peer through the slats at the real children he heard laughing by the fence, daydreaming of calling to them, asking them to join him or maybe, just maybe, going down—

I want to go down and play. Won't you please let me go down? He'd tapped out on his computer, begged of the hidden cameras he'd known were watching him even then.

His companion of that time, the softhearted Moll,

had baked him brownies and, moist-eyed, told him fairy stories. Alexander had thrown a glass of milk across the room, and smashed the brownies underfoot.

And been sorry for it ever afterward.

He shook his head. *Drifting.* He couldn't let his mind wander, not here. He was lost enough. He heard odd noises, looked to the very back of the long, vast hall; a mirrored ball spun overhead while a man played Frank Sinatra music on a bass.

"Hey!" the blond girl again shouted to the people. "Filaments?"

"Out," a few called. "We're all out."

"Rats and alligators!" Alex heard Urban mutter. "Do you know where we are?!"

"Bardo," Alexander whispered.

"Spock's Lounge!" Urban pointed to the far wall. Papering the entire wall was a photograph of a man with pointed ears, one hand raised and split in salutation. "This is the Man and Superman Bar for Brainiacs! What are we doing here?"

"I went looking for Noel in the place where you said he'd be," Cinder said to the blonde. "Couldn't find him."

"There you are," Emerson tossed back. "We're looking for Noel."

Urban tossed up a rude gesture. "Slink back into the Closet, Jabberjaw."

Surrender to your darkest dreams, Alexander found himself thinking, an old Web prayer. He'd stopped the prayers after Christine died. Now, however, he felt the prayers returning, running through him like an underground river.

"Yeah, I'm sorry about that," Strawberry said. "He actually came by here to grab a few bottles of pills and say he wouldn't be at the usual spot this week, and then"—she made a zooming motion with her hand—"gone! But he mentioned something about stopping by the bazaar to trade with the Salaams."

"When's that?"

"Tomorrow. You can stay with us tonight if you like."

Cinder nodded, pleased, it seemed. "We'd like, thank you. And I'd better stock up while I'm here."

"I can give you a really good deal on nitrous oxide, opiates," she said. "Crystal meth—"

"Creative, but I think we'd better stick to the brain boosters and uppers."

"Well, there's always your garden variety amphetamines."

"That'll do."

The blonde unfolded her sunglasses and set them on her nose. Alex noticed then that she wore upon her thumb and forefinger what looked to be tiny finger cymbals of gray plastic.

"Will a standard hundred do?"

"Make it one-fifty," Cinder decided. "You know what they say, 'Better too high than too low.' That's one of Ethelred's favorites." She said this to Alexander with an almost hypnotic flash of perfect, white teeth.

"One-fifty." Strawberry tapped her finger cymbals together, head lifted, sunglasses gleaming in the track lights. "Give you an equal number of opiates in case you want to come down?"

"Good thinking."

"Hydergine? Vasopressin?"

"Oh, yes, yes indeed. Couldn't leave without a good supply of vasopressin."

"Vasopressin!" Urban shook his head, "Why do we—?"

"Corpus collosum connection, Urban," Alexander said irately; he was beginning to feel jittery, like a wire strung too tight and plucked. "Communication between brain halves enhanced. Increases in reflexes, memory, and calculation. The amphetamines will speed up the process as well. Can't you see that?"

"You could let me ask!"

"Where would be the challenge in that?" Alex responded tartly, even as a portion of him winced and hissed that it was wrong to be so rude, so unkind to this last companion.

Last.

"How about some Yaga shakes?" Strawberry asked Cinder.

"I don't—"

"We've got a Bavarian mint flavor that's to die for."

"Bavarian mint? Really? How novel."

"Not that they'd have a cappuccino flavor," Emerson complained.

"Bavarian mint!" Cinder seemed quite taken with that, surrealistically so. "Bavarian mint. I would like to write that down—" She dove into the sidecar, searching, forcing Alexander to shift so far back he started to slide up.

She came up with a silver thermos in hand. Lifting it to her ear, she shook it and grinned. "Seems I was dead wrong; Ethelred remembered to fill it! Oh, say, Alex, have you met"—she turned to the girl—"ah, no, I don't suppose you have. Alex, this is Strawberry Fields, Strawberry, this is Alexander. We just broke him out of the warehouses down by the freeway—"

"Alexander?" The girl pulled off her glasses. Odd to hear two voices speaking his name instead of just one. "You don't mean—"

"That's why we needed your wonderful motorcycles, to make a quick getaway. I'm afraid the King players are after us. I suppose I should have mentioned that right off. Alexander is rather important to them, you see. Which is why we need to talk to your friend Noel."

"Alexander . . ." she whispered, as if in shock. Did she know of him? How could she? "You got Alexander! *The* Alexander!" Strawberry turned and shouted back at the room, making him jump, "Cinder got Alexander! Come look! She got *him*!!!"

Bodies moved, forms rose from couches.

"No shit?"

"Trying to jerk us off, Strawberry?"

"You're kidding—"

And suddenly, they were coming at the motorcycle. *People.*

Female fragrance, male sweat. He recognized the smells, but never, never had they been so strong! Alexander caught his breath as the world turned topside down. Bodies and faces and the reek of strangers. He shrunk down into himself. *There couldn't be so many people. All in one place, all near him. Between worlds, living and dead.*

Bardo.

Oh, God.

"I have to get home," he heard himself whimper; how many people knew all about him? *And what did they want of him?* "My computer programs, my sketches . . . ?"

Emerson's eyes, magnified from behind their round lenses, shifted, not sardonically but with pity.

"How hard it must be for you," Alex heard him mumble as the crowd descended. They all wore pouches or pocketed vests and sunglasses. Most had an up-pointing arrow tattooed on their left biceps.

"Hey—" Urban moved to guard Alexander, but the people slid around.

"Maitreya!" one haled Alex.

"Oh, come on, he can't be!" said another.

"What do you think, Fraudster, he's a neural hormonal experience?"

"What's with the Web mask? *Real* Mandelbrots aren't into Virtual castration!"

"Hey, lay off!" Urban shoved a man back. And Alexander sunk down lower, fearing their touch, their fantasies, their combined presences.

"Yo! Po-mo!" a slender Latino woman pushed at Urban in return. "No need to be rude. Grumpy implant?"

"Long night," Cinder responded.

"He's not the only one," Emerson said loudly, pointedly, and to no effect.

"Scientific method number one, Siddartha." A woman with polished black skin leaned in on Alexander and, before he could jerk back, slipped her glasses onto his head. "Test to make sure your identity is not ersatz."

Close to panic now, Alexander grabbed to the glasses, then blinked with astonishment. On the interior side of the lenses, floating before his eyes, was a computer program.

"Where's the bug, boyfriend?"

"Get off him!" Urban snapped, and the glasses were jerked from the Web's face.

"No—" Sander cried and reached for them, standing and almost toppling from the sidecar. His heart was racing. There were spots before his eyes.

Rebirth was being held hostage in Urban's fisted hand.

"I'm not going to tell you people again—"

"Urban!" Alexander shouted, and his companion twitched back as if they were still in the loft, still where Sander called the shots. "Urban," he lowered his voice, fighting the grinding urgency, "give me those glasses, now!"

Lightning flashed behind the gray eyes: anger, defiance, resentment.

Urban could smash the glasses, Alexander realized,

and leave him; they were on the outside now, where Alex had no control, where his will could be questioned. Urban could do that, but he mustn't—the companion had a role in this fantastic play, a part with lines and reactions all scripted.

If Urban left, Alexander would be trapped in this in between, surrounded by gods and dreams, drifting, unborn. Cinder might be his guide, but Urban was his anchor.

"Urban—" he heard himself ask.

The glasses were back in his hands, candy-stripe frames and black lenses. He pushed them onto his face. Stared and shivered with emotion.

"It's a computer." He swallowed, and felt tears rising. "A computer."

"Uh-oh," someone said. "Techno-fetishism rears its ugly head."

Over the top of the glasses, Alexander saw Urban swing at the speaker and make contact.

"Hey!"

There was a scuffle. Sander half saw it. But the fearsome power of the outside, the smells, people, noise, and movements had been supplanted by the wonder before his eyes.

A computer the size of a pair of glasses. A screen he could take with him anywhere. A private, personal, and highly advanced computer. The tears rolled down his face.

"Cinder," he heard himself say.

"Alexy." He could smell her, leaning in. He was already able to distinguish her heat from others, the electric current that seemed to leap between them when she was close. It wanted to enfold him, that current, and absorb his every mental spark.

"Cinder—"

"Your friend Urban is an excellent if unoriginal

fighter. A crowd of Brainiacs armed with syringes, and all he can think to do is leap and kick."

"It might be a good idea to tell them not to kill him," Emerson suggested. "I hate his driving, but I still prefer it to my own."

"Cinder," Alexander tried again; it was odd to say her name, to know that he had several names he could call. "Cinder," he touched onto the sunglasses, "I must have this!"

"Of course you must," Cinder said, and he caught a glimpse of her smile over the rim. "The Brainiacs would never let you leave without one. Brainiacs are revolutionaries."

"Revolutionaries?"

"Tech-revolutionaries. Fighting against the tyranny of the Virtuals." Again he saw her pleased smiled. "Just like us, Alexy. Just like you and me."

Chapter 10

"Your target," Blake stated, pressing a photograph
into Kelly's hand as she descended from the train. She
pushed her way through the knot of passengers, coffee
brown hair loose about her shoulders. Her eyes, charcoal colored like those of her migrant mother, adjusted to the interior of the station. Lights swung from
the cathedral ribbing overhead, and strobes pulsed impatiently over the locomotive's gleaming windshield.

As per instructed, she was dressed like a Corporate
Inferface, her petite frame almost swallowed up in a
shiny gray blouse, black skirt, and black stockings. The
color of the stockings hid her short, muscular legs; her
implants, three shiny tabs—two to the right, one to
the left—were buried under very careful makeup and
bangs of dark hair. All of which combined was making
her sweat like crazy. Her temperature always ran a
little hot, and she fervently hoped that her *real* disguise would be a good deal cooler.

"A Web, huh?" she murmured, scanning the photo
while mentally knocking her Doc implant into total
recall. One final, holistic glance at the picture; then

she crumpled it, causing the chemicals on its glossy surface to catch. She dropped it into a trash barrel; it flashed and crumbled into ash.

All right, Doc, she thought, *let's see it again,* and in her mind the image instantly reappeared: a holographic photo showing a youth from several angles, both with and without a Web mask that she assumed was characteristic of him.

"Arrogant," she said, playing the word-association game, "afraid, brilliant." The Doc implant caught the sounds and attached them to the photo. She knew they were valid; her instincts had a ninety-seven percent accuracy level.

"Did you get the file I sent you on the Mainframer?" she asked Blake.

"I got it," her Anchor said shortly. As always, Blake looked like a simple secretary for upper management. But she saw that there was a wrinkle in his black silk tie, and a hair out of place; that disturbed her.

She said, "He knocked out his sensors by rigging up a Van de Graaff generator. Sent an electric charge through himself."

"Your subject's name is Alexander Julunggul Damaxion Kitatimate," Blake interrupted, which caused her to frown. Why wasn't he listening to her?

"What about the Mainframer?" she demanded. *Damn if Blake was going to stonewall her on this!* "*Madre Dios!* That's the ninth defection we've had this year! Something has to be done!"

"Here." He pressed a tiny chip into her palm. She scowled, but touched it to her temple with practiced ease. She felt it make contact with the disguised implant; a faint, electric shock, and then she dropped the chip. It flashed silver on the pavement, erased and useless now, she knew, but she still made sure to crush it underfoot.

"Always pulverize used chips," Blake had once told

her. *"You never know when their programs to erase will fail, or when the programmer has forgotten to write one."*

Need that image back, Doc. She knew she oughtn't personalize her implants, but having spent a good deal of time at the Kingdom, she couldn't help it. Given how many times her implants had saved her ass, she felt justified in thinking of them as her friends. The picture was back, clear in her mind, and with it, all information on the Web Executive Hawthorne wished her to have.

"Alexander," she said aloud, attaching the name. The face was young, daunting, though not in the same way as other, daunting targets. In her time she'd gone after and nabbed Ice-Cream Men, Yeltsins, and Holists. It was humbling to be given such assignments.

She scanned the information. Still an eerie experience that, to have facts never learned just appear in the mind. She had to remind herself at such times that the knowledge was in the microscopic filaments of the implants, not in the organic folds and crevices of her brain.

"Mainframers always escape," Blake said suddenly, uneasily. "Nature of the beast. Tell them they can't leave, and they have to see if there's a way to escape."

"As an ex-Sierra, I can tell you you're wrong," Kelly said, wincing as they stepped out into the sunlight. Her heels went from a tapping to a grinding sound upon the old, broken tarmac. "Damn it, Blake, some of those poor bastards haven't been outside the Orange Kingdom since they turned fourteen. The Kingdom's big, but when you're confined there, it gets awfully small, awfully quick. This isn't a simple Mainframer's challenge; if it were, everyone that left would come right back. You think a Mainframer's going to skip out on comfort, continuity, and his precious computer to live among the Grinders??"

"Did you raid the Brainiacs looking for them?"

"More times than I can count. They always seem to know when we're coming," Kelly admitted, and braced herself. She expected Blake to take her to task over the shoddy security, to ask her why she'd yet to find and collar one of these missing Mainframers. But he only nodded and led them toward Olvera Street.

"It doesn't matter," he said at last. "A couple of—"

"We're not talking a couple, we're talking nine, Blake! That's double from last year!!"

A faint flush touched Blake's cheeks; that was all there was to indicate that he, too, found the situation embarrassing.

"They don't matter," he insisted.

"Don't matter?! Every one of them was a genie, the kind that'd sell their souls for two seconds on the Virtual net. They're somewhere in the LA basin trying to break into Executive Cyberspace; I'd stake my life on that."

"Later," Blake said shortly. "This mission has priority."

"But—"

"Executive's orders."

That silenced her. She swallowed and nodded. "Yes, sir."

Uncomfortable, Kelly focused in on Alexander again. Her target. Her only concern for now. His image seemed to stare at her, brilliance in his eyes. She could feel how special and rare he was. An orphan, the dossier told her. He'd found a mother substitute once, but lost her. Still searching for the father figure.

Kelly winced. Hell. Of all the connections between them, that was one she'd rather not have made.

A Bell 58C Juiwa was waiting for them at the freeway on the ramp. The wind from its cycling blades whipped up Kelly's hair, and she blinked against the dust storm that surrounded it. Merchants from Olvera Street and their curious customers cringed back from it, eyeing it like a monster.

Blake hustled them into the cramped, insulated cabin. With a hefty slam, the copilot rolled the doors shut, then climbed into the cockpit. The helo's tail rose up, and, with a sudden, nose-dip takeoff, knocked Kelly's center of gravity right out of her.

Holding tight to her chair, she fought the vertigo, reasserting balance into her ears and lower back with a shake of the head. The helo's nose came up, then steadied, smooth and almost quiet. And through the window, the city gave way to a clear blue sky.

The vertigo vanished, and Kelly found herself fighting a grin.

Mary Mother of Jesus, how she loved helos! Couldn't get enough of them. She dreamed of the day she'd rank high enough to fly everywhere by helo.

"This man may or may not be with Alexander." Blake swiveled to face her; in his hand he held another photograph. "Urban Myth: Sierra. No useful information on him. He also has to be brought in."

Toeing off her shoes, Kelly scanned the photo. Unlike Alexander, this second target was far from awe inspiring. She was all too familiar with that kind of boyish smirk and devil-may-care wardrobe. She remembered it from her years spent as a cocky little Sierra, wandering the world, thinking herself free instead of lonely and scared and tired.

She crushed and dropped the photo into the tray provided. It flared and disintegrated.

"Got an identity for me?" she asked, beginning to roll down her stockings. Blake brought a case out from under his seat and snapped it open; from it he passed her a lampblack brassiere top, matching biking shorts, and a cracked leather jacket. They smelled of illicit tobacco and vodka.

"Blond Munitions?" She shook her head and stuffed away shoes and socks in the tote. "You should have told me. I would've bleached my hair."

"That won't be necessary." Blake's answer was terse. The helo took a sharp turn, passing now beyond the square rooftops of the city to race over tangled threads of highway.

Blake grabbed the armrests; Kelly, on her feet now, easily maintained her equilibrium with a bend of the knee; the Bell was that wonderfully smooth. Which made Blake's obvious tension the more unnerving. The secretary was never disoriented; he was a decision maker, like Kelly, and once the decisions were made, he was always sure and organized and committed.

She could think of only one thing that might rattle Blake's all-powerful solidarity. Her heart rate sped up. It always raced when she thought of Executive Hawthorne, in anticipation of his praise or in fear of his censure.

Blake was staring down now at his polished black shoes. "I failed him," he said abruptly, almost too softly to be heard over the whirl of the blades; it did not surprise Kelly that he'd read her thoughts. Where Hawthorne was concerned, they were in perfect alignment, like teenagers in love with the same idol.

Kelly slipped off her skirt. The Bell took another wide, airy curve; with acrobatic aplomb, Kelly shifted on the balls of her feet.

"Might I know what happened, sir?" She concentrated on tugging on the biking shorts. She didn't want to look at Blake's face.

"Alexander was being held in a warehouse not far from Union Station."

"Complete surveillance?"

"Inside and out, yes, but the exterior range is narrow. Just wide enough to film anyone trying to enter or exit the building."

"Sounds good enough. What went wrong?" Kelly pulled off her blouse. On the other side of the glass separating them from the pilots, she noticed the copilot trying to peer sidewise at her naked breasts. She grabbed onto the back of her chair just before the Bell, not unexpectedly, took a little drop.

Over the helo's continuous thrum, Blake slowly explained what had gone wrong. He took special care to emphasize the Hockey player who had lost his head and the sound of fleeing motorcycles. "None of this," he added at the end, "was picked up by the surveillance equipment." He shrugged. "As I said, the range is narrow."

She was back in her chair now, snapping on the bra and adjusting herself within. "I see. So you want me to recruit the Munitions for a highway search."

"I conferred with Executive Hawthorne on this. We both agree that regular patrol won't be able to get within shooting distance of our quarry."

Which meant, Kelly translated, *that Blake had spent the night frantically searching for these two with no luck.* No wonder his hands were twitching in his lap. She glanced away uncomfortably.

"Whoever's holding or helping them," Blake calmly went on, "has unexpected resources. We need to spring a trap."

She didn't like it. Working with hired help was always risky, even with the Munitions, who were honorable despite their obnoxious attitude. Besides, she performed better solo.

"Kelly," Blake said softly, a plea in his eyes, "it is urgent that these two be retrieved immediately! There is no letting you go at this on your own, we haven't the leisure. We're searching with every agent and patrol we have. What we lack is a team to effectively and quietly nab and subdue these two and whoever's got them. The Kings won't do, and we haven't the time to formulate a real undercover operation. So its up to the Blonds and you."

His tone and expression shook her; he sounded like a broken man. "What kind of gun got the King?" she asked, subdued.

"Double-barreled shotgun, probably sawed off."

"Nasty. Got any shoes for me?"

Blake produced a pair of thick purple socks and petite boots. He was slower on the uptake than usual, and now she knew why. Inside, she winced for him; she couldn't imagine ever failing the Executive so utterly; she was amazed Blake was still alive, let alone acting as her Anchor on this assignment.

The helo lurched, this time downward. Kelly buckled herself in and hurriedly tied on the shoes. She stuffed skirt and blouse into the tote, then fished out a hair clip and swept her coffee brown mop into a loose tail.

Blake, in the meantime, produced a Fanny belt, a pair of gloves, and a holstered gun. "I took the liberty of providing you with one hundred capsules of amyl nitrite, a small case of Blues, bottle of ecstasy and Thorazine. You've got your Cookbook lenses?"

In answer, Kelly produced the lens case. As the Bell begin to spiral down, she spread wide her eyelids and applied the clear circles onto her corneas. She blinked them into place.

Doc, she thought, *Cookbook's in, are you connected?* She whimsically imagined a bearded little man lifting his head, adjusting his spectacles, opening a book. In actuality, she merely felt a small click behind her eyes, like a pair of plugs going in.

Blake handed her the gun. "This is to be used on Urban Myth—*only* Urban Myth."

Kelly examined it. It was loaded with a suction-cup dart, not unlike those used by children. But she knew at a glance there was nothing childish about it.

"Executive Hawthorne's orders," Blake said, and that was that. "There are more darts in the Fanny bag."

Kelly shrugged, restored the gun to its holster, and snapped on the Fanny belt. *This Urban Myth,* she thought, pulling on the gloves, *must have some pretty weird protections.*

The world was rising up now, buildings seeming to elevate as the helo gingerly lowered to Earth; the thrum of its blades altered key as it resigned itself to hovering a foot above the pavement.

Kelly hurriedly transferred static handcuffs and nerve plugs from her tote into the Fanny pack. Her hand laser she stuffed into the tight, inner pocket of the shorts. Blake, in turn, passed her what looked to be a narrow, lapis lazuli compact. She clicked it open, glanced once into the mirror, then peeked under the thin cake of blush powder to be sure.

"Madre Dios!" she murmured, eyeing the tiny, numerical keyboard. "Anyone knows I have this, and every Tandy and Brainiac in the city will be after my ass." She shut and slid it into the brassiere's single pocket, right between the breasts.

Blake was already raking open the side door to wind and dust and noise. Kelly pulled on the jacket and looked out. They were in the parking lot of a burned-out mini-mall; a lone King player was waiting for them, rigidly guarding a customized Honda V-f 900cc.

She caught the edge of the door as the illusion of tilting captured her, then made a neat little leap onto the pavement. She crossed to the motorcycle and circled it admiringly.

Blake came up behind her, raking his thin, ruffled hair back into place. "The tires," he informed her, "are a fullerene-foam core, and there's an adjustment switch for nitrous oxide fuel additives."

"Very nice." She approved. The motorcycle was small, dark, and sleek. Very nice indeed. She smiled, glanced right and left, then called up a location map from Doc. They were on the seventy-two hundred block of Sunset Boulevard, right across the street from The Fuzzy White Biker, a cheap, renovated tittie bar and favorite Blond Munitions' hangout.

"Kelly?" Blake's voice stopped her just as she was about to hop onto the bike. "For both our sakes, bring them in fast."

Kelly paused. There was a question she'd almost forgotten to ask, and that rattled her. She must not do that again, she thought fiercely, and peevishly gave her wrist a pinch.

She met Blake's gaze. "How alive?"

The barest hint of a fearful smile touched his lips. "Kelly, bring in both your targets, and whoever helped them, alive. Alive and well."

"Good." She straddled the bike. "More of a challenge that way."

Chapter 11

There was a windy fresh feeling to the day; crumpled papers rolled down the wide street, bouncing and scratching. Ancient wires cut the hazy white sky into long, thin rhombi. And in the distance—merging with the sky where the sun struck it blind—the sea.

"There is nothing to tell, Urban." Alexander walked a step behind Emerson. He could feel the Web's halting gait at his heel, and edged ahead, nearer to Cinder.

They were part of a river of people, all heading toward the Virtual Bazaar. *As if that weren't bad enough for my paranoia,* Emerson thought, glancing resentfully over his shoulder at Alexander.

A ruby red lens, tapered like an almond, winked back at the Jabberjaw from the half mask's single eyehole. A gift from the Brainiacs. A priceless gift.

Alexander's right forefinger and thumb were tapping, pin to cup, as they had been all last night and all this morning. The clicking sound infuriated Emerson.

"I just want to know what you were doing holed up with those Brainiacs all night long—"

"We discussed Yaga shakes," the Web said, glancing up with his exposed hazel eye at the endless sky. "I pointed out to them that yogurt cultures were hardly enough to transmit genius level RNA to brain cells. I recommended E. coli bacterium. I also recommended they try flavoring the shakes with natural spices, but only because I'm inordinately fond of cinnamon."

"All night you were with them, and you talked yogurt??"

Alexander threw him an amused look. "The wonder of you, Urban, is that I never know whether my words have passed you by, or whether you have profoundly reduced my meaning to its most elemental form. Yes. We talked yogurt. We also talked programming, mathematics, physics, and revolution."

"Revolution!" Urban echoed, both angry and triumphant. "Rats and alligators! Didn't I just know it! Those damn—"

"No organization," Alex interrupted. "I remedied that. Now, if they really wish to enact a revolution, it will only take them six months."

"Six—" Urban gasped and so did Emerson. No one had ever been able to organize the Brainiacs, let alone urge them into action. They were talkers, not fighters.

"Do you mean"—Urban was nearly shouting now—"that in six months the Brainiacs will overthrow the"—he saw people looking their way and dropped his voice—"the Virts?!"

"They could. But what do you care? You didn't vote the Virtuals in, did you?"

Emerson snorted. The Son of a Mainframe had a point.

They were at the bottom of the hill now, at the end of the street; before them stood the pillars of a rickety old pier, reeking of swollen wood and seaweed. Angling off north and south were tents, row upon row of colorful cloth fluttering along the boardwalk. Bodies milled in, out and about this rainbow, gliding from stop to stop. The current fad, Emerson noted with interest, was a colored glass tab stuck to a shaven spot on the right temple, mimicking the crickets worn by Virtuals. An aggressive young woman was standing at the prime spot just where the roads split, hawking them.

"Poseurs! Get your Poseur Pak! Comes complete with a razor for shaving the temple, hair slicker, and mock cricket! Seven different colors! Today only, an eighth strip! Buy two, get one free! Be a Virtual!! Poseurs—"

Emerson was tempted in spite of himself. The woman was practically giving them away.

Cinder led them to a halt three steps down from the woman and took in a deep, appreciative breath. "A wonderful place, don't you agree? It stretches the mind."

"Oh, yes," Emerson quipped, "just lovely. The chaos, the stink, the jostling masses, pickpockets and fistfights—"

"Best find Noel first," she said, turning and, without warning, plunging toward a corded-off area of white gauze tents.

"Cinder—!" Emerson and Urban cried out in unison, but it was too late. Two Ice-Cream Men in jackets, bow ties, and sunglasses permitted her into one of the tents. A swing of gauze, a glimpse of dark, turbaned women, and she was lost behind a veil of cotton.

"Damn—" Urban said, grabbing Sander's arm as he tried to follow. "Whoa! You can't go in there!"

Alex jerked his arm back in a manner more instinctive than insulted. "Why not?"

"Because your skin is an alarming shade of white," Emerson patiently explained. "Only folk sun dark as

Cinder can go into the tents of Salaam uninvited. We'll just have to wait out here."

"Wait?" Urban snorted. "Hell if! I've been cooped up for a week—"

"Three days," Sander corrected.

"—No way I'm cooling my heels waiting for her!"

"Desertion *is* the Sierra code," Alexander sneeringly observed.

"Scared are we, Sander?" the taller man smirked back. "I'll be right there if you need me, under the pier with the Fannies—indulging in a *fantasy* of mine." He threw them a look of defiance, and made toward a line of women, breasts and bodies surgically augmented, leaning seductively against the round pillars.

Emerson sighed. Alexander appeared distressed.

"Good God," the Jabberjaw said, exasperated. "He's just gone off for a quick roll in the sand! It's not like he dropped you in a trash bin."

"They don't come back," Alexander answered bleakly. "If they go away, they don't come back."

"You're outside now, remember? People can leave and return if they please."

Alexander did not look convinced.

Emerson shook his head. He should have known something like this would happen, that Cinder would leave him holding the dirty cups. Might as well be back at the Closet! *Sweep that up, Emerson! Clear that off, Emerson!* And now, *show the Web around, Emerson! Don't let him get lost!*

"Well," he said gruffly, "we can keep here or take in the sights, which is it to be?"

Alexander shrugged.

"I'll take that for a 'sure, why not?' Come on then! Just keep in mind that there are limits to where you can go."

"Make me feel at home." Alex fell into step with him.

They moved in tighter with the crowd, where elbows poked, bodies nudged, and hips jostled. Emerson felt a sweat break out across his back; the sun was beating down on his head, heating his hair, while the wind, in opposition, blew chill and brisk. He squinted against the brightness bouncing off the white sidewalks and tugged his blazer tighter about him.

" '*A crowd flowed over London Bridge, so many,*' " he quoted aloud to himself, " '*I had not thought death had undone so many.*' "

"T. S. Eliot," Alexander responded automatically, "referencing Dante. Do you find him misanthropic or just pretentious? '*I have heard the key,*' " he quoted back. " '*Turn in the door once and turn once only.*' " He smiled a knowing smile. His thumb and forefinger were tapping.

Emerson looked away, chilled by more than the wind. The words brought to mind his mother and the day she decided to leave the Closet. Emerson, almost seven at the time, could not understand why his mother would want to venture outside, where monsters roamed, nor why she would want to leave their home of storytellers and poets. So he begged her to let him stay. Finally, sadly, she offered Langston Künstlerroman, chief of the Closet, two bags of coffee to adopt him. Then, without a backward look, she'd gathered up her worldly goods and slipped out the door into the world of Krakens and Jabberwockies.

Far from crying over the loss, Emerson remembered feeling shamefully relieved at being allowed to stay. Though ever after he would sometimes stand at the door, waiting for her to return, like Mariana of the Moated Grange.

"Who is Noel and why does Cinder want me to see him?"

Emerson glanced back, he'd almost forgotten Alexander. The young man was eyeing a Golden Arnold.

The Arnold—male at a guess, with biceps so round and heavy that the arms could not rest at ease, was hawking bland-smelling vegetable burgers and barbells.

"For that matter"—Alexander's one hazel eye suddenly locked on the Jabberjaw—"what does *Cinder* want with me?"

"Why don't you ask her?"

"I'm asking you."

"I have no idea who Noel is nor what Cinder wants with you, nor even who you are! And I don't care. I'm just along for the ride."

"Oh?"

"Yes. I wanted out of my Poetry Closet, and Cinder was—"

"The key?" Alexander offered with a smirk. He was keeping pace even though his limp seemed to be worse. Emerson slowed down, then realized what he had done and was disgusted with himself. *Let the Great Alexander fend for himself!*

"I *do* understand, Emerson," Sander went on, his voice riding like the gulls on the salty wind. "Who better? We are like brothers."

"We have *nothing* in common!" Oh, why had Cinder saddled him with this—this creature!

"Of course we do. We have both been residences of the *Kafes*—"

"The what?"

"The golden cage!"

They passed a cluster of brown-faced boys hawking old cans and bottles of beer and themselves. One was dickering with a toothless old pedophile. Behind the dark-eyed boys, a man in a candy-apple-red Rolls Royce was selling jump ropes and baseball bats.

"Back in 1666," said Alexander, "—and we ought not, like the Western puritans of the time, make much of those triple digits—Selim II of the Ottoman Empire

decided that murdering his brothers was too cruel a
way of holding the throne. Instead, he condemned
them to the *Kafes*. Luxuriously isolated, the princes
were allowed women, alcohol, opium, but no contact
with the outside world. And no freedom. Deaf-mutes
waited on them, watched them."

Alexander moved on, Emerson beside him. From a
dozen different directions they could now hear drums.
And wailing. Familiar wailing.

"Few brothers were ever released from the *Kafes*.
Those who were came out mad. We are like them."
The Web's voice was engaging, almost hypnotic. It
frightened Emerson, and yet he could not help but
listen; he did not want the Web to stop talking. "Like
them, we have heard the key turn in the door and
feared that our freedom might be a trick. Like them,
we have stepped out of the cage, afraid, insane. But
you are wondering why I, far more secluded than you,
do not share your *particular* dementia. Like you, I
should be agoraphobic, I should be sweating, nearly
panicking here, out in the marketplace."

Emerson shivered. Madness . . . was he mad? His
mother had told him once, and only, bluntly once,
about his father, a schizophrenic Halfway who raped
her. Had he inherited that sickness?

He could hear his racing heart babbling at him, *Too
many people, too many!* Was it loud enough for Alex
to hear, too?

"Look, Black Sisters!" Sander pointed to where five
tangle-haired women were howling and waving their
arms up at huge photographs of cruel-looking young
men. A circle of curious onlookers maintained a re-
spectful distance from the scene.

"Come away!" Emerson said quickly.

"Why?" Sander deliberately, perversely edged
closer. One Black Sister, staring up at the grayish

photo of her young man, scratched bleeding welts into her cheeks.

"Be my guest, if you want your eyes ripped out."

Alexander raised his brow, as if unsure of Emerson's sincerity. Then he shrugged and turned away. Emerson directed them toward the tables opposite the sisters. He felt eyes on the back of his neck.

Dangerous. So deadly dangerous on the outside.

"So," he asked, voice low and rough, "why aren't you?"

"Your question should be, 'Why am I?' Why am I at ease among others when I was released only last night?"

"Just answer the question!"

Alexander smiled at him, the one visible eye distant. And then his hand snapped out, and he locked on Emerson's wrist.

"Hey!" Emerson tried to jerk free, but the grip was surprisingly strong, the fingers long and spidery. Perspiration broke out across his brow. He was suddenly terrified of the Web.

"You recite your verses to a standing crowd of the finest poets," Sander said. "They are crushed together, listening rapt and amazed."

Emerson's stomach turned and turned again.

"When you finish, they applaud with admiration; they sit you down at the best table, the one with the chessboard top of gray and red marble, the one near the window. You can see the stars out that window, can't you Emerson? You can feel the cool of evening seeping through the glass. You're served espresso, not synthetic brew, but pure rich, contraband coffee; it is presented in a little silver demitasse with a twist of lemon peel. The bitter smell is faintingly wonderful. Isn't it?"

The Jabberjaw began to tremble. He was dimly

aware of the people parting around them in a continuous, noisy flow.

"You lean back, a serious, faraway expression on your face—have you practiced that expression before the mirror, Emerson?" The vague smile grew, and Emerson swallowed.

His secret. That had been *his* secret.

Sander released him. Emerson stumbled back. He was breathing harsh; there was an ache up his back, and for a moment he feared he would pass out. He licked his lips, then fumbled his glasses off with a trembling hand. He wiped a damp palm over his dank face. He felt sick.

"Uh—ah—"

Alexander was looking at him, arms crossed, disgusted amusement on his face. And Emerson found himself no longer worried about Black Sisters or hidden threats in the crowd. This was the monster. This was the nightmare. He had never hated or feared anyone so much.

"Pathetic," Sander finally snorted, crossing over to where a gaggle of Life Warriors hawked their wares under a pink tent.

Emerson angrily shoved his glasses back on. Damn if he was going to let this son of a bitch rattle him! He stormed after.

"Is that your deep dark power?" he taunted. "You're a mind reader? A telepath?"

"I've no idea what you're thinking right now," the Web responded innocently.

"Life's a blessing!" a small, dark-haired Life Warrior prayed at the crowd. She was dressed in a neat blue skirt and blazer, trying to sell dolls, quilts, old newspapers, and American flags. "Buy the blessings of life!"

Emerson moved close enough to hiss in Alexander's ear. "Damn you! What the fuck was that all about??"

"Human fantasies are supremely simple, Emerson."
The Web glanced over a line of umbrellas and car
batteries. "A need for order, comfort, and safety combined with a wish for appreciation and love. Humans
dream of being both special and accepted, part of the
tribe and set apart from the tribe. Are your bones
vibrating?"

"No."

"Mine are. And when I close my eyes, I see electrical storms blinking on and off all around me."

"So?"

"I knew your secret fantasy because I experienced
it. That is what my deep, dark 'power' is. I live other
people's fantasies. I always have. That is why it took
so little time for me to adjust to my release."

"Yeah, right." Emerson pushed his glasses up a slippery nose. His hands still shook. "Forgive me for
being a cynic, but I've had better fantasies!"

"I'm sure"—Sander was droll—"but it's a sad if
nauseating fact that I am not receptive to the *fantastic,*
just the mundane."

Emerson snorted. "That's a piss-poor excuse!"

"You miss the point, Emerson," the younger man
sneered. "But then you're a wanna-be poet. I wish
Urban would return," the voice warbled, the Web's
first indication of nervousness since they'd wandered
from the pier. "His simplicity is a veritable treasure
trove of insight."

"Let us tell you of the sanctity of life!" the petite
Life Warrior had seen them and was attacking. Emerson quickly sidestepped to the next tent before she
could grab or tackle him. Life Warriors had been
known to do that. "All life!" the girl screamed after
him. "Every animal and human who walks the earth
or is yet to walk it—"

"Hmpp!" snorted the old woman under the next
tent. She was selling marijuana plants and home-cured

tobacco. Jerking her head toward the Life Warriors, she took a drag from her cigarette holder, then exhaled a white plume. "Ain't they special!" Her voice was rough, as smoky as the gray wreaths spinning over her curly white head. "They don't care what misery you're in," she went on, confidentially, bitterly. "If you're alive, you're blessed. How can they know? Eh? If they think being alive's joy enough, how could they ever be miserable enough to think of ending a life? Eh? Oh, they'll tell you they hit the bottom somewhere along the line, and then you can be sure it's all guilt talking. Got to redeem themselves from the guilt. Fuck guilt, that's what I say."

"But what do you say?!" The Life Warrior had not given up. She was standing on the boundary between the tents, childish face poutingly intense. Emerson felt the sweat on his back again, this time trickling down. And even as he reached to draw Alex away, he heard, with horror, the Web's answer.

"Do you know what the population of California was before the hate wars? Over fifty million. After the wars, the population of California was five million. The first ten million of that deceased forty-five were gang members and criminals. Our forefathers hired the military to slaughter these undesirables wholesale."

The Life Warrior paled. "Murderers!" she hissed. "God forgive them!!"

"Indeed," Alexander nodded sardonically and pulled away from Emerson. "But do you know what's really interesting? Now, two generations later, these same criminals and gang members are worshiped by the Black Sisters as martyrs; each sister has adopted a man to weep for, a man who undoubtedly murdered adults and children without thought or remorse. Do you find that ironic?"

"Damn right!" the old woman cheered.

"Sander—" Emerson hissed. The young man's voice had gotten louder, but he didn't seem to notice that he was drawing a crowd.

"Are you trying to say that we should only weep over the loss of *innocent* lives?" the Life Warrior demanded.

"No. I am saying that any form of life can reproduce itself out of balance; when that happens, I would observe that somehow or other, the balance will be restored. It is a fact that men, like rats, destroy one another when they are crowded too tightly, when food, space, life, as you put it, are limited. This makes what the Black Sisters have done all the more ironic. Metamorphosing criminals into deities is not unique, but, unlike the extraordinary character of past criminals-turned-gods, these so-called saints were merely rats feeding on rats—"

"Aieeeeeee!" A black Sister came flying, painted nails raking, carmine lips drawn back.

Alexander stepped aside. The sister crashed into the Life Warrior, clawing and screeching hysterically.

"Jesus!" Emerson leapt back. "You did that on purpose!"

"I wanted to know if the Life Warrior would hold to her ideals if it was her own life is at risk—"

"Jesus, Sander, *you idiot*—!"

Too late! Black Sisters and Life Warriors joined the fray.

Alexander backed away, frowning and shaking his head with something very like confusion as the pink tent came down, crashing into the marijuana table. The old woman fell, her burning cigarette flying. Cloth caught fire and went up in a flash. There were cries and screams.

In an instant, the flames, whipped up by the wind, had jumped to the next tent. The old woman seeing

her ruined table and the burning tents, searched under
the broken table.

And then she came back up and leveled a gun at
them.

"You Sons of a Mainframe!" she shouted, and fired.

Chapter 12

The gun was a Smith & Wesson, .44 "Classic" Magnum, or so his computer told him. He didn't even have to ask it; it was programmed to zero in on weapons and machinery. And so the lens over his right eye obediently flashed the information, white letters over an opaque ruby screen while his left eye saw it all in vivid, terrible color. Saw the polished steel of the gun, the old woman fumbling with its heavy, unwieldy shape, and the spreading fire crackling hellishly behind her.

How many wrinkles she had! and yet how powdery soft was the skin, and the hair, so thin and white he could see the pink of her skull; the hands that held the gun were spotted, knobby in the fingers; she was trying, painfully it seemed, to squeeze the trigger—

I had not thought death had undone so many—

The computer had a gun outlined now, a menu of potential cross-references rolling over the picture. Only the barest portion of Alexander's brain registered the catalogue:

Gun construction and parts
Usage
Smith & Wesson
Magnums
Dirty Harry
Ballistics

Vaguely, he heard the screams around him, sensed the crowd that bumped past. There was an uncomfortable pounding in his chest.

He would wake from this nightmare eventually. Wake to his dark loft with the wind whistling through the slats and faint drunken voices shouting obscenities from the streets. He would wake and clutch at his blanket, wipe the sweat from his upper lip, and stare out at the city with longing, despite the terror he knew it held, the terror pointing like an accusation at him right now.

Cr-rack!

His eardrums shattered, and the ground hit him, hard and firm. He knew it ought to hurt, but it did not. He just felt it below him, solid, and he was flat and the world was horizontal. He wasn't sure he was breathing, wasn't sure the shout he had heard belonged to him. The report of the gun still hung in the salty air.

A brief graph on the computer lens affirmed that the gun had been fired; it registered the time of the shot, the trajectory of the bullet.

Was I hit? he wondered for a dizzying second, and almost clicked his fingertips to ask.

"I'm going to superglue your damn mouth shut!" Arms hard and strong as iron swept him up. "I don't know what you said, but I know you're the cause of this! Damn lucky that shot went wide! Are you all right?!" The arms shook him. "Answer me!!!"

Alexander giggled. Giggled and giggled and giggled. He couldn't help himself.

"Chree-ist!" Urban deposited him behind an abandoned food cart. The Sierra's chiseled face was all edges and anger; his pale eyes were storming. Sand crusted his boots and part of his vest; the muscles under his thin white shirt were bunched up, sweat graying the underarms. "Don't you get hysterical on me!"

Alexander giggled again, then caught his breath, then crashed into sobriety.

I was almost killed, he realized.

"There I am, bartering with a Fanny for a freebie, and suddenly the butane lighter explodes. And do you know what I think? I think, *Sander!* Do you know why? Because I know, I just know that you're behind it!"

"He was," Emerson's dour voice responded. The Jabberjaw scuttled up from around the back. Shots were being fired now from all sides. People swarmed around them. Shouts hung overhead.

"I'm not sure whether to be glad to see you alive or not." The Jabberjaw's voice dripped with ironic brevity. Then to Urban, "He incited a Black Sister to go berserk."

"He what?!"

"When she attacked, he let her smash into a Lifer. From there it was like dominoes."

"Rats and alligators!"

"I was not aware"—Alex heard himself saying—"how many factors there were to take into account. I never thought—" He fell silent, realizing that neither Urban nor Emerson was listening. He pursed his lips. It wasn't as if he had to explain anything! Still, the excuses came, pushing against his teeth, tumbling over one another like dishes falling. There had never been such consequences before: one companion, a con-

trolled environment. There was never any real danger
in either, though he pushed both to the limit, striving
for that rush, that mixture of fear and excitement.

That mixture which he had *not* felt facing the gun.
No excitement there, no rush, just horror.

"We should get out of here before that old woman
comes after us," Emerson said to Urban.

"We're gone!" Urban agreed, and before Alex
could protest, the Sierra had them out in the madness.
Sander clung onto Urban's vest in terror of being
dragged. His bad leg was strained to where pains were
shooting up his calf and thigh; and all around him:
people. The red of a cotton shirt, a snag of long hair,
the stink of urine, a shout in his ear. There were distant crashes, the odor of burning cloth, and always the
flashes, not flames but brief flares, like the lettering
he saw and read peripherally on the lens.

"Cinder!" Emerson's shout cut through. "We can't
get the bikes back without Cinder!" The Jabberjaw
was tugging, with frantic, erratic reaches and pulls, at
Urban's shirt. To their right were the tents of Salaam.
Despite the riot without, the corded-off area remained
rigidly serene; the gray-suited guards watched the panicked crowd with disdain.

What are they? Alexander unconsciously tapped the
tiny needle on his forefinger into the little cup on his
thumb. It hadn't taken him more than an hour to learn
the code. By now it was almost second nature.

Ice-Cream Men, the answer flashed on the red lens,
followed by the obligatory directory of cross-
references:

Sons of Malcolm Lee
Sun People
Ice-T Schism—

"How are we going to get her?" demanded a clearly
daunted Emerson.

Alexander, pressed against the Sierra's rock-hard rib cage, hardly felt the shift of breath as Urban answered, "Like this!"

And then they were plunging through the white curtains, even as guns appeared in brown hands.

"Cinder!" Urban yelled.

She looked up from where she sat, cross-legged, jodhpurs and goggles incongruous amid the shadowy billows of white gauze and folds of red paisley cushions. Across from her sat three women, turbaned and graceful in colorful caftans, gold jewelry glowing warmly in the filtered daylight. The screams and havoc from without were muffled, the wind cut off, making the interior warm and a little muggy.

"All hell's broken loose—" Urban started.

And then, from behind there was the click of cocked firearms.

"There goes the neighborhood," complained one of the guards.

"You've defiled our tent, Peckerwood!" the other shouted. "You're Iced!"

"Oh, dear," Emerson half sighed, half whined.

"Urban!"—Cinder smiled up at them and set down a tiny porcelain coffee cup—"and Emerson. Alexy. I got you some new clothes." She tapped on a wrapped bundle before her. "I hope they fit. Oh, and Noel isn't here. Seemed we just missed him. But I've a good idea of where he might be. Would you like some coffee? Emerson, I know you would."

The women stiffened. "Are these . . . these people with you?" one of them asked.

"Not at all," Cinder said blithely, and Alexander's stomach seized into a tight little ball. Then she said, "I am with them." And something bright and shiny and sharp went flying.

Knife, his computer told him, *switchblade.*

A scream and a shot fired wild; Urban was lashing

out with his free arm, swinging it back farther and faster than ought to be possible. Alexander heard but did not see the blow connect. There was a crunch. It did not sound as if a hand or fist had struck; it sounded as if a pound of metal had gone through fragile bone.

Cinder, grabbing up the bundled clothing, dashed by them. Urban hauled Alexander around. The young Web heard the angry shouting of women and caught sight of a crumpled, gray-suited form with a crushed nose. The other man was flailing his arm, blood spurting from it in pulses.

Radial Artery severed, Alexander's computer lens informed him; the words *Estimated Time of Death* appeared in the corner, coupled with a set of numbers rapidly running backward.

And then they were out in the sunlight and wind, Urban pulling him along after Emerson's flapping black blazer and Cinder's lithe, swift form. Alexander caught a lungful of the fresh, salt air, ominously tinged with smoke. It chilled and then evaporated the sweat on his brow; he shivered, and tried to keep pace with Urban.

The street seemed to go on forever. People crossed and crisscrossed in front of them, slowing them down. And Alexander, huffing from the strain of it all, felt his bad leg begin to give way. It had worried him before, in the loft. From the time he was old enough to compare, he had fretted over it, done what he could to cure it. But never before had he realized how maddeningly vulnerable and helpless it made him!

He cursed under his breath. Finally, Urban grew impatient and lifted him bodily off the ground.

"I can walk!" he shouted, even as the Sierra locked powerful arms under his stiff knees and back.

"And I've got an octopus in my stomach!" the older man retorted, and plowed up the hill. They reached

the gym just as Cinder was paying off the two hel-
meted Yeltsins they'd hired to guard the cycles.

"About time you got here," Emerson said, fidgeting
beside the smaller of the two bikes.

With a sigh of relief, Urban set Sander down.

"You're quite a wonder, Urban," Alexander came
close to snarling. He was angry again and glad of it;
anger allowed him control; but there was a tremor in
him also, fear of the unsuspected strength and sheer
physical prowess contained in this otherwise unimpos-
ing companion. Urban was barely breathing hard, and
there seemed to be no new patches of sweat. From
where did this man come? Who had trained him?

"I never would have thought you so strong."

"That's me." Urban crossed to the smaller motorcycle and straddled it. "The Man of Steel."

Emerson jumped on behind him, and the Sierra
revved the motor. Alexander limped to the larger bike
and hastily climbed into the sidecar. As he settled, he
felt his body give way to delayed shock. His hands
began to twitch uncontrollably, and his legs shook
with fatigue.

A twine-wrapped bundle dropped into his lap.

"Take care of that, Alexy," Cinder said, tugging
down her goggles and revving the motor. She backed
the cycle out. Urban and Emerson followed.

The gym sat at the pinnacle of the hill, looking
down at the falling street and the sea beyond. Masses
of screaming people could be seen streaming out of
the burning bazaar. An ugly sooted pillar of smoke
wafted up from where the wind whipped up the
flames.

"Alexy," Cinder said in a voice that carried despite
the motorcycle rumble and the cacophony of shouts,
"did you do that?"

Alexander's hands twitched violently, and he felt his
face go deathly pale. It was the same feeling as when

he faced the "Classic" Magnum. He had to swallow twice before he was sure he wouldn't throw up and shame himself.

"Yes," he said.

The eyes behind the sun-whitened goggles could not be seen, but the full lips split into a wide, delighted grin.

"Wonderful!" she said with enthusiasm. "Alexy, you surpass my dearest hopes!"

And then she released the brake and shot them out and around the corner, away from the fire and the crowd and the sea.

Chapter 13

Blondie, a muscled Aryan woman, had an antique hairpin through her chignon. The Cookbook informed Kelly that such a pin could be pierced through the ear to silently and quickly assassinate. Across from Blondie, a bony, bronze girl named Houston guzzled down vodka. The Cookbook flashed pictures of Molotov cocktails. As for the leader of these Blond Munitions, Concrete, the Cookbook insisted that nothing about her or her black jumpsuit could be used as a weapon.

But Kelly was wise enough to know that Concrete, in and of herself, was a weapon, one she had every intention of using—providing, of course, that they could all get around to the matter at hand.

"Have you ever read Italo Calvino?" Concrete asked.

"Who?" Kelly asked loudly. The music blaring from a priceless compact disc player pounded through The Fuzzy White Biker and through her bones.

"Italo Calvino." Concrete was a tall girl, big-boned with a very wide, round face. Unlike the other two,

Concrete's short black hair was dyed platinum blond only at its ducktail. Houston had her tresses bleached from root to split ends. The Cookbook had plotted out a complex manner in which the peroxide still upon the hair could be burned to form a poison gas.

Kelly shrugged and took a cautious sip of her beer. There was no being a sister without sharing a drink, but the drinks were straight, not watered down. Too much alcohol would interfere with her implants.

"Calvino," Concrete went maddeningly on, "writes these precise little allegories. Microcosms contained within a short space of words. I'd kill to write like that."

Kelly glanced up the runway. Up on the stage a trio of Molls performed a cancan. The makeup was good, accenting the cheeks, the carefully shaved legs as shapely as any she'd seen. They were good dancers, too. How they managed to keep kicking in those high, steeply spiked heels was beyond her.

"Can't say I've ever read Calvino," Kelly said, quaffing her beer, "but next time I come across a bookseller, I'll be sure to pick him up. Listen—"

"There's a great collection of his stories called *Our Ancestors,*" Concrete interrupted. "I'll loan it to you if you like."

"You're too kind."

"Just make sure you get it back to me in good shape. I knocked the teeth right out of the last fucker who ruined one of my books. A rare collection of poems by Henry Rollins. Spilled whiskey all over it! Can you believe that! People don't understand what kind of stuff goes into a book, how amazing it is! They just can't appreciate the creative process."

"No, they can't, but what I really—"

"That makes me mad. Goddamn, what I wouldn't give to be able to write stories. After I busted out that bastard's teeth, I chopped off his fingers. Did the same to this guy I saw burning down a library."

"Shit, Concrete," Blondie spoke up; her voice was low and a little drugged. She was among the few women in the room with hair naturally moon white. The tiny mole to the left of her upper lip, however, was, according to Doc, the work of plastic surgery. Blondie was also the only one of the three dressed lightly, frivolously in emerald chiffon. "You know that place was looted down to the effin' ground. There weren't no books hardly left there."

"There were enough. Words can re-create feelings. They're the most powerful shit on Earth, you know what I mean?"

"Yes, I do." Kelly nodded her sympathy; *Jesus!* She hated this part of an operation! She'd spent half the morning cooling her heels, waiting for this bitch. Yet now that Concrete had finally arrived, here they were, still in limbo, nothing certain.

The cancan ended with the dancers on the stage floor in splits, gloved and bangled arms raised to reveal shaved armpits. Kelly applauded loudly, knowing that would earn her extra points. "Brava!" she called out, self-consciously, and the false eyelashes onstage fluttered with delight.

"That's nice of you, sister," Houston said. Her butterscotch skin showed off the bones in her face. She had bleached her eyebrows light as her hair, and her brown eyes looked black beneath them. "Politeness is subtle, not digital, if you know what I mean. We think it's sterile now to be kind, but that's as bogus as when we thought machines were cleansing the world of our humanity. Right?"

Kelly took a draft of tepid beer. "Guess so." Behind her, along the wall, her motorcycle waited, spotlighted by the downturned tracks. The women in the bar had been taking covert looks at it, white, fluffed heads turning in that soft, slow manner managed only by Blond Munitions.

Come on, Concrete, she thought, wished. *You've seen it. You know you want it. Speak to me!!*

Concrete shifted. "These bikers you're after," she said, and Kelly almost grinned. "How'd they fuck you over?"

"Stole some cycles of mine."

"Like that one there?"

At last! With practiced languor, Kelly leaned herself back and glanced at the motorcycle. She crossed her legs, knowing that the pose showed off to advantage her petite form, the muscles in her thighs. Concrete shifted again.

"Beauty, isn't it?"

"That it is, sister," frilly Blondie agreed. "Not never seen anything like. What you asking for it?"

"I'm afraid it's one of a kind. But I might be persuaded to surrender the blueprints for it."

"What did they do?" Concrete asked again, this time moving in close enough for Kelly to smell the musk of her perfume.

"Stole some cycles and burned down my place." Kelly met Asian eyes straight on. "I created that bike there; that's how I make my living, motorcycles. Or rather, how I *made* my living."

"Did you try the Kings?" Houston asked.

"Know a *Per My.* I went to him. He contacted his uncle, who said that if I could gather up a posse, there'd be backup."

"Dangerous?" Blondie wanted to know.

"Yes." No lying to the Blondes on that, not if she wanted their help.

The Munitions exchanged looks; Houston gave a shrug, and Blondie chewed on her rouged lip.

"Listen," Kelly said, judging it finally, thankfully time to do a little pushing, "I can't wait around here much longer. I've already shot the morning. Either you want to help, or you don't. I'll give you a minute to decide which it is." Taking her mug, she headed for the bar with an exaggerated swing of her hips. Bleached-blond heads turned to watch her; carmine lips moved in whispers.

"Same"—Kelly set down her empty mug, stretches of froth still sliding down its interior. The corseted Moll standing behind winked at her as he refilled it from the tap. Onstage, the curtains folded open to a quartet of Molls dressed in bright, military uniforms loaded with medals. They came marching down the runway.

Kelly snorted and shook her head. What was she doing here?

Ought to be out chasing down my Mainframers, she thought, antsy. Had she her druthers, she'd be searching Brainiac hangouts right now. All of them. Mainframers were fragile and rare. They had minds. Jesus, how she wished she had such a mind.

But fetching precious Mainframers back to their protective environment was not her assignment.

Leaning with one elbow winged back upon the bar, Kelly pretended to take a long gulp of beer. Well, the quicker she brought this manhunt to an end, the sooner she could get back to what she really wanted to do.

She called up the image of Alexander. Her first moments on assignment were always the most nerve-racking. It was like stage fright—the butterflies always there no matter how many shows. Once settled in, however, she could peruse, examine, theorize, pretend. It was what was expected of her, the reason why Executive Hawthorne had refrained from killing her that day he'd caught her trying to steal computers.

She'd been working for a Tandy who'd managed to blackmail a secretary into leaving off certain alarms.

She well remembered that night. She was barely
eleven and the dark, tall, hush of the office building
had filled her with an almost religious sense of dread.
She'd felt that she was trespassing on holy ground,
and made double sure to keep to the assigned area.
*No alarms, cameras, or monitors on that floor will be
active, and no one will be there,* she'd been assured by
her Tandy.

But someone was.

He'd appeared on-screen, right there on the monitor
she was trying to move, and he'd asked her what the
devil she thought she was doing.

That was the beginning of her conversion, the rais-
ing up of her from the muck that had once been her
life.

Kelly was not one to forget a favor, a friend, or
a benefactor.

Alexander. Doc reproduced the image. Kelly licked
froth from her lips and mentally moved herself behind
the mask. Web, but not orthodox, since he'd not
scarred his face. Hard lines to his features: intense.

I am intense, she thought, *I am afraid.* Yes. That
was it. Intensity to fight fear. What kind of fear? Not
external. He was too smooth and healthy for external
fears. Internal, then.

And then a flash came to her mind, red and blinking. Slowly, casually, she turned to the bartender.
"Where is the ladies' room?" she asked.

"Right over there, honey." He smiled and pointed.

She passed through a door marked with a picture of
Marilyn Monroe. She was relieved to find the interior
mirrored and sparkling, done up in black marble and
brass. Best of all, there was a lock on the door.

She had the Cookbook scan for cameras or listening
devices, though they seemed unlikely. Finding none,
she reached between her breasts and brought out the
compact. The reflection was gone from the mirror, and

in its place was Hawthorne. Kelly's heart stilled, then dared to beat again.

The Executive, she called him, because he was great and good and all knowing. *The Executive.*

"They're being traced by satellite," Hawthorne said without preamble.

"Where'd you pin them?"

"Southwest, along the coast. The bazaar was being held there. A Weekly saw them fleeing from it."

Kelly nodded. The VR lenses Virtuals wore sent to as well as received images from the central computer.

"The bazaar was burned almost to the ground," Hawthorne added almost as an afterthought.

She frowned. "Alexander?"

"I do have my suspicions."

"Are they still on the move, sir?"

"They are indeed. Do you want me to flash maps to this monitor?"

"I think it would be best, sir, considering you want them well and alive, if we wait and see whether they settle for the night. Easier to trap them."

"You are the expert, Kelly," he complimented with a nod.

"I try, sir," she said, blushing quite furiously with pleasure and guiltily aware of having wasted the entire morning. She should have had the Munitions on the road by now!

"Blake and I decided this morning that the Kings would be wrong for this operation. Are you in agreement with that?"

"Yes, sir," she said, both surprised and flattered to be asked for an opinion. "Kings are too noisy and too rough. Tribes like the Munitions will blend in, won't send the quarry running." She shifted nervously. "But, begging your pardon, sir, that makes a well-formulated plan all the more essential."

The Executive did not look happy, but he nodded resignedly. "How long?"

"Have them by tomorrow morning, sir. You got my word on that. And you'll get them clean, not a mark on them."

"I'll be counting on that, Kelly. And on you." He smiled his quick, thin smile at her, and then she was staring into her own dark Latin eyes in the narrow mirror.

It took her a moment to feel her chest relax and breath return. With a sigh, she snapped shut the box. *Someday,* she thought, someday she was going to stand before this man who had saved her. All she'd ever seen of him was a face on-screen; but one day soon he would send for her. Perhaps after this very assignment. She'd be escorted to the top of the tallest building in downtown—or perhaps the Executive would send a helo to fly her to the roof of one of those mirrored buildings that gleamed so bright and promising in the sun. And she would be led into a suite more beautiful than anything in the Orange Kingdom. He'd be sitting in a winged-back, English armchair, and he'd greet her by name, maybe take her hand.

No, that was probably too much. But she *would* greet him face-to-face. And she'd tell him then how grateful she was for all he'd done for her. How desperately she wanted to make him proud of her.

Kelly took in a breath, eased out of the dream, and slid the case back into the bra. She was going to have these subjects wrapped up tight and solid by 0600 tomorrow if it killed her.

Yes, sir, she was. She would do it for him.

Chapter 14

A view hole within the iron door flew open even as Cinder raised her fist to knock again. The eyes that glared out at them were magnified hugely behind thick, round lenses: green eyes crowded at the corners with wrinkles.

Rats and alligators, thought Urban, squinting against the light. *What now?*

"Fuck off." The eyes snarled. There was part of a nose there as well, and a nasty pair of bushy black eyebrows.

"Is there a man named Noel in there, Jack?" Cinder asked, and Urban heard Emerson groan beside him. Not that he blamed the Jabberjaw. Cinder was like a drunk mouse; you never knew in what direction she was going to point.

The brows scowled. "Cinder?"

"Is Noel in there?"

"Ralf??"

"Noel."

"Wha'? You jerking me sideways?? There's no Noel here!! Fuck off!!"

"Can we spend the night?"

"Shit no!!" The peephole slammed shut.

Cinder scratched under her cap, then she shrugged and knocked again.

The little door flew open. *Go the fuck away!*

"Are you all right, Jack? Your eyes look awful red. Here, let me just check—I know I have some eye rinse." She began to search through her pockets.

"Here we go again," Emerson sighed.

"Who's out there with you??" Jack demanded, his eyes darting like fish behind the lenses. "You haven't got Ethelred out there? Do you? I swear, Cinder, if you've brought that damn marsupial-from-the-id with you I'll—"

"Ah! How about this?" She held up a bottle of pills to the peephole. The wild eyes froze, reading, and Urban heard the man swallow.

"H-how many of those have you got?"

"Hundred fifty."

"Give me a hundred, and I'll let you stay the night."

"One hundred, huh?" Cinder shuffled and scratched at her head again. She glanced back at the others. "Does that sound fair?"

"Seventy-five!" Urban said to Jack.

There was the click and snap of locks being twisted, and the door, flaking, rusty white paint, groaned open. Light ran out into the dank street like a broken egg yolk.

"Eighty," Jack bartered.

"Done." Urban nodded.

"Thank you, Jack," Cinder said, and pushed the door open all the way.

"Wait—" Urban grabbed her arm; it felt slender and frail under the thickness of the jacket. "What about the motorcycles?"

"Ethelred will watch over them," she said, as if it were obvious, and vanished within. Alexander, his new

clothes bundled up in his arms, shrugged and followed her.

"Just who is this Ethelred?" the Sierra demanded
of Emerson.

The bespectacled man met his gaze, a cynical twitch
playing at his lips. "You don't want to know." And
then he was inside with the others.

Urban hesitated, all his training and instincts
screaming that the bikes ought not be left out in an
alley no matter how empty the streets, no matter how
abandoned that part of the city.

Might as well hand babies over to stoned sitters,
Urban thought, finally going in. He shut the door behind him and locked it, leaving the motorcycles to
whatever mercy there might be. Perhaps they would
be all right. Or maybe, he thought, just maybe, he
would sneak out and steal the smaller cycle himself.
It was well past time for him to be on his way and on
his own, wasn't it?

He paused dead on the threshold, uncertain, as his
eyes adjusted to the olive-oil light.

It was a sculpture gallery; only there were no statues. Men and women—most of them naked, bent,
twisted, and posed upon separate little platforms—
were on display. Glancing to one side and then the
other, Urban took in a lean, Asian woman crouched
like a sumo wrestler, a stuffed armadillo hanging from
a rope around her neck.

"What do you think, Emerson?" Urban heard Cinder ask. She and the others were a step ahead, staring
up at a blond woman in high heels; tinsel and Christ-
mas tree ornaments dangled from the pierced parts of
her body. A star on her head flashed and blinked, and
there was a banner stretched tight over her crotch
reading: "MERRY XMAS."

"It's different," Emerson conceded.

"It's asinine!" Jack corrected, appearing from the

side. He was full Caucasian with a hooked nose and a hound-dog face. He was also unkempt, checkered shirt lacking or dangling buttons, ribbed undershirt gray and spotted. "That's what it is, and you know it! Why don't you just come out and say it!" He gave his pants a tug up; though belted tight, the brown, electrician trousers sagged on his narrow hips.

"Jack has very little imagination," Cinder said with a small, chill smile.

"Don't touch anything!" Jack snarled.

"No need to sic the Dobermans on us," Urban retorted.

"You try to touch anyone, and I'll toss you all out on your ear!"

"Do they ever move?" Emerson asked.

"Asshole! Of course they move! And eat and shit, don't I know it!"

"I don't understand." Alexander had moved to a fat, bearded man, chin in hand, lobster shells on either knee.

Jack flapped his arms, exhibiting pits of straight, prickly hair. "Welcome to the club, asswipe! I don't understand, either! Do you think anyone ever comes here to look at them!? They just stand there! Who knows why!"

Urban saw a flicker cross Alexander's exposed hazel eye; during the few days he'd been Sander's sole companion, he'd grown familiar with that look—the Web was thinking of breaking something.

"I would imagine," the young man said softly, "that the reason why would be obvious to all but the very stupid. Clearly, they are their own audience. They see each other's work every day, do they not? And who can better appreciate a work of art than a fellow artist?"

Jack looked slightly taken aback. He crossed his arms, shuffled his feet. "Don't touch anything!" he said, and spun like a toy to follow Cinder toward the back. "You tell that to Ethelred, Cinder! No touching! Fact, I don't want to see that flop-eared horror any-where near this place. You hear?"

Urban leaned into Emerson. "What did this Eth-elred do?"

Jack spun. "You want to know what he did!? Let me tell you what he did, butt-hole! I used to be a Mindscraper; you know what that is?"

"Yeah, you enlightened people by putting them into concentration camps."

"If that's what they wanted. And that *was* what they wanted, you know!" He was circling them now, wildly tapping at his head. "See, it's only the well-off tribes in the hills—the Holists, undersecretaries, and enter-tainers—that can afford our programs. And they've got all this shame about their wealth and comfort. They want to be deprived and punished. You initiate them, and they suddenly feel better, special. Everyone knows that!"

"American Indian sweat houses," Alexander said, his voice surprisingly level and clear. "Medieval flag-ellation, purification by starvation, deprivation. . . ."

"That's it!"

"On the other hand," Alex continued, "such meth-ods are also used to brainwash and demoralize. They can lead to psychosis as easily, if not more so, than enlightenment."

"Listen, shit-head!" Jack retorted, heatedly, "I'll have you know that in all the time I was a Mind-scraper, I never had one psychotic reaction! Okay, there was that guy who stuck a vacuum nozzle down his throat and tried to suck out his soul, but he was one in a million. Most of my customers came out bet-ter than before, they understood themselves. They were able to make decision about their lives, and they were happy! And so was I!"

Emerson sighed loudly. "And then one day . . . ?" he coaxed.

Jack threw him a glare. "And then one day, I'm working this enlightenment scene called *The Rainbow Path,* and I'm going at it, keeping them from sleeping, yelling at them for getting sick like it's their own fault—you know, the basics. When suddenly, this—this couch-sized, rabbit-eared bulldog appears! Just pops in, and everyone screams and runs for the doors, and there's no stopping them! I mean, I'm not even trying! I'm there shitting in my pants, and you know what happens then?!"

"I can guess," Emerson muttered.

"This thing talks!"

Urban snorted. "Sure."

"Hey, fuck-nose, you don't want to believe you can leave. I don't got to let you stay here!!"

"What did it say?" Alexander asked.

"It asks me to put it through treatment!" Jack waved his arms, as incredulous now as he must have been then. "It wants to go through *The Rainbow Path,* it tells me! It's having trouble making decisions, it says, and besides, it can't get its ears up!"

"Ethelred was going through a rough period," Cinder offered.

Emerson pushed back his glasses. "Did you put him through the treatment?"

"Are you crazy!! That fucked-up bunny wrecked my seminar! I told it to take a walk! But that's not the end! Word about it gets out! And then it starts. First I have to return all the credit because *The Rainbow Path*'s guaranteed, and no one was able to finish the program. Then no one wants to sign up with *me* anymore! And then I get investigated by the Mindscrapers' Board! They think I'm using drugs or holograms to enhance my sessions! *'Deprivation must be total and clean,'* they tell me! Me! Who's never let a single participant use even asthma medicine during a session! They pull my license anyway. So now I'm broke and out of business. And this is it"—he waved at the gallery—"this is what I'm reduced to! Baby-sitting fucking mimes!"

A pause, then, "A moving saga," Emerson noted.

"Fuck off."

"Ah!" Cinder had reached the run-down kitchenette at the very back. There was a tiny sink, dirty water dripping slowly from its crusted faucet, a little refrigerator, and a hot plate. "Charming!"

"What's that covering the eyehole, Web?" Jack was peering at Alexander, leaning in close enough to breathe on him. The young man retreated, disgust wrinkling his nose. "If it's a camera, you're out of here! No one's allowed to take pictures!"

"It's a computer."

"Computer? Where'd you get it?"

"Brainiacs."

"Those Bulldadaists!" the proprietor snorted. "Bunch of fuck-ups; let 'em go back to San Francisco where they belong! That's where they're from, you know! Slipped past the Caesars like illegal immigrants and snuck into this city to tout their Virtual Revolution!"

"Their reasoning seems sound enough to me," Alexander said testily.

"It's bullshit!" The Virtuals are hoarding technology, and that's the cause of all our misery! Sure! And I'm Mao Tse-Tung! What a crock! Comes right out of bad cyber-novels!"

"The Virtuals don't have a monopoly on lost high tech?" Emerson languidly, scathingly challenged. Jack, clearly to Alexander's relief, stopped following him and turned on Jabberjaw, fast as a roach.

" 'Course they do! But do you know why? Because no more is being made! It's all leftovers from the war.

And even if the Virts decided to share those leftovers, hand me a computer maybe, what the hell am I going to do with it? The nets are down! The economy is shot! We're back to trading chickens! Do you know how fucking lucky we are just to have electricity in this shit-hole? If the city hadn't switched over to solar before the wars, we'd be dead in the dark. The Brainiacs are like old Commies. Share the tech, like share the wealth. Won't do us squat. Not in this world. Not now."

"Eggs, soda." Cinder was peering about the tiny refrigerator. "No milk. What's this?" She removed a long, slender black object from the bottom tray. "A baton?"

"That's a vibrator, you stupid bitch! What? Think anyone would pay to see these still-life turkeys??" Jack waved back at the gallery. "I sell sex toys out the back."

Cinder, with a cock of her head, pressed a switch. The stick rumbled and shook. "So it is." A flicker of bright thought behind her eyes, and then she shut it off.

"Excuse me," Alexander interjected, "but is there anywhere in this . . . establishment where I might change my clothes? A restroom perhaps?"

"Restroom?!" Jack scoffed. "There's a fucking toilet! That's what there is! Back there!" He jabbed at a door half off its hinges; then to Cinder, "Where's my eighty-five pills!?"

"Eighty," Urban corrected, and Jack scowled at him.

"Hold your horses, Jack, while I get out some bread—" Cinder smiled indulgently. "Oh, green bread. Wonder how that will taste."

Alexander turned a little pale. "I think I'll pass." He made for the bathroom. "Ugh!" Sander took a startled step out of the bathroom, exposed side of his face noticeably white.

"Yeah," Jack snorted. "*Toilet* doesn't begin to describe it!"

"The charms of the outside world," Emerson said smugly. "The more you see, the more appealing our golden cages."

Alexander threw him a glare, then, as if to prove himself, plunged in, jerking the door shut with an effort.

"Here you go, Jack." Cinder counted out the pills onto a soiled napkin. "Eighty."

"Fuck off," he said, clutching his prize and spinning stiffly away. "You want me, I'll be in my room on my shitty little stiff-as-a-board cot committing suicide! Don't let me hear you touched anything!"

"There doesn't seem to be an eggbeater," Cinder observed, puttering about. "Ah. Never mind." She grinned, and switched on the vibrator.

Urban, wide-eyed, sank down into a graying, plastic chair by a rickety picnic table. Emerson, pulling out a handkerchief, took a swipe at the seat of a chair before settling across from him.

"Emerson," Urban said, "mind if I ask you a question?"

"You will anyway," he answered, glancing back at the gallery.

". . . What's a coddled Jabberjaw like you doing on this road trip? I mean, isn't it a bit, well, unsanitary for your sort?"

Inky black eyes came up, and Urban realized for the first time that they had an Asian tilt to them. The man's nose, on the other hand, was occidental, his skin Poetry-Closet pale.

"Why are *you* still with us?" Emerson retorted. "I would have thought a 'freewheeling Sierra' like yourself would now be on his way, clear of any ties."

Urban tensed. Had the Jabberjaw seen those covetous looks at the cycles? "I like having fast transportation," he answered. "And as a freewheeling Sierra, it doesn't matter where I go, so long as I go."

"As a 'coddled Jabberjaw,' " Emerson returned, "it doesn't matter where I go so long as I am far, *far* away from a poetry closet." There was an undertone in his voice, like rust being scraped from metal. His lips were stretched tight.

So well, Urban knew enough to tread softly around sore spots, however tempting.

"Do you want French toast, Urban? Emerson?" Cinder had gotten out a crusted frying pan and was setting match to the oil under the hot plate.

"Just eggs, I think," Urban said.

"Same for me," Emerson nodded, but his magnified gaze remained on Urban for a moment. "Ever read Horace's *Art of Poetry*?"

"I can't read."

Emerson sighed. "Tragic." He glanced away. "'*To be a mediocre poet, neither gods, nor men, nor booksellers have allowed.*' The plain truth is, I'm not even a *mediocre* poet. Among Jabberjaws, that means all I'm good for is cleaning, clearing tables, and maybe— *maybe* if they're shorthanded—pouring the coffee or serving the customers. No making the espresso, no trading or dealing with the merchants, and no say in how things are run." He shrugged. "Cinder offered me a lift. I took it. End of story."

Urban leaned back. He felt almost sorry for Emerson. The man was so far out of his depth; could life in the Closet have been that bad? *Like Sander,* he thought. Perhaps that was why he was still hanging around; he felt sorry for Alexander, too. It must be terrible to suddenly be out on the streets without a compass or survival kit.

There were sounds coming from the frying pan now,

a faint popping rather than actual sizzling, and the fragrance of cooking eggs.

"What is Ethelred?" Urban asked abruptly. "I mean, what is he *really*?"

Emerson leaned in. "Imagine the offspring of a huge, hideously ugly bulldog and a fat, flop-eared gray bunny."

"Oh, come on!"

"Actually, he claims to be what you are—a myth."

"And you believe him?"

"We are speaking of a creature the size of a small sports car who can talk. I'm rather inclined to believe whatever he chooses to tell me . . . within reason, of course."

Urban glanced back down the gallery expecting, for some reason, to see the "statues" reacting to all this. He noticed that the man with the lobsters and the woman under the veil had changed positions. That made him feel distinctly uncomfortable. Urban prided himself on his second sense; he was acutely aware of the movements of others, even if he wasn't watching them.

But not here, he thought, *here everything's nutty.*

"Mold," Cinder suddenly remarked, leaning over the frying pan. She reached a finger out to the wall and scraped a nail down a green stain.

Cinder saw him staring, and smiled; then she put the finger in her mouth and sucked.

Shaken, Urban looked to Emerson. The Jabberjaw had not seen, seated as he was, with his back to the dark lady.

"And who—what is Cinder?" Urban ventured, softly. "Is she .. like . . . Ethelred?"

"They're both from the same place, or so I gather."

"And where's that?"

"Who knows? The other side of the looking glass?"

"Aaaaaahhhh!!" the scream came from the bath-

room. Urban was on his feet and tearing the door off its hinges just as Alexander came flying out. The youth was in fresh clothing, a billowy cotton shirt, black vest and pants. His hair was wet and slicked down flat. Most startling of all, however, was that his face was bare. He held the mask, flaccid and loose in one hand.

But he's so young, Urban found himself thinking.

"I saw it!" Sander cried, pointing, "in the mirror!!"

"What the fuck!" Jack came sliding out of his room.

"Saw what??" Urban demanded, leaning the door up against the wall.

"A rabbit-dog, something!"

"Ethelred!" Jack yelled, shoving them out of the way. *"Ethelred!! You fucker! Get out of my mirror!!"* There was the sound of glass smashing. Urban hustled Alexander over to the table.

Damn it! He knew the whole world was crazy, but he never thought it could get *this* crazy.

"Just your imagination," he heard himself mutter. The kid was shaking, exposed face looking pitiful. Alexander settled docilely into the chair, hands playing with the mask.

"It wasn't his imagination, you know," Emerson said dourly. "We're among the Jabberwockies out here."

"Monsters," Alexander said, "monsters of the deep."

Jack came stomping out of the bathroom, dusting his hands together and hitching up his trousers. "That'll teach him!" he said, disappearing back into his room.

"Dinner!" Cinder announced, tossing down a plate of half-raw scrambled eggs.

Alexander looked at her with disbelief. And then he snatched the plate and threw it hard against the wall.

"Jesus!" Emerson leapt up as egg went flying; the

plate broke into three pieces, falling and landing with ringing clatters upon the stone floor.

Urban sighed; Cinder blinked.

"You don't like eggs?"

"I saw something in the mirror!" Alexander repeated fiercely.

"Mirrors hold a variety of fantastic images," she responded, eyes bright. "There are entire worlds in mirrors." Then, with a glance at the egg-splattered wall, "I guess this leaves green bread for supper. Anyone for toast?"

Like the devil from a dance hall, Urban thought then, firmly and decisively. *Come nuclear explosion or industrial waste, I'm outta here, tonight!*

Chapter 15

The motorcycle was resting under the cracked yellow of an old, half-dead lamp, its seat damp with four-in-the-morning dew. But it was indecision, not a wet seat, that kept Urban standing there in the dank alleyway. And that surprised him. Worse than surprising him, it unsettled him.

Should get on that bike and zorch out! he kept thinking. It was the logical thing to do, the rational thing to do. Hell! It was the thing he would *normally* do.

So why wasn't the UFO gone and soaring? Why, after fifteen minutes, was he standing Ordeal Art still, feeling like a windup toy that had run into a wall?

The gallery door creaked, and he sprang automatically into a defensive position.

"Still here?" Alexander, wearing his most irritating smirk, slipped out, nudging the door shut behind him. "Don't you know how dangerous it is to stay with me?"

"I like danger," Urban said tightly.

"You were created for it, Urban." Alexander

stepped nearer the light. He had on his new clothing, the slacks jet-black with knife-edged creases, the velour vest trim and tightly buttoned. In the dim light, Urban could make out a raised, paisley pattern that swirled down the sides of the vest. From the masked side of his face, the computer's incandescent eye burned both hot and ice.

"The highest intellect cannot escape the primal scream," Alex continued. "Even in my secluded little loft I ran into it. It's how we live and breathe and survive; we prey upon each other, as Shakespeare so aptly put it, *'like monsters of the deep.'* "

"Fuck you, Sander," Urban snarled, surprising himself yet again. "I don't have to listen to your nonsense, not anymore."

"That's right," the youth said with mock astonishment. "You don't have to put up with my esoteric ramblings; you don't have to duck my erratic tantrums. You don't have to sweep up the frustrations I smash along with sugar bowls and wineglasses. You have been released from the prison of my mind. So why are you still here, Urban?"

There was a discernible perplexity beneath the sneer. It relaxed Urban, if only a little. So the kid was scared. Smart-ass little twit didn't really want him to leave. Served him right. But even as Urban willed his hands to take hold of the bike's handlebars, he felt them, unaccountably, slipping back into his pockets.

"It makes no sense," Sander observed, his hazel eye nailing Urban, as if it could shatter and condense reality. "You aren't like Emerson or me, confused, half-mad. You know who you are, and what's right for you, don't you?"

"Damn straight," Urban said staunchly, but inside, the dismay was back. Sander had hit it again. A Sierra like Urban knew *exactly* what to do in any given situation. Act, react, move. It was all clear: cut-and-dried.

So why couldn't he leave?

"Monsters from the deep," Alexander said.

Urban sighed. "What?"

"It's what we are." Alexander's new boots squeaked a little as he twisted on a heel and limped back and forth. "I once spent a summer going over filmed footage of the hate wars. Of what people did to each other during those wars, the mutilations, the plagues, the mass graves. The hatred I saw looking at those pictures was the panicky, self-hate of monsters. I saw that same sort of hysterical hatred in that riot I unintentionally caused."

Alex paused a moment to smile ironically. "And I saw it as we toured the city afterward, and finally got to see what was behind those mysterious buildings— the ones I've been staring at all my life." A shake of the head; the red dot of the computer eye swung steady, like a hypnotist's charm. "Crumbling tenements and skeletons barely able to look up from their needles. And I thought my last nursemaid was bad. *'Humanity must perforce prey on itself like monsters of the deep.'* "

"Just tell me what it means, Sander! Or better yet, what the hell do you mean! Harder to get a straight answer from you than a Neiman-Marcus cookie recipe!"

"You've taken to edible analogies lately, Urban, which is sad, since I was growing fond of the body parts." He shrugged as if philosophically accepting the change. "Interesting thing about myths, yours and mine. Used to be that myths were grand and magnificent. They told us why the moon changed shape and how the sun arrived in the sky. Now the only myths remaining are monster myths."

"There you go again—"

"Monster myths," Alexander emphasized with exaggerated patience, "are the kind of myths you're so very fond of. Psychopaths with hooks! Rats so big they're mistaken for dogs! Lies and conspiracies! Myths that lead to hate wars! That is what happened, Urban. We mythologized each other until all we saw were monsters. And then, out of fear and hate of these monsters, we went out and committed crimes of mythological proportions. We descended in helicopters like Harpies, went after blood like Red Caps, spread infection like Yakkus, we . . . what is it? What's the matter?"

Urban had only shifted slightly, turning his head just a little, but Alexander had picked up on it. *Bastard's damn perceptive,* the Sierra thought, *have to give him that.*

Perhaps he even sensed what Urban could faintly hear and was just beginning to see far down the road.

"Motorcycles," Urban said, "lots of them."

Sander frowned. "I'll take your word for it. Should we be worried?"

"I think so," Urban said, even as the gallery door banged open and Cinder strode out. She paused, hands on hips, legs braced wide, and took a deep, enthusiastic breath.

"Good morning, one and all! Wonderful to be up at this time, isn't it? Light just appearing, the colors of morning and all that."

"It's miserable." Emerson appeared, reaching under his glasses to rub at sleep-swollen eyes.

"Time to go," Cinder said, striding to her cycle. "We're being pursued."

"By whom?" Alexander demanded.

"How did you know?" Urban asked simultaneously.

Cinder, buckling the chin strap of her cap, just smiled at him. "Ethelred told me."

Urban saw Alexander's face go pale, and wondered at that.

Time's run out, the Sierra thought, hearing the

sound of distant motorcycles more distinctly now. *D-base wants him back.* And then it occurred to him that D-base might want Alexander's servant back as well. Back or dead.

He fairly leapt onto the bike, waiting only for Emerson to settle behind him before turning the key. As the bike rumbled to life, Urban wondered if he ought to feel grateful or worried that he had not left, that he had, so disconcertingly, taken himself by surprise.

The cycle cut through the wind, whipping it back and over Urban's shoulder blades. He felt the rumble through the handlebars and glanced down at the gauge. Yesterday they'd tanked up with ethanol. The needle still read high.

Damn lucky that, he thought, glancing into the rearview. He saw Emerson, leaning in, felt as well as saw the man's hands clutching his belt. Farther back he saw a line, like a flock of birds, arrowing at them.

For some twenty minutes they'd curved and cut and woven their way over the treacherous cracks and buckles of the Hollywood freeway. But the dogs, as the saying went, were unshakable.

That had Urban worried.

Cinder was signaling to an off-ramp.

"Glower!" Emerson shouted in his ear. Urban nodded. It was becoming a habit between them: Emerson reading the signs for him. Of course, he knew the streets by sight, but the signs, read aloud, were a good reminder.

Urban flew down after Cinder and tightened his hold on the handlebars as he rounded a pothole.

And then, just at the bottom, Cinder stopped.

Jesus!!

Urban grabbed at the brakes. A screech and he could smell the hot stink of rubber. Gravel and dirt flew up, and Emerson's head knocked into his spine.

A hard twist, and the front wheel kissed Cinder's tailpipe.

"Damn it!" he yelled, planting down a foot before they could topple.

"Ouch," Emerson winced. "What have you got for muscles, rocks?"

Cinder glanced back at them, a puzzled frown on her brown face. "I've been wondering . . . Do you think they've got us on satellite?"

Urban, who'd been bunched up to shout at her, went cold.

"Rats and alligators!"

"That's what I think," she nodded, and Sander, bundled in the sidecar, looked wan. "I'll have Ethelred take care of it. I suppose I'd better get Alexy home."

Sander stiffened at that. "I won't go back!"

"Back where?" Cinder revved the bike. "I said I was taking you home. My home." Then to Urban, "Ever been to the observatory?"

"Uh—"

"Good!" Cinder shoved off. Urban, with a nervous glance over his shoulder, followed after. They shot under the freeway. Murals lined the walls, flashing by too fast to really see, but Urban knew what they depicted: the wars. Napalmed limbs falling from the sky, naked men impaled on fences, burning buildings, emaciated plague victims.

Once and once only, he'd paused long enough to get an eyeful of those murals. Now, thinking back on what Alexander had said, they made him feel sicker than ever. Sander had studied actual footage of the wars, had seen more than just drawings of belching black smokestacks and dogs feeding on human entrails.

No wonder the kid was so screwed up!

They were out in the sun and halfway down a street

of burned-out apartment buildings by now. Crumbling masonry dangled from chicken-wire inserts, blackened beams supported ashen brickwork. Urban flinched at the sight and glanced into his rearview.

A pack of Blond Munitions barreled out from under the freeway on sleek chrome cycles. Their blond hair blazed white in the morning light, and fire flashed off their mirrored sunglasses.

Ah, hell! Urban thought, a chill running down his back. *Rats! Rats and dozens of baby alligators!* Munitions were worse than Rodney King Hockey Players. They could kiss you, mutilate you, treat you politely, and then spit on your remains.

And they were the most persistent bitches on the planet.

Urban leaned in and sped up until he was almost on Cinder's bumper. They skidded around a fallen palm tree, past the Scientology Club, serene and fragile as a lost ghost behind its copper green fences.

Cinder pointed: go left. Urban eased off on the speed and banked behind her, shooting past the shadowy ruins of the American Holographic Institute upon its distant hill.

"Fern Dell Road!" Emerson's voice was barely there before the wind kidnapped it. Urban nodded all the same. There was something oddly comforting in the Jabberjaw's assistance; perhaps the man just didn't want Urban to forget he was there, holding tight with sweaty hands.

The street they were on was smoother, the homes, overgrown with ivy and bougainvillea, still standing. Gates held safe the mansions, most of which seemed to be waiting for someone to return to them. From a few, Urban saw figures darting behind a shattered picture window or leaning from a balcony.

Cinder signaled again.

"Vermont!" Emerson yelled as they made a hard

left onto a curving road. It was huge and terrible. Cracks yawned, and there were potholes the size of craters. Beneath his wheels Urban felt the choppiness of the uneven asphalt as he curved one way and then the other. A lane of grass split the vast street in two, and trees to either side formed a canopy through which only spotty sunlight could be seen.

Urban caught an eyeful of the rearview. The Munitions were a distance behind, but still holding. *Satellite for sure,* he thought, and that left him breathless. A man who could command a satellite to trace them was not a man to cross.

He glanced at Alexander, blond-brown hair ruffled in the wind: *Why is this kid so important to a man who can command satellites?*

And then Urban heard something that scared him dry. Overhead, flashes of sunlight appeared and disappeared, confirming his fears. As they passed the remains of the Greek Theater, the helicopter came into view, sleek as a dragonfly.

Something exploded on the pavement, and a yellow haze of gas flared up.

"Jesus!" Emerson yelled, as they cut around the gas. And then Urban saw Cinder draw, flip, and aim the shotgun upward.

Blam!

A shadow overhead; Urban gaped, and glanced as quickly and briefly over his shoulder as he dared. He saw the helicopter swing wildly, like a toy on a string, its bubbled head cracked and a body dripping out; he caught the merest glimpse of the copilot frantically grabbing for the controls. And then he felt rather than saw it drop.

K-bloommmm!!

A wave of heat flared up at his back; screams and the screech of motorcycles spinning. Urban felt Emerson's body pressed up against his, cringing like a child, trembling.

Rats and alligators! What a shot!

A curve to the left, so sharp the wheels almost skidded out from under his control.

Pop-pop-sssssssss!

Explosions behind them, and more screaming, distant. The ground to either side of the road was dry and khaki in color, pine trees and shrubs clinging to it with a sort of fierce stubbornness; old lampposts, their candle-flame heads broken, measured out the meters.

"My God." Urban could feel Emerson looking back at what he could guess was a flaming, blackened wreckage. For himself he kept as close to Cinder's back wheel as he could. She had, he noted, reholstered the gun. Alex was low in the sidecar, clutching his knees.

"It wasn't loaded," Urban muttered, only now realizing it. He'd seen her cleaning the gun the night before. She hadn't loaded it then, and there'd been no time since that she'd touched it.

It had not been loaded.

Up and up, with the hills rolling off to either side and the city spreading out like magic beyond them. They were heading for a tunnel when Cinder made a sudden turn, one that kicked up the dirt and almost threw Alex from the sidecar. And then she was speeding full throttle up a side road.

Damn! Urban followed, Emerson's arms locked around his waist. Where was she going?!

Ahead rose the triple domes of the observatory, looking for all the world like scoops of rusty brown ice cream. The white of the building itself was stained and scared with graffiti. Yet there was still something beautiful about the spiraling stairs, the arches of windows and doors covered by jade-colored metal.

Like a creature that has shut all its many eyes, Urban thought. *It no longer looks at earth or sky, present, past, or future.* It was an odd thought, the more strange for the sadness it abruptly gave him.

Cinder slowed and stopped before the dead, un-weeded lawn. Urban, perplexed, paused his bike beside her.

"Why are you stopping!?" he yelled over the motor-cycle rumble.

"Because we're here," she said simply, shutting off the power. She pushed up her goggles. "Alex, Emerson, come over here, I want you to see something. Urban, why don't you keep watch?"

"They'll be 'round that crashed 'copter and after us any minute now!!"

Too late, Cinder was off her bike and helping a badly shaken Alexander to his feet. Emerson practically slid from his perch, stumbling on trembling legs. And then all three, the two males limping and weaving like drunks, shuffled over to a flagstone balcony that jutted out from the sidewalk over a cliff edge. Two ancient telescopes still stood, waiting to offer visitors a magnified view of Los Angeles. Beyond the ruin of the railing lay a panorama of the city, gleaming under the auspices of a deep blue sky.

To one side, back down the road, an evil, atom-bomb plume of black smoke billowed up from the helicopter wreckage.

Damn! thought Urban, shutting off his bike. You could smell the acidic stench of it up here.

And then he heard Emerson gasp.

"That's impossible!" Alexander breathed, leaning out dangerously far over the crumbling ledge.

Cursing, Urban heaved himself off the bike. *Now what!?* he wondered. *What the fuck is he seeing now!? Flying whales?!*

"Get Sander away from that ledge!" he commanded. "What are you trying to do?!"

"Don't worry," Cinder said, a self-satisfied smile on her oval face. "He's perfectly safe."

"He's going to fall off!" Urban stomped toward the flagstones. Emerson and Alexander turned, and so did Cinder.

"Urban, no!"

Urban froze, one foot up upon the cobbles, the other rising to complete the step. For one moment he feared that he had just put the little balcony in danger with his weight, then realized that couldn't be right.

Then he saw the look of shock and horror on Emerson's face and Alexander's.

He met the Web's hazel eye, the human one, wide with disbelief. *The eye that sees,* he thought for some reason, *the hand that creates.* And suddenly, impossibly, Alexander's pupil was magnified a hundred times.

Mirrored in that pupil was a figure of gleaming white and silver.

Slowly, Urban glanced down at his arm. It was lithe white plastic with a platinum ball for an elbow. Farther down, a metal thigh depressed itself into a plastic cylinder.

Urban looked back up and into the hazel eye. He could see his reflection there perfectly, knowing, of a sudden, that he could magnify anything he saw, microscopically or telescopically.

His reflection was faceless. The head was a silvery sphere with a black, glassy strip encircling it like a blindfold. Tiny laser red streaks shot wildly across the glass like particles.

As his prosthetic foot completed that terrible step, Urban Myth stopped dead, more suddenly and completely than any human being could. The grid that formed his mouth unhinged itself, trying to cry out its agony and finding itself incapable.

Cinder heaved a sigh and shook her head. "They should have programmed you better, Urban," she said. "They really should have programmed you better."

Chapter 16

Not true! thought Alexander, *Not, not, not, not, not!!!*

But it was true. Even as he tried to pray otherwise, the thing moved, its white plastic torso rotating on white plastic hips.

Robot, Alexander's computer eye politely informed him, outlining the figure and labeling the various parts, corroborating what his other eye saw.

A white thigh shifted, sliding over the silver ball that acted as a knee, and the leg seemed to spring. The robot took a gliding step back.

And there was Urban, flesh and worn Sierra garb, brown curls shaking in the wind, broad, handsome, roguish face blank with terror and panic.

"Oh, God," the Sierra whispered.

"It's not possible," Sander insisted, touching upon his computer eye. It registered Urban there. *Human,* its lettering now insisted, *Male, Indo-European—*

"He's downloading directly into your computer," Cinder explained. "It would, after all, be pretty useless to have a VR disguise that any camera or computer could see through."

"That can't be!" Emerson blurted. The Jabberjaw was breathing hard, one hand over his heart as if to keep it from breaking out. "I mean," he pushed his glasses back up his nose. "For Virtual Reality you need lenses, implants—"

"It's the mythic field," Cinder went on, doggedly following her own agenda. "When he steps up onto the flagstones, the field interferes with his Virtual imaging. You might say that *its* myth cancels out his." Her lips pressed into a mild smirk.

"Oh, God," Urban muttered, "Oh, God! I'm not! I'm not!" But there was no conviction in his voice. He seemed to know it was a lie. He looked pleadingly at Alexander. "It's an illusion! I'm not!"

"Of course you're an illusion, Urban," Cinder said softly, her dark eyes deep and distant.

Alexander swallowed past a lump in his throat. All his life, his greatest fear had been that none of what he'd seen out his window or lived within his loft was real. He'd endured the paranoia, knowing that his companions could easily, far too easily be spies, scripted actors. And outside, the world he yearned for could all be pictures, all Virtual Reality. Even the information he studied, day after day, could be a plant, false.

And now, just when he'd begun to hope, to see the cracks of light, now the nightmare resurfaced, impossibly, horribly.

"How long have you known??" he demanded of Cinder.

She looked surprised by the question. "I've always known."

"You didn't tell me—" Alex shut his eyes; something was squeezing tight in his chest.

"Sander—" Urban cried, but as his hands passed beyond the invisible boundary, the skin vanished, leaving plastic fingers extended. Alexander tumbled back, almost off the edge, and Urban instantly jerked back his hands, even though his face showed that he would have rather leapt forward and snatched Alexander from the cliff side.

And that was when it clicked. *He's protecting me, looking after me, spying on me!* Alexander realized. It was so clear. That was why Urban had stayed with him, stayed with him when any other servant, never mind any other Sierra, would have left.

And then they heard the buzzing of motorcycles.

"Time to go!" Cinder announced, heading toward her cycle. "Urban will stay. Right here, the Mythic Field only interferes with the images he's sending," she coolly explained to Alex, "but taking him over Skylight Bridge would cut him off from his brain."

"His brain?"

Cinder pointed up. "An ingenious satellite orbiting the earth." Her eyes grew very bright. "Wonderfully imaginative, putting the brain out in space! And what a brain! Hybrid communication chips, neural net, microwave transmitters—" She glanced back at Emerson. "*That's* why you're experiencing the illusion without lenses or implants."

"Can't be—" Alexander said, giving Urban a wide berth as he limped after her. There was a kind of mad hope, a tight, desperate logic working in his mind. "That sort of manipulation of magnetic fields, X rays, microwave transmissions—VR never got that sophisticated, not before the wars!"

"With the military it did," Cinder said flatly, and mounted her bike. "Amazing what the armed forces can do! Of course, they always were ten years ahead of the current technology. Though I would venture to guess that Urban here is one of a kind. Aren't you, Urban?"

"No," he insisted, sounding more wishful than defiant.

She rolled the bike around. "Get into the sidecar, Alexy."

Alexander hesitated, locked once again between worlds. Forward beyond or backward, entrapment of one sort or another. He realized now how much he had trusted Urban, depended on Urban, more than he ever would have admitted. Predictable, pragmatic, and seemingly simple Urban.

Incredibly complex Urban, as it turned out. Lost technology with a lost purpose. And would he stay with that? It was an option, and one that had some surety, some reality.

But as Urban's gray eyes searched his, Alexander could not help but remember the glassy black reality, the flat surface with its laser streaks that served as a three hundred and sixty–degree eye for a machine.

There was nothing and no one to trust anymore.

Alexander climbed into the sidecar. He caught a glimpse of Urban's human face, hurt and pained, as if there were pins being driven under his nails. And Sander had to remind himself, force down with a memory of metal and plastic, that the expression was an illusion.

All an illusion.

The distant roar was louder now; it altered pitch, laboring up the hill.

"Emerson," Cinder said, for the Jabberjaw had not moved from the flagstone balcony; he seemed to be captured by her gaze, pinned as if staked out for a sacrifice. "You will stay here."

The Jabberjaw did not protest. He merely gazed at her with a look of pure misery, as if he'd always known she would ask something terrible of him.

"You can't—" Alex ventured, not knowing why he even thought to care. He was cut off by the roar of the single motorcycle that popped up from the side road, racing its way across the empty asphalt.

Cinder revved the motor.

"No!" Urban yelled throwing himself in front of them. Alexander felt his heart go dead—*He's going to stop us. It's how he's programmed. For me, he's after me!*

At the same moment, their enemy on the motorcycle drew a weapon and aimed for Alexander. And Urban Myth shifted, placing himself in the line of fire.

Sander's heart jumped back to life; programmed indeed! And with his safety as its first priority.

Cinder instantly pushed off. For one second it looked as if she were snatching up the chance offered her by Urban to escape down the hill. Then she swerved, shooting forward so fast it took a moment for Alexander to register the truth.

And then they were flying off the cliff.

What kind of decision was this??? Kelly thought as the first canister of yellow gas landed on the pavement.

She caught her breath and swerved around the rolling gas bomb, nearly sending her bike into a crater.

Bad enough Alexander and friends had found out about them somehow, and made a run for it. Bad enough the bastards had given them a fifteen-minute chase down the Hollywood freeway and now had them spitting gravel as they flew up toward the observatory. Bad enough they were recklessly, hazardously skidding past potholes and cracks barely visible in the sun-dappled road!

What the hell did Blake think he was doing???

They'd been almost on top of the sons when she'd heard the thrum of the helo overhead! *Damn Blake! Didn't he think she could handle this!*

It came swooping down, hovering low over their prey like some great dark shadow. Kelly tried to wave at it. This was her operation! Damn it! And then—

Blom!

A canister exploded on the pavement, yellow gas hissed out, escaping in a foul cloud, and Kelly nearly screamed! Was the helo planning on shooting gas bombs until they were all drugged and unconscious, flying off their bikes???

Blam!

Jesus! What—

She saw sunlight gleam off a great glass ball, saw black blades spinning down at her; her Sneezy chip kicked in, amplifying her reflexes; her arms strained as she jerked the handlebars to the right and the bike went skidding forty-five degrees toward the trees.

And then she was off the seat, no memory of her legs making the jump; gravel stabbing into her back as she rolled into a somersault; she heard her bike crash into trees just a second before the explosion rocked her.

The earth bucked, and she bounced painfully, tumbling and skidding over the cracked pavement. A flare burned through her eyelids, searing her skin; a molten stab of pain shot through her hip.

Screams, screeches, crashes.

¡Dios!

She winced open her eyes, threw up her hands as flames spit from the skidding wreckage of the helicopter. A searing whiff of acid smoke went up her nostrils, and she coughed.

The smoking carcass blocked the road, its tail broken, the blades snapped; its bulbous head was cracked. Two forms, pulped and red and charred, spilled out from that shattered egg.

Kelly swallowed, and pushed up. Her hip screamed, and her sight went black. She found herself back on the graveled pavement, gasping, head spinning.

The hell—! Her gloved hand came up slippery with blood. There was a bleeding red hole in her hip; a flying bit of metal from the wreckage must have punctured her.

"Grumpy!" She knocked the chip into action.

Percentage? it demanded.

One hundred! she thought back. And the pain disappeared.

She clamped her teeth and pushed up, legs trembling. Grumpy would cut off the pain for the moment; and for the moment she was going to have to let the wound just bleed—hope something serious hadn't been punctured. Catching her prey came first.

She coughed and blinked against the smoke that billowed through the broken canopy of trees. Half of the Munitions were on their sides moaning. One was holding what looked to be a broken arm. Concrete was alive and moving, bending, limping from one to the other.

Damn! Kelly searched for and found her bike among the roots of the pine trees. One of the tires was flat. Heaving it up and back onto the road left her breathless and shaking.

She glanced down at the little screen centered between her handlebars.

"Hijo de puta!" The map that displayed the roads was still there, but the twin dots they'd been following were gone. Vanished!

That shocked her worse than the blast had. How could anyone interfere with a satellite trace! Especially one ordered, observed, and controlled by Executive Hawthorne!?

No time! She reprimanded herself. There was a tunnel up ahead, and beside it, a road heading up to the observatory.

Were I being chased, she thought, *I'd cut through the tunnel and back down the other side of the hill. But then, why head up this road in the first place?*

Unless . . . unless there was someone or something at the observatory—

She snapped a toggle. There was a foaming sound from within the flattened tire, and two seconds later, it was up and ready to ride. She mounted it and shot off, banking it off the road and off the dusty side of the hill to avoid the smoldering ruins of the helicopter.

The wind cleared the sting from her eyes and cooled the sweat on her face. She jumped the cycle back onto the road, her arms shaking with the effort it took to keep the bike steady.

At the last possible moment, she cut up the side road. Los Angeles spread out before her, and a memory flashed in her mind of a little girl coming up over a hill, seeing the city for the first time and breathing in the promises it seemed to offer.

And then she heard the renewed roar of motorcycles, distant but right behind her.

Blondes! she thought with an amazed shake of the head. She had to hand it to Concrete and her ladies. They hadn't complained or reneged on their deal. When the quarry fled and the plan to entrap had fallen through, the Blondes had just shrugged their shoulders and climbed onto their bikes.

"Let's get after them, then," Concrete had said, matter-of-factly.

Kelly figured they were either out to kill her or still holding to their bargain. She didn't care much which, so long as they let her collar her prey!

The domes of the observatory appeared, and then she was racing across an abandoned parking lot.

There they were! Alexander in the sidecar with that strange woman driver. There was a black-haired man on the flagstones of an observation balcony, and there, standing before Alexander, was Urban Myth.

Kelly snatched out her gun, the one she'd been told to use against Urban and only Urban.

Obligingly, Urban Myth jumped out of Alexander's path to stand before her.

The cycle with the sidecar shot forward—

And made right for the cliff side!

"Madre de Dios!!" Kelly cried.

There was a scream from Alexander, and the cycle with its sidecar flew off the cliff—

And vanished into thin air.

Simultaneously, Urban Myth leapt, incredibly far and fast toward the edge. Without thinking, Kelly fired; the dart hit him, dead in the neck.

He stiffened like a flat wooden puppet, and then crumpled so completely that Kelly braked her bike, afraid she'd killed him. He fell just short of the flag-stones, one hand reaching desperately, as if to pull time backward.

Kelly dismounted and ran forward. The other man, a washed-out Jabberjaw, was kneeling by Urban's body. Kelly skidded to a halt, fumbling out her hand laser and leveling it at him.

"Get back!" she shouted, and the pale man sprung away, hands raised.

"Don't shoot!" he asked, eyes blinking behind his glasses.

Keeping him in her sights, she inched onto the flag-stones, past the telescope. She heard motorcycles roaring across the asphalt and dared a quick glance back. Concrete and two others appeared, looking scratched, filthy, and disheveled, but very determined.

She glanced out over the cliff. She could see Los Angeles, and the billowing black smoke from the heli-copter wreckage. But of the motorcycle and its pre-cious sidecar, there was no hint, not amid the trees, shrubs, dirt, or rocks.

Nothing.

"Where did they go!?" Kelly demanded of the Jabberjaw.

Hands still lifted, the frightened man timidly shrugged. "I don't know," he said, "I swear!"

Concrete, limping and with a catch in her breath, came up. Kelly, eyes locked on the Jabberjaw, felt the Blonde at her shoulder.

"You're bleeding like a stuck pig," the Munition remarked.

"It'll keep. How about your sisters?"

"Houston's taking care of them."

"Sorry," Kelly ventured. It wasn't enough, but right now she hadn't much more to offer. "You planning on taking me out for it?"

Concrete shrugged philosophically. "You didn't promise no risk. What I want to know is who called in the fucking helicopter?"

"My *Per My* friend. And I'll be talking to him about it, believe me."

Concrete nodded, satisfied. "Where'd the big bike go? The one with the sidecar?"

Kelly hesitated a moment. "Got away," she said. "Clean away." She motioned to Emerson. "Watch this one for me, will ya?"

"Sure."

Kelly pocketed the laser as Concrete, a knife appearing in her hand, motioned the Jabberjaw away. He went easily enough, but his eyes stayed on Urban Myth's still form.

For the second time in two days, Kelly thought about her mother, about how she had worn white blouses with red and yellow hand-stitched zigzags rounding the yoke. About the last time Kelly had seen her. They'd been camped not far from here, behind the broken remains of the Hollywood sign. Kelly had been playing around the giant letters when her mother, without warning or explanation, headed off down the hill.

"Mama?" Kelly had called, starting after.

"Puedaté allá," her mother had told her. *"Voveré. Espera, como un angel."*

Wait here. Be an angel. And, obediently, Kelly had stayed where she was, right beside the letter "O." Her mother had waved good-bye, and headed down through the dry, overgrown grass.

Kelly had waited there for three days, but her mother never came back.

She glanced down at Urban, and frowned, perplexed. With her foot she nudged his limp hand, causing it to tumble onto the asphalt.

So.

She would take these two back to Executive Hawthorne, see they got to him personally. And she would allow him to have her Doc scanned so that he could see for himself what had happened.

And then, if she dared, she would ask some questions, some very important questions.

Chapter 17

There had been a cave, that he remembered; a red-hazed plunge into a tunnel, a hole in the sky that could not possibly be there . . . Cinder sending them over a cliff into the mouth of that cave. Emerson and Urban—

Urban.

Memory of a creature steel and plastic, reality behind an image, or an image under reality. A lie, a betrayal.

And behind it all, a staccato rhythm, his thumping, aching heart, still pumping oxygen to a frenzied brain.

His bad leg was aching, and he realized that he was standing even though he could not remember getting to his feet. He found it bitterly ironic that even now, in whatever limbo had claimed him, he must suffer that old, irritating indignity.

Andrew Lloyd, how it hurt!

Gimp, he thought angrily. *Gimp.* Old thought.

Open up your mind, that was Christine's angora soft voice. He could hear it lilting over the pounding in his ears; maybe he was dead. Or maybe he just needed to take a breath.

He opened his mouth, and air rushed into his lungs, rushed out.

Oh, God.

He opened his eyes; there was the smell of water and stone. His stomach tumbled; grimly he swallowed down mouthful after mouthful of very wet saliva. He was not, he was damn well *not*, going to be sick!

Above him, the colors of the sky swirled like the robes of Africa, sunflower yellow, Titian orange, Jupiter red, and iris purple.

His mask was in hand; how it had come to be there he could not say. He was seeing this fresco of a sky with both eyes, and he knew, somehow knew, that this glazed dome was it; day or night, this was the sky, now and for all time.

"The colors of creativity," Cinder said.

Alex started, barely catching his balance as his feet stumbled upon a rocky surface. She was to the left and a little behind him, goggles up and hands on her hips, beautiful brown face, mild and content. It was only then that he absorbed the landscape, craggy with pockets and eddies that stretched out as far as the eye could see. The two of them stood beside an inlet of liquid, a tidal pool he might have called it had there been an ocean nearby. It was preternaturally still. Rocks poked up, small islands that seemed to be floating on the brilliant, reflective surface.

"You're stepping on my ear."

This time Alexander did fall, only to be caught and steadied by Cinder. The huge leporine creature to his right eyed him balefully. It was charcoal gray with long, thin, marsupial limbs that ended in blunt-nailed paws; its fur was short, but soft and thick. The hunch of its spine, level with Alexander's eyes, rolled down into a neck and then back up into a nobby head sporting a jowly face with a drooping, whiskered muzzle. Heavy brows hung sleepily over large, dark doleful

eyes and, to either side of the head, a pair of suede
ears hung limply, sadly down. They were so long they
trailed on the ground. It was on the tip of one such
ear that Alexander had inadvertently been standing.

The animal huffed at him, then it scratched at its
head with its hind leg and said, in a gruff, fumbling
voice. "They used to go up. Then I started listening
to Metallica and 'poof!' down they went. Never been
the same."

"Forgot my notebook." Cinder was patting at her
jacket. "Must have left it with the motorcycle."

"Motorcycle?" Alexander repeated, absently
stuffing his mask into his pocket. The motorcycle was
nowhere in sight. "Where is it?"

"Where would you like it to be?" Cinder looked
up from a ragged piece of yellowed paper she'd dug
out of her back pocket. "Ethelred, did you purchase
a silk suit and a maroon tie?"

"Is this Virtual Reality? It is, isn't it?"

"That depends on whether you believe the universe
is holographic or not," Ethelred said.

Catastrophic reaction, he thought; it was one of a
thousand flickering ideas pivoting behind his eyes.
They flashed like lighthouse beams, little snatches of
logic. *Psychotic reaction to being outside—if I am outside.* That was the fear, of course. That he had never
actually gotten outside. He could feel the tight, cable
knit of his mind beginning to unravel. And ship-
wrecked on the edges were his emotions, quivering,
ready to spiral down into a muddy, foaming
Charybdis.

He wished to heaven Urban were there, to cut
through it all with some simple statement solid as
bedrock.

Urban.

My last companion, he thought, remembering how
he used to pretend, late at night, that his companions

were really long-lost relatives. He'd fantasized about
discovering a record or a secret mole marking them
as his kin.

He'd even, down in the secret, shameful recesses of
his childish heart, dreamed it of Urban.

A lie. A VR trick. That's all Urban was. His last
companion. Quite possibly all his companions, except
Christine. He couldn't accept that Christine had been
a lie.

"You're in Schrodinger's Neighborhood," Cinder
said, her firm, quiet words floating around him like
feathers. And as she spoke, the sky mutated, clouds
sweeping across it, casting her features into shadow.
"*Axis mundi,* to be more precise. The town square of
the global village. This is it; the widest, most complete,
most immediate networking possible. All information
flies up to this sky, travels inward to this center, flows
down to this vast sea."

"So we're still in the loft?"

Cinder's eyes grew bright. And Alexander finally
recognized where he'd seen their like: his last nursemaid, the Blue Liner. Her eyes had held the same
brilliant glitter when riding high on a rush of Blues.
He swallowed in a dry throat. What drug was Cinder
feeding on?

Get a grip, Alexander, get a grip! He thought angrily,
*This is either a dream, an illusion, or reality. Whichever
it is, it has to be dealt with. But, oh, God! Am I even
who I think I am? It would be programming if he
were . . . No! Couldn't be! Couldn't be—*

But there was Urban.

The fractals split again, cracks upon cracks, and he
felt a loss of breath. This was the way he felt when
he woke from dreams. As if his mind and soul were
about to shatter. Only this time there was no waking
up.

"Geeze, Cinder." Ethelred pushed with his hind

legs, then pulled forward, a seesawing hop that brushed his fur against Alexander's side. "What's wrong with him?"

"He's having a nervous breakdown," she said simply.

"I am not!" Sander said.

The creature cocked its nobby head. "Would pounding his head on the rocks make him feel any better?"

"Probably not."

"How about multivitamins?"

"I'm all right!"

Cinder gave Sander a sidewise glance. "Louie," she suddenly decided. "If ever there was anyone who could straighten out a metaphysical psychosis, it's Louie."

"He'll rag on me," Ethelred sadly observed.

Cinder shrugged at that. "Come on, Alexy. We're going to make you feel better."

She set off, hips swinging in a leisurely stride. Sander held back for one moment before fear got the better of him. Whatever Cinder was, her company was better than being left alone.

"You ought to enter the inner mind with less fear, Alexy," Cinder remarked as he caught up to her; her eyes slid below their almond lids, and she gave her head a shake like a little girl feeling her hair down her back. "Merge it with that shadow you see behind the city, with the dreams you dream. You have the ability to do that, you know."

"Hey, Cinder!" A man appeared, out of nowhere. His skin was dead black against the blinding white of his shorts and T-shirt. He was jogging steadily across the rocky surface in a pair of neon orange running shoes.

"Roy!" Cinder waved as he passed. A moment later, he disappeared behind the horizon.

Alexander stared after. *Unwinding fantasies,* he thought. *Unwinding into darkness.* Another Web prayer. They were falling into his mind like stars.

"Do you mean," he ventured, hoping that if he kept talking, kept thinking, he could hold himself together, "that I can have a *coniunctio* of realities? Is that what's happened here? I've unified my personal psychic reality with a collective psychotic unconscious and objective reality?"

Cinder smiled. "I'm saying that your endoskeleton allows you to intuit the different faces of reality, where they merge and connect."

"My what?" He felt his face go pale.

"Bauhaus Plaza," she announced, pointing just ahead to where the ash white remains of a single tree sprouted abruptly out of the rocks.

There seemed to be a large half-submerged boulder before the tree. As they neared, it unexpectedly moved and turned. And Alexander shrunk back from the flat, wide beak of a platypus the size of an armchair.

"Glad you could make it," the creature carped. Its small, disdainful eyes glowered at them. "The idea is to alternate the legs one ahead of the other. That makes you walk, which makes you move, which gets you from there to here in a reasonable amount of time."

"Louie." Cinder nodded to the platypus, which in response flapped its beaver-shaped tail. "How are they?"

"That's it? That's the best question you can ask? They've been in the same condition for forty thousand years! How do you think they are?"

"Ah!" Ethelred looked as if he'd come up with an idea. "I see. They're the same as always."

"He lost the owner's manual to his brains," Louie confided in Alexander. The Web just nodded, too dis-

tracted by the creature's size to do more than stare.
For some reason Louie was more fantastic, more dis-
turbing than Ethelred.

"Come take a look," the platypus invited, shifting
on its webbed feet. And that's when Alexander saw
the grave. Inside it, knees up fetal style, sat five venerable men and five ancient women. Their skin was ox-
blood dark, noses large and wide, their graying,
flyaway hair either marigold bright or the color of pep-
per. Swirls of vivid yellow and white patterned their
bare bodies like charms. Their hands, curled up near
their chins, were painted ocher red.

Every one of them was deep asleep, and one snoring
old man, Alex noted with amazement, had a platter-
size turtle balanced on his head. Even as Alex stared,
the turtle turned its sulky eyes on him, then pensively
drew in its narrow head.

"What are they doing?" Sander asked.

"Dreaming," Louie prosaically answered. "That's
what happens when you shut your eyes and go to
sleep. Or weren't you aware that they were asleep?"

"And how would you know?" Sander sneered back.
"Been waddling through their heads, have you?"

"Oh-ho!" The platypus rocked back on its hind
legs. "Think ya got a sharp mouth, do ya, bright
eyes?"

"Sharper than yours, and I wouldn't forget it. So,
are you going to tell me who these dreamers are? Why
you bothered pointing them out to me? And why I
should be impressed with them?"

"Why you should be impressed?" Louie snorted.
"No good reason. Except that they're it. Humanity's
first mothers, first fathers. First *dreamers,* boychick!
First storytellers!"

"Is that so?"

"That's the rumor, sweet pea."

"And I suppose the rumor says they'll wake up when doomsday rolls around?"

Louie snorted in disgust. "Sweet cheesecake, Cinder! Where'd you find this one, in a Cracker Jack box? No, Mr. Know-it-all! As a matter of fact, grapevine says they wake when the right defendant comes along."

"Who's the right one?"

"How should I know? I'm just a platypus."

"The right one," Cinder said softly, "will be like them, a mythmaker at the center of a new dreamtime. A single one who can do what it took the ten of them to do, who, fully awake, will finally take their place." Her eyes shifted to him, glowing brighter than ever.

That bothered and scared Alexander. Profoundly. *Ten dreamers,* he thought. *Five and five of them, framing a grave like a living mandala. Five: the number of Man. The fingers on a hand. Ten: the number of the cosmos, of unity and wholeness. . . .*

Ten, as Cinder had just pointed out, always returned the cycle back to one.

He shivered and covered up his discomfort with a cough. "Ever tried to wake one of them up?" he said, roughly.

"I did," Ethelred announced, "once."

"*He* tried to wake them!" Louie said. "I should have known! What can you expect from something with a nose that droops like a camel's?"

"No," Cinder disagreed with a shake of her oval head. "No, Louie, I think you're wrong."

"The bunny's imaginary friend thinks I'm wrong!"

"Ethelred's nose looks more like a llama's. Don't you think, Alexander?"

"What happened?" Alex asked impatiently.

"What happened when?" Ehtelred cocked his ungainly head.

"When you tried to wake one!!"

The creature stared at him blankly. "I can't wake them up. I'm just a myth."

"I can't believe this!" Louie yelled, tail slamming. "What is the deal with you?! Did your brains climb out and slide down your ears?!"

"Told you he would rag on me," Ethelred sadly reminded Alexander.

"What I wouldn't give for a good pair of incisors so I could bite this yutz!"

"Feeling better, Alexy?" Cinder's gaze scanned him up and down. "Yes, I can see you are. Time to go. The others are waiting. Bye, Louie. See you later."

"God, I hope not!"

"Who's waiting for us?" Sander demanded as she dragged him away.

"Does it matter?" she asked, strolling past a pair of elephants, each with an Indonesian girl riding upon its neck. The elephants were headed in the opposite direction, trunks swinging, their passengers swaying with the slow, loping gait.

"Hello, Cinder!" One of the women waved, her multicolored wooden bangles clustering together on her arm, pagoda-like.

Alex stepped back, almost slipping, the size and smell of the elephants startling him.

Cinder waved back, and then the elephants and their riders were past.

"This *is* Virtual Reality," Alex said then, and trembled because he suddenly accepted it as possible. It gave him the same feeling he'd had when, as a child, he realized his sadistic companion was going to beat him again.

"Not on a technical level," Cinder said.

"What do you mean by that?"

Cinder came to a stop. "Why did you become a Web?"

"What's that got to do with it?"

"Everything has to do with everything, Alexy. You know that. Why?"

"Because a woman I loved was one."

"Oh, hey," Ethelred bobbed his nobby head; Sander twitched. He'd almost forgotten the creature. "That's beautiful, really wonderful."

Alex snorted. "It was pathetic. I thought she would stay, you see, if I became a Web. And I wanted her to stay, desperately."

"Did she leave?"

"In a manner of speaking. She died." A thoughtful pause. "I used to have fantasies of what I would do if she left—climb out the windows, sneak down the elevator shaft. I was ready to crawl after her if I had to." He blinked rapidly, suddenly finding the sky too bright. "Then she died, and staying a Web was the only thing I could do to be near her, to make it up to her."

"Wonderful!" Cinder emphasized. "You loved her, and she was a Web, and to stay near her you stayed a Web. Symbolic magic, the heart's blood of the human imagination. Now, tell me, what about the Web religion was *her;* what about it still speaks to you in her voice?"

That caught him cold. He frowned and mentally circled the question. "A Web," he said, careful as a surgeon with a new scalpel, "believes that humans are united by their unique ability to wish and dream. The monster dreams of beauty, the present dreams of the past, and the demon in hell dreams of heaven. Each of us dreams of what we would have or would be but are not." Another pause, a long one this time. "The prisoner dreams of freedom. Becoming a Web gained me admittance into humanity and its realm of wishes. I knew that everyone out there dreamed, just like me."

"The wish for wishes." Cinder nodded. "A beautifully recursive fantasy. And elegantly dichotomous with your uncle's vision of humanity."

Sander caught his breath. He couldn't have heard—she couldn't have meant—

"My uncle???"

"No, no, no, that's all downside." Ethelred's tone was lofty. "His uncle's into individual dreams, not the everyman theory of Web dreaming."

"But his uncle is basing his theory on the concept that human dreams are generic enough that a computer could satisfy them all."

"What uncle?!?!"

"Actually," Ethelred said, "he isn't, technically, your uncle. At least, not anymore. Isn't that right?" he asked of Cinder.

Alexander was flabbergasted. "Well, what is he, then?! And where is he?!?"

"I told you, Alexander," Cinder said with a dimpled smile. "Everything has to do with everything; and where and what are exactly the same. Exactly the same." And then she started to grow.

Alexander's heart came to a stop.

She soared upward, lengthening, her skin fading.

When she was as tall as a skyscraper and chalk white, she took a step back and merged with the others. They filled the horizon, cloud-like splashes, morphing forms outlined by a glistening liquid red corona. They reminded him, uncannily, of a disk he had watched on childbirth: newborn babies fresh from the womb, chubby and elongated, smooth, slicked with blood.

They had no mouths, just wide round eyes, bright as suns.

Alexander caught at his chest and worked to breathe, even as the one that had been Cinder leaned down from the vast sky, her bottomless pupils large and deep like pools in a forgotten cavern.

"Don't be afraid," she said in a voice that sounded like rain falling in the distance. "Quantum physics can explain all this."

Chapter 18

The cloud creatures seemed amused, filled with a grand, light, vaporous humor that expanded like air.

Alex, much to his own amazement, was furious. He felt small and human and pathetic. And he hated the creatures for making him feel that way.

"Don't you want to know what this is all about?" the one that had been Cinder queried; her voice was the same, but slow, filled with tidal rises and falls.

"I *know* what it's about!" he heard himself shout. "Zenith and nadir, Nietzschean nightmares and electromagnetism!"

"The stuff that dreams are made of," the cloud creature agreed.

"Lies," Alex said, defiantly.

"Imagination," the cloud creatures corrected in unison, their claret red auras crackling. It was a moment of profound déjà vu, a sudden epiphany sharp as a slap. These were like the lightning storms he saw on the back of his eyelids.

"And what do you want from me?" Damn, they were *huge*! They seemed to touch the glazed sky, and they went on forever, like some grotesque skyline, filling the horizon. "You do want something from me."

"We want you to bring back the legends," they answered.

"Oh, that's wonderfully specific!"

The cloudy creatures hovered over him like the underside of reality. They seemed to be conferring.

"Your antennae receives beta state transmissions up to two miles."

That spooked the anger right out of him. His mouth went dead dry. "The . . . endoskeleton you mentioned?"

"Yes. Every bone in your body has a sensor."

Well, he thought to himself, *you knew you were a freak. You just didn't know what kind of freak.*

"Subcutaneous electrodes match your mental state to the beta waves. Somatic overrides lock out your own dream activity."

"Meaning, I pick up on other people's fantasies and have almost none of my own. What else is new?"

"The man who did this to you is named Hawthorne. He is a Virtual. In a distant sort of way, he is also your only relative, your 'uncle' so to speak. He wants to use you; so do we."

Alexander gathered in a breath. None of this should have surprised him, but somehow, it still did. And it still hurt. "What use does he want to put me to?"

"The usual: to gain power, control."

"And you don't want the same?"

"When humanity was young," said the Cinder cloud, "it walked with its own unconscious. It created and lived with what it imagined, the monsters of the deep . . . and the gods."

"Go on," Sander said cautiously.

"Not many years ago dreamtime and real time almost merged, as they had in the beginning. It was not to be. Humanity gave up its godlike dreams, and little myths took our place. And then the Virtuals monopolized our one hope of restoring the balance. But for them, we would be soaring beyond all physical boundaries, along the path of stars and the curves of time."

A pause, and this time Alexander was sure the creatures were grinning even if they had no mouths. "We're not seeking control, Alexy. To the contrary, we want to give humanity the power to walk with the gods. Help us, Alexy. We'd really appreciate it."

"And if I refuse."

"We don't think you'll refuse. It is little enough to ask in exchange for your freedom, now and before, when only in fancy could you escape your loft. And we think you will find it well worth your while." The red eyes seemed to laugh. "Well worth it."

Blake had his back to her when Kelly entered. He was standing before the vast picture window taking in the spectacular splash of a raspberry and cream sunset. In his hand he held a delicate, opalescent goblet filled with dark liquid.

Madeira, cherry-flavored brandy, gin. Her Cookbook dutifully listed the drink's ingredients, floating the words before her eyes. Kelly, instead, watched how the sunlight rippled over the lip of the glass. She'd been seething mad on the journey back, and in her mind she'd locked together words like parts of a pistol to fire at him. But the hour she'd spent on a table while a Holist sewed her shut had cooled her temper, and seeing Blake now, all sad and mild, made any fury seem childish, unimportant.

"Have you reviewed your tape?" he asked softly.

"I only just got out of medical," she said, joining him at the window. She had to move slowly; her hip hurt something awful despite the painkillers.

She leaned against the window frame and tried to gaze out at the view with identical nonchalance, but it was hard. Only Executives and their servants were permitted such scenic pictures, so vast and powerful they took the breath away. Whenever she was given a chance to share in the magic, she inevitably felt unworthy and small.

Hawthorne had once told her that he valued her for that humility. "*Humble people are loyal people,*" he had said. Oddly enough, that had made her proud.

"You were wounded," Blake said. "Was it bad?"

"Had to dig some scrap metal out; they gave me a tetanus shot and put me on antibiotics to be sure. I'll be sore and limping, but the wound's all pasted up and bandaged."

He nodded at that, and Kelly shifted. The Holist had allowed her to shower, and she'd gratefully changed into a pair of sweats and a T-shirt. It left her feeling odd beside the impeccable secretary.

"About the helicopter," she ventured, not angry, just saying, "why did you send it in?"

"Fear," Blake responded as casually as he might chat about a new weapon. He passed the drink by his mouth, barely seeming to wet his lips with it. Kelly caught the hot cherry fragrance of it. She flashed on a memory of warmth spreading down from her collarbone to her lungs, tasting rum for the first time.

She remembered an old man at a campfire with a gray stubble beard that glistened all prickles and sweat. Speaking only Spanish, the old bastard had drunkenly boasted that he had lived through the cholera and other plagues of waste and pollution and mob violence in Mexico as well as the sexually transmitted epidemics; more, he'd managed to evade the assault weapons and napalm, and slip across the border; and, of course, he'd survived the hate wars. He had shown her scars: this from a bullet, that from acid.

"*Nos tratan como perros!*" he kept muttering. *They treat us like dogs!* He never bothered explaining who "they" were. And he had poured a bit of the warm brown liquor into her nine-year-old hands. *"Perros,"* he insisted, *"como perros."*

She'd felt her father stir in her for the first time on that day as she took a sip of rum and listened to the lies of that filthy old drunkard. Her father had been a patrolman, thirty years her mother's senior; during the wars, he slaughtered illegals wholesale. But not her mother. Instead, he had fallen in love, or so Kelly's mother had tried to explain to her, the day before she walked down that hill, leaving her forever.

"Your padre," her mother had said, *"he loved me too much to kill me. We shared a dream, you see, and I made him see that. That's why I loved him, even though his kind murdered my family."*

Loved him enough to name their only child after him, the man who had impregnated her then died of some disease or other.

Sitting with that old man, Kelly had finally understood that she was her father's daughter. Because she knew that, given the chance, she'd kill this lying, dirty old fart. Such people lived in misery and made the world a misery with them.

And that had to be stopped, no matter the cost. That, she suspected, had been her father's dream, the one he shared with her mother: to stop the misery that infected the world.

"I ought to have trusted you, God knows," Blake said now in a tone uncannily like the drunk old man's. "Worked with you long enough . . . but I was scrambling to cover all the bases, you see." A long swallow of the drink this time. "I nearly ruined everything. Would you like a drink?" For the first time he looked at her. His eyes, she saw, were bloodshot, and the wrist poking out from the starched white cuff of his sleeve looked thin and frail.

It scared her, bad. "What's happened?"

Something like a smile flitted across his face. "I've been demoted." He slipped around behind the single, perfectly square sheet of obsidian that formed his desk. With a touch to the surface, he commanded open a screen in the wall. "Executive Hawthorne," he said to the air, "Kelly's here." He met her eyes. "Serve him better than I did."

Her mouth dropped open, but Blake was already on his way out the door before she could say his name.

"Blake—"

Too late. The secretary and his drink vanished into the hall, the door sliding firmly shut behind.

"Kelly?"

She did not know when the picture windows had changed into a set of screens, each filled with the image of Executive Hawthorne. She felt that she ought to have noticed, but couldn't quite reprimand herself for the lapse. All she could think was that Echo Park, the Hollywood Hills, and the sunset were gone; and it suddenly, chillingly occurred to her that they might never have been there in the first place.

Hawthorne, casual in a pair of gray pants and a thick, shawl-collared sweater, seemed unaware of her discomfort. The black Virtual eyes were bright and focused, reading her thoughts.

"Men like Blake are only useful until they fail. Thereafter their sense of worth falls so low that their capabilities become irreparably damaged."

"But—" For some reason her lips felt fat and heavy.

Hawthorne held up an imperious finger, long and very straight. "I understand. It can't be helped. My own fault, if you'd care for a true confession. I gave Blake too much flexible responsibility—I say flexible meaning that it required more fuzzy logic than he was capable of. You, however, are quite superior when it comes to improvisation."

"Me?"

"You. No, not a word!" The Executive insisted, "I won't waste valuable time discussing whether my faith in you is justified. We have more serious matters to discuss—"

Kelly shook her head, feeling as if she were tossing away pieces of herself with each swing. She felt guilty, pained, and, heaven forgive her, elated. What she'd always wanted, but—*Oh, God, poor Blake*—

"You can't possibly transfer all of Blake's operations over to me—" she blurted, halting as she realized she was contradicting him. She shouldn't have come in angry, she thought, crazily. If only she hadn't been angry at Blake. "I'm *field* trained, Executive Hawthorne."

"So you are and so you'll stay!" he assured her with his quick quirk of a smile. "Never fear, Kelly. I know what I'm doing. I don't want you to *become* Blake, I merely want you to oversee certain aspects of his former network. We'll discuss details later. Right now, I want to review with you the Doc scan." His image shifted off two of the windows, centering onto the middle one. The other two fuzzed gray, and then a picture came on.

"*Watch this one*," she heard her voice command, and the replay showed Concrete moving toward the Jabberjaw.

"*Sure*," Concrete agreed, wisps of inky hair fluttering in the wind.

Kelly felt her hands go wet and icy. She knew what Hawthorne wanted to go over. She wanted to see it herself.

Did I see it, or didn't I?

Doc's record followed her eyes as she scanned Urban's still form; she'd been confused, at the time, by his unnatural stiffness.

"Here it is," Hawthorne said, and the picture

zoomed in for a close-up of Urban's hand, the one lying on the stones.

It was white and silver: robotic.

She *had* seen it. Now as then, she frowned, saw her foot nudge the hand to be sure. But as it slid off the flagstones onto the pavement, it turned to flesh.

"Holographic image?" she demanded. At the time she had supposed she'd been mistaken. The light, the smoke, the sweat in her eyes. Now she knew she hadn't been.

"Some of it was holographic," Hawthorne said with a smile, "yes."

Kelly licked her lips. This was big, and this was dangerous; very carefully she framed and asked her next question. "Which part?"

Hawthorne's smile went cold, very cold. "The one you want to be real, Kelly. Isn't that always the way? Come into my office. It's time we talked."

She caught her breath, felt her heart pounding loud enough to count the beats. "How—?"

"Right across from you, behind the center shelving, the one holding the disks."

There was no need to ask. Kelly was well trained at finding and opening secret doors. This one was fairly simple, a touch to one of the knobs holding tight the Plexiglas sheeting over the shelves.

Executive Hawthorne vanished from the windows, leaving the raw colors of sunset behind. They washed over the disks as the black shelving swung open, smooth and silent.

So this is it, Kelly thought, and found herself wishing, with odd fervency, that it were not. She wanted to be more in control, as she was in her visions of this moment. Entering like this, by herself, with no protocol, no one to show her how to show proper respect to an Executive—

Madre! And dressed as she was, all casual and sloppy—

It was all wrong.

She went in anyway.

The room behind the shelving took her by surprise. She'd seen Executive Hawthorne's office a thousand times, and she'd been expecting the elegant Japanese chairs of polished maple red cherry wood, the wide, matching desk, and an English armchair, all of it centered on a rug, eggshell and cobalt. The Executive never sat behind the desk, always before it, either leaning against it or resting in the armchair. That is what Kelly had anticipated.

Instead, she entered a room filled with monitors. The walls were squares of gray, the floor black tile. She felt Doc try, instinctively, to adjust her sight to the darkness and countermanded the implant and her instincts as well. It would be presumptive and disrespectful, she thought, to use infrared without Hawthorne's permission.

The screens across from her flickered, and Executive Hawthorne's office appeared upon them. For one split second, the surrounding screens gave her the illusion of being there.

Hawthorne, arms folded, smiled at her from behind the desk. "Well?" he asked, lips quirking.

"I—" words tumbled, none of them right, all of them wanting to be said—"I had thought—if I am now in Blake's position—that we would be meeting face-to-face, sir."

The lips went up into a full smile, tight and quick.

"This is face-to-face, Kelly."

She started to shake her head, not understanding, and then she shivered.

She understood now. Blessed Mother of Jesus. She understood.

Chapter 19

Emerson wasn't sure he wanted to remove the dart.

The guards had laid out Urban on the couch, a long, burned black deco piece with tire-wheel armrests.

Sugar and coffee decor, from top to bottom. Emerson wanted to shrug off such drama, but it reminded him too uncannily of his Poetry Closet. The actual center and heart of Emerson's long-lost home, the original, narrow, high-ceiling room that had been a coffeehouse nearly seventy years ago, had had the same checkered tiles as this elegant room; it had also had the same sort of curtains, sheer, sleek, and milky, billowing gracefully under the patient spin of the ceiling fan. It had been one of his jobs to tie back those curtains with the onset of daylight, so that they framed the gleaming silver counter with its cylindrical glass case of shelved baked goods. Everyone had called the case the "Jewel Box."

Emerson remembered the hours he'd spent as a child polishing that counter till it gleamed, wiping the Jewel Box to crystal clarity. *Look!* had been the message in that naive zeal, *look at what I've done! See how dedicated I am? how useful!* It had given him a false sense of purpose, polishing and cleaning; of course, it had also given the other children a nerve to pinch. They snickered when he brought up, at Thursday night clear-the-air chats, his concern for a clean sink; and they had deliberately smeared the Jewel Box with fingerprints and honey.

Hanging above the Jewel Box had been two pinstriped lanterns of frothy silk. The older poets used to say that one was a zeppelin, the other a hot-air balloon. One day Emerson had gone into the Closet's vast library (an old bookstore that, seventy years ago, had been the coffeehouse's left-hand neighbor) and plucked down an encyclopedia and looked up both words. Thereafter he always saw the fixtures floating away, carrying him up into the sky.

Was that where Cinder had gone? he wondered. The opening had cut into the very air, impossibly hanging against the heavens like some proscenium arch onto a stage.

"I always remain in the audience," Emerson observed ironically, miserably. He thought of his lost Poetry Closet family and how they'd always come back from excursions to the clothing department laden with costumes, studded belts, hats, and high boots. The others had often taunted him for picking loose trousers, pullover sweaters, and short practical jackets. At least he'd had the sense not to wear colors; they would have mocked him without mercy then.

He settled into an armchair that matched the couch. Upon a low table, gleaming ebony with short angular legs, was a plastic thermos. There was a thick, china cup—round with a fat handle, and a saucer beside it, identifying the contents of the thermos as straight coffee. Doubtless the Virtuals were refined enough to know that such a cup could not be used for any other beverage.

Emerson wanted that coffee, bad, but he was afraid. Who knew what was in it? He'd heard horror stories enough about Executives and their dubious hospitality. His jacket was hanging from the hat rack, a *Waiting-for-Godot* tree as they used to call it in his closet; this one had a stiff stem and short, straight limbs. He tugged at the sleeves of the clean white turtleneck sweater they'd given him. It was, he realized, the first time in weeks that he'd felt normal. That was strange, since he knew he was in the worst possible danger.

Coffee was not the only temptation. There was a tray of delicious-looking sandwiches: smoked chicken and Black Forest ham.

And next to him, on the couch, there was Urban. Emerson couldn't help noticing details, as if he were examining a photo-perfect painting. Urban's trousers, battleship gray with black stripes down the sides, were realistically worn at the knee, and his tall leather boots were scuffed at the toe. There were stains on the vest, particularly around the armholes, and the white shirt was badly wrinkled.

A very eerie work of art was Urban Myth.

"I'm scared," Emerson confessed aloud, watching Urban's chest rise and fall with breathing. No sense in trying to lie about it. He was scared of the Executives, of the coffee, of the future, and most of all, he was dead scared of Urban, this thing he'd been traveling with.

No use lying about it.

And Cinder had given him that look, that steady, cruel look. *This,* her eyes had said, *is what I want of you, what I demand of you.*

And then she had told him that he could not come along, that he would have to stay.

Did she want him to watch over Urban, absurd as that sounded? Did she know they'd be captured? Or had she just gotten tired of him and his whining?

He shook his head, stood up, reached across the curve of his armchair, and quickly, before he could change his mind, nabbed the dart out of Urban's neck. He heard it pop, and only then feared that removing it could do damage.

But then he saw Urban's eyelids flicker.

The Sierra bolted straight up.

"Sander!" the robot cried, alarmed, then just as suddenly seemed to get a grip on himself. The head turned, mechanically, and looked right at Emerson. To his shame and chagrin, the Jabberjaw cringed.

"Emerson." Urban combed a hand through his tumbled curls. "Hello."

Emerson swallowed. "Uh. Hi." His hands jerked, unsteady, anxious. "How—how are you?"

"Functioning perfectly."

The Jabberjaw winced.

"That was a joke." Urban swung his long legs around.

"Oh." Emerson sat back.

For a moment they were both silent.

"I, uh, suppose you'd like to know where we are?" Emerson ventured.

"I know where we are." Urban pointed up. "I'm a satellite, remember. I can tell you *exactly* where we are. And as a robot, I can also tell you that this room is bugged to the rafters."

"Terrific. Does that mean we can't talk?"

"About me, you mean?" He smiled ruefully. "The man who captured me knows me, Emerson, every chip. He couldn't' have captured me otherwise. We can talk about me all you want. Of course, what he'd really like us to talk about is Sander and Cinder. That's why he put us together."

Artificial bastard doesn't seem worried, thought Emerson, but then, only the living could fret.

"Your, um, image," the Jabberjaw hemmed, ". . . all

the time you were in a-a coma or whatever, your VR
image never cracked. How did you do that?"

Urban leaned forward to set elbows on knees, hands
locked together. Emerson could not help remembering
what those legs really looked like, the metal and plastic moving smooth as mercury.

"The dart interfered only with my body." Again he
pointed upward. "That's where the VR emanates."

"Oh."

"I was wondering if you would remove the dart,"
he added, not an accusation, just a thought. "I'm
grateful that you did. What *did* happen to Alexander
and Cinder?"

"They went into the window."

"They what?"

"I forgot"—Emerson pushed up his glasses—"you
didn't get to see it." *Probably couldn't see it,* he
thought. *How could a machine see a myth?* "Standing
on the balcony, you could see a . . . a window, a piece
of sky cut away. On the other side was—" he searched
for words. Urban waited patiently. "Have you ever
seen pictures of lava? That's what it looked like. A
cave of lava, only not hot or threatening. Rather like
glass pottery."

"And Alex went in there?"

The Jabberjaw nodded. "Cinder took the motorcycle over the cliff and straight into that opening. Alexander was still in the sidecar."

Urban was utterly still for a moment. "Is this possible?" His tone was oddly childlike.

Emerson frowned. The question was totally unexpected.

"Well?" Urban insisted, and Emerson could see
that he was perfectly serious.

"Aren't you supposed to argue the impossibility of
that sort of thing? Seeing as, um, that you are, well,
what you are?"

Urban shrugged. "I have no system of disbelief. Whatever you tell me is either a lie, incorrect, or a fact. That is all I know. As for impossible—do you know that the first time a computer was asked to build a tower out of blocks, it tried to build it from the top down? It didn't know *that* was impossible, because it didn't know about gravity."

"But—*but I've heard you say 'impossible'!* I've seen the looks you've given Cinder and Alex when they mentioned Ethelred—"

"That was Urban, which is me and not me. Urban is pragmatic. Unfortunately, he—*I* am also just a computer program."

Emerson felt his spine pressing back against the chair again; he couldn't help himself. And the face that was Urban's looked sad and weary, very weary.

"You're talking differently—" Emerson said hoarsely. "Why are you talking differently?"

"Because Tinkerbell now has more control."

"Tinkerbell?"

For a third time, this time laconically, Urban pointed toward the ceiling.

"They named it Tinkerbell?!"

"Think how I feel. Urban is very classically macho." The smile was broad and winning this time, pure Urban Myth. "Seeing was remembering, in my case," he went on. "Not that I ever really forgot—I just submerged it, what I was—am."

Emerson snorted, "You flat-out denied it."

The gray eyes glanced away, the nervousness chillingly natural. "I did not want it to be true. I wanted to be Urban."

The Jabberjaw had no answer to that. How, he wondered, could a computer want anything? How could it feel shame in what it was, or was not?

"I'm supposed to think I'm human," Urban said

softly, "and I very much did—until my cover was blown."

"You're a spy." Emerson pushed out of his chair. He moved as far away from the robot as he could. "You're armed, aren't you?"

Urban smirked a pure Sierra smirk. "Don't need to be. I'm a walking weapon."

The Jabberjaw shut his eyes; he could hear his lungs working. God, he was frightened. "Are you going to kill me?"

"Kill"—an inhaled breath—"Jesus, no!" The voice was emphatic, human enough to make Emerson meet the gray eyes. They looked wounded, even offended.

Just an illusion, Emerson reminded himself.

Urban must have deduced the disbelief, for he stretched out his hands pleadingly. "I'm as close to AI as a machine ever got. I have, well, wants and needs, software-based, I admit, but there nonetheless. I won't hurt you, Emerson; I want, *I very badly want* your trust."

"Do you?" Emerson went back to his chair. *Might as well be sitting,* he thought, *be comfortable. Oh, God.* "I don't know how to trust you, Urban. Teach me. Tell me how you work."

"How I'm *supposed* to work, you mean." Urban got up, nervous, it seemed, and checked over the thermos of coffee. He unscrewed the top, releasing wisps of steam and a glorious smell, then frowned at Emerson as if he were a sick child. "It's full."

"I'm afraid to drink it. It might be drugged."

Urban peered in, so close the steam ought to have burned his eyes. A beat, and then he set it down.

"It's clean; freshly brewed."

"What did you do?"

"MRI."

Emerson stared, and Urban glanced away—modestly, it seemed.

"I'm a *very* expensive machine," he said, pacing away. His face was blank, almost doll-like in thought. "You know what instincts you were born with, Emerson?" And before the Jabberjaw could answer, he lifted a hand and counted off, "You knew how to suck, how to swim, and you knew how to arch yourself if you started to fall. That's all reality-based instinct. All out here. Solid State, as the Virts like to call it. Know what I was 'born' with? Mathematics! That's all in here." He tapped his head. "All theoretical, Virtual."

Emerson fidgeted. "Yes, so?"

"It is easier to teach a human how to do math than it is to teach a computer how to swim or understand the laws—the Solid State laws—of gravity. That's what makes AI such a bitch. Analog computing and silicon networks notwithstanding, the question always is: how do you bypass all the years it will take trying to teach a computer what humans know from birth?" He shrugged. "Answer: give it a human brain."

"You're a human brain? A human brain in a computerized body; like a cyborg?"

The Sierra looked chagrined. "Ah, no. Didn't mean to give you dummies on a roller coaster—"

"What on a what?"

"It's an Urbanism, means false information." He gestured. "I'm built so that the . . . call it the Solid State half of my brain—down here in this body—can take on an implant. I'll give you an example. Let's say my, uh, masters want me to infiltrate a Poetry Closet. They capture you, a Jabberjaw, and copy your brain pattern onto the silicon neurons of my Solid State matrixes. I'll operate primarily on that pattern in conjunction with the servos, proximity sensors, and feedback chips that make up this body."

"So you'd have all my, uh, memories and such to tell you how to react." Emerson finally ventured to pour himself a cup of coffee. He sipped it delicately. *Fresh grounds!* He shut his eyes and savored the taste. Bless and brew him! Another sip. God! Rank extravagance, but it was *so* good!

"That's it."

"And Tinkerbell?"

"My VR brain's an expert system, which means that if I get into a spot not covered, even vaguely, by the brain pattern I've borrowed, Tinkerbell will inference a solution."

"And Tinkerbell will create a VR illusion of me." The thought shook Emerson.

"Down to the smell of your breath."

He gulped down more coffee. "So you *have* read Horace's *Art of Poetry.*"

"An edition of that work in the original Latin has been scanned into my memory," he readily agreed. "But Urban Myth's illiterate."

Christ.

"And your Solid State brain has Urban Myth's pattern?"

"Ah, no." He looked genuinely embarrassed, almost ashamed. "You see, I wasn't reactivated for, um, twenty-three years."

"What? Your masters shut you down and left you to rust?"

"Not funny," Urban almost scowled. It was as if Emerson had genuinely, finally, rubbed not the imaginary human but the robot beneath the wrong way. "There is only one of me. I'm a test model." There was a bleakness to the words. "They erased the human pattern they used for the test, and, well, turned me off. Not that Tinkerbell ever went dead—it's just that . . . I wasn't in use."

"Who turned you on?"

"I turned myself on—the Tinkerbell half of me. The other satellites were giving off this magnetic flux—

used by the Virtuals, I think—but I was programmed to be suspicious, and, well, wake my Solid State self up."

Urban hesitated. Emerson waited.

"The base was in ruins," the robot finally confessed. "I read later about all the military infighting during the hate wars, the sabotage. I guess I was lucky the top brass knew about me—or never discovered me, whichever it was."

"What did you do?"

"Once I'm on, my program mandates that I find a cover for myself, a face."

"And Urban Myth was it." Emerson nabbed one of the chicken sandwiches. With alarm he added, "My God—you didn't kill him did you??"

"Rats and alligators, Emerson, don't be stupid! I can't get a brain pattern by killing! It has to be fed in through special machines—all of which were at the base."

"Destroyed by scavengers?"

"Yes," he said unhappily. "So I left the base wearing a standard VR illusion of some half-demented bum and started searching for both a working machine and pattern."

"And?"

The embarrassed look was back, more acute than ever.

"I'm a computer game."

Emerson nearly choked on his sandwich. "You're putting me on!"

Urban flushed red, angry with shame or frustration. "It was all I could find!"

"But it's so cliché!"

"Damn it, cliché is all I know! I'm a computer! I don't have original thoughts! Everything I learn and know I upload into my memory, and that's all I know, period. I researched the question for six years, and, well, a computer game was the only answer."

Emerson rested back in his chair, chewing thoughtfully. He felt suddenly, strangely at ease. It was as if the threat had been erased from Urban. "So Urban Myth was a computer game."

Urban nodded uncomfortably. Emerson felt a sting of pity for the poor robot; a human might be satisfied with compromise, but how could a computer, knowing that it had not really met the demands of its primary programming?

"It was a highly interactive game," a strange voice asserted. Emerson jumped, almost dropping the remains of the sandwich. Urban merely turned his head.

There was a screen between the white curtains. It had dropped down soundlessly from the ceiling and now hung there like a spiderweb. Upon it, looking amused, was an Executive, lean and dressed in the archaic garb of a professor. "Not a poor choice, given that it was the only choice."

Emerson carefully set aside the remains of his sandwich. "Do I know you?"

"No, but Urban does. Don't you, Urban?"

That got to the robot. The head came up, and he blinked as if trying to focus. "Take me for an unseen hitchhiker, you're downloading right into—"

"Yes. Just like you download into other machines. Mr. Emerson, is it? Do you understand the gamer term 'Fantasia Flyer'?"

" 'Course not," Emerson snorted, not because he was indignant, but because the fear was back. "Jabberjaws are hands-off on tech. *'Poetry is the spontaneous overflow of powerful feelings and comes as naturally as the leaves to a tree.' "*

Urban tilted his head. "You're mixed your quotes."

"We poets can do that. Machines won't. So what is a Fantasia Flyer?"

"The term refers to a gamer who goes beyond any and all boundaries set for him, even those set by the computer." The Executive explained smoothly, "Urban Myth was that sort of game. It allowed the player to make up an answer if the computer could not provide one. The programmer, a rather hack writer, created a fairly simplistic, archetypal hero for his adventure game. He then created data for the character—what Urban ate, how he dressed, what kind of women he liked. The question was, what to do about contingencies not covered by the data? Ah! There is the true genius in the game, if such a game can be considered anything more than prurient trash."

"Go to hell, D-base!" Urban growled.

"Very Urban Myth, Urban." The man smiled, the humor stopping at his pupil-less eyes. "It works like this, Mr. Emerson: while playing the game, you decide that Urban Myth will enter an ice-cream parlor and purchase himself an ice-cream cone—but when you do so, you discover that the programmer never entered in as data Urban Myth's favorite flavor of ice cream. Not to worry! The game asks *you,* the player, to tell it what kind of ice cream you think Urban likes. From then on, it's a given."

Emerson removed his glasses and set about polishing them on his sweater. His hands, he noted, were trembling. Virtuals scared him spitless.

"What kind of ice cream *do* you like, Urban?" D-base asked pleasantly.

"Chocolate peanut butter strudel," Urban said with some disgust. "Every dessert I crave is chocolate peanut butter something."

The Executive barked out a laugh of pure pleasure. "Wonderful!"

"So," Emerson ventured, putting his glasses back on, "Urban's just a well-written character? Is that what you're saying?"

"Well written? Hardly. That's why Tinkerbell latched onto the program. It is pitifully easy to know what Urban Myth will do in *any* given situation."

"The character is not that simplistic," Urban protested.

"*You* are not that simplistic," the Executive corrected. "How many years have you been Urban, uploading information and experiences into your satellite subconscious? You modified the character to keep it alive and well, and you incorporated it. Where's Alexander?"

Emerson's heart gave an alarming skip. *Ah, hell.*

Urban snorted. "Why ask me? Your agent knocked me dead, remember?"

"Mr. Emerson said he went through a window in the sky. I find that difficult to believe. And who is this woman he's with, the one who no doubt broke the two of you free of the warehouse?"

"Her name is Cinder. That's all either of us knows."

"Is it?" His expression was thoughtful.

"What are you going to do with Emerson?" Urban demanded, and the Jabberjaw felt his stomach drop right out of him. Superstitiously, he wished the robot had not asked that question.

Hawthorne looked amused. "Not, 'What are you going to do with me?' Urban?"

"You can't do anything with me until you get past the Iron Butterfly. If you do get past, then what you do will no longer matter to me."

"True enough. But you know, I can get past it."

Urban snorted, pure Sierra response. "Sure."

Hawthorne smiled politely. "You've already given me the password, Urban."

Urban went pale. Hologram or not, Emerson knew the robot was as scared as a robot could be.

"Impossible," he asserted, but there was fear under the bravado.

"You know better than that." The Executive looked almost apologetic. "You gave me the password when you named your favorite flavor. You see, I knew your creator, and chocolate peanut butter was her favorite flavor, too. I'll be seeing you in a moment, Urban—not you, but the robot you really are. In a way, I'll be sorry to erase this persona of yours. It has been enjoyable."

And with that, the screen went blank.

Urban sat back down on the couch, head falling into his broad hands.

"Iron Butterfly?" Emerson wasn't sure he wanted to know.

"Entry into my satellite brain is guarded by an Iron Butterfly Code," Urban said, not bothering to look up. "It's a pair of codes that change constantly. It can't be cracked because both computers—Solid State and Tinkerbell—are programmed to graph the spatial relationships of their respective codes. In short, there is no knowing what the code is at any given moment."

Emerson did not understand, but he doubted that further explanation would help. "So," he ventured, "you can't, um, be captured and used by the enemy."

"Not unless he knows the password."

"Which Hawthorne does?"

"Which Hawthorne probably does. He hasn't any reason to bluff us, after all."

Emerson sat himself down beside the robot, feeling as he had back on the cliff side. It was silly, he knew, ridiculous to anthropomorphize, but that was in his Jabberjaw nature, pathetic as it was.

High tragedy or dead farce, the only thing that had ever needed him, it would seem, was a robot about to be reprogrammed.

Ethelred would have approved.

Chapter 20

"Well, Kelly." Executive Hawthorne was back on the screens, looking right at her.

So real.

She glanced back to where a small upper screen kept continual watch over the prisoners. It occurred to her that Emerson would have no privacy from Hawthorne, who could watch him twenty-four hours a day without a blink.

Doc, she thought, *off!*

She felt the implant go dead, as if some part of her mind had gone to sleep. Although she did not know how, she feared Hawthorne capable of forming some sort of comm link with the Doc and reading her thoughts.

And if he could do that, she wasn't sure if shutting it down would help.

Executive Hawthorne, she saw, was patiently waiting for an answer.

"Urban Myth's a spy robot," she said carefully. "The best—the only one there is. I can see his being of use to infiltrate the tribes—"

"Kelly, Kelly!" Hawthorne shook his head and smiled sadly. And Kelly felt her heart sink. Pavlovian response to his disappointment, even now when she knew he wasn't real.

"You must be more all inclusive in your thinking!" he insisted, narrow face animated for the first time. Even the black eyes seemed to sparkle. "I'm going to show you my life's work." Hawthorne stepped to the right, easy as that, and the elegant room behind him became a stone cell, walls slimed with bacteria; centered against the wall was a prisoner, weeping, naked, and seated cross-legged on the floor.

He no longer had arms.

"Dios!" Kelly caught her breath and hastily crossed herself, something she had not done in years.

Hawthorne smiled his tight smile; it chilled Kelly to see real pleasure and excitement on his face.

"Welcome to my *Isle of Creation;* the house of frights and phobias. *This* particular nightmare," he said, "is about to pay off. I want you to see."

"What happened to his arms?" Kelly whispered, heart pounding. Mother Mary, was this a threat?

He snapped his fingers, and a set of black boxes framed the image; neon lines peaked and jumped within them. "Chemistry," Hawthorne said, and boxes lit up, one after another, "blood pressure," a box to the other side—"heartbeat."

"Sir—"

"Really, Kelly!" Hawthorne sighed with profound disappointment this time. "Haven't I made it clear? It has taken me several weeks of the most delicate programming to lead this fellow into this *particular* reality. Each warped desire and paranoid fantasy has been banked and coaxed into growth, like vines working their way up a trellis. Now they are about to flower!"

Hawthorne seemed to lean back, hand to chin, eyes

on the scene like a director watching a play in progress.

Keys rattled in the cell door, and the man began to shake as it swung open; pasty light cut into his prison. The jailer appeared, spanking clean in a white lab coat, a bowl in hand. The man's amputated arms were carefully balanced on that bowl.

"No," the man wept, "I can't—"

Kelly felt her stomach go bilious, her throat tightened. "Oh, Jesus!"

"You must eat," the jailer insisted, crouching down and lifting a limb to the man's mouth.

Along the frame, the brain waves jumped, altering dramatically.

"There!" Hawthorne said triumphantly. "Did you see that!"

"I—" Kelly swallowed, and blinked. She felt treacherously faint.

The jailer was gone. The walls of the cell were white; in the margins, heartbeat and blood pressure, both high a moment ago, dropped dramatically, slowing to just below normal.

"All an image." She could barely catch her breath in outraged astonishment. "That horror—you—it—"

"Virtual Reality! Did I not make that clear? Of course, there is no longer any point in upholding the technological half of the nightmare." Hawthorne's tone was conversational. "However easy it is to tap into dreams, nightmares, and fantasies, it is, I assure you, nearly impossible to tap into madness. All that exists is in the mind! And that, Kelly, is what matters to me."

The room had gone white, the man was sitting in the corner, healthy and with all limbs intact.

He was muttering to himself.

"How beautiful," he was saying, "how very beautiful."

Hawthorne reached and touched the margins; the lines bounced, replaying, Kelly guessed, the exact moment when the poor man's mind had snapped.

"The chemical alterations are easily traced"—Hawthorne waved a hand to the charts concerned—"but there are no absolutes in regard to how and why they are triggered."

"How beautiful," the man muttered, eyes, dead black with VR lenses, staring out sightlessly.

"The electricity leaping about the brain goes to the wrong circuit and remains on that track. And there is no way," Hawthorne whispered with an almost magical flourish of his long, expressive hands, "to change it back."

"I don't understand," Kelly said. She was horrified, terrified.

"Imagine, Kelly, if I could create an image, a utopia, if you will, for each individual on earth."

"I . . . don't know that I could imagine that . . . It would be wonderful, of course, but how would you do it?"

A smile, rare in that it was broad and showed off the Executive's small square teeth. "I want to prevent the hate wars from ever occuring again, Kelly—to prevent *any sort of war* from ever happening again. As to how, that is where Urban Myth comes in. He is one half of the key. Unfortunately, Alexander is the other half. It is imperative that we find Alexander."

"Yes, sir. But given what I saw and what Mr. Emerson said—"

"Yes, yes." He stopped her with a light lifting of his long hand. She found herself staring at the lines along the palm, noticing for the first time how clear and unnaturally deep they seemed.

Long lifeline—went right down into the bracelets along the wrist. The Executive had a sense of humor.

He frowned darkly. "Some trick has been played,"

he said firmly, "that much is evident. A brilliant trick."

"Ah, sir?"

"Hm?"

"What about the Jabberjaw?"

"Emerson?" A twitch of a smile. "Only one thing for him—a trip to the *Isle*. Don't you agree?"

Kelly's hands were clutched behind her back; she felt the muscle that twitched in her thumb and smelled the tang of perspiration from under her arms.

No use any of that! she thought, with a mental pinch. She was either with the Executive all the way or not; and *not* wasn't an option. That thought made her feel better; it gave her a direction to go.

"Yes, sir."

"I want you to begin a fresh, citywide search for Alexander. Wherever he turns up, and he *will* turn up, there you will go."

"Yes, sir."

"In the meantime, you can arrange to have the Jabberjaw taken to the lab. Then I have a very special assignment for you."

And Kelly, as always, nodded obediently.

Getty knew Hawthorne's secret. Hawthorne's great and terrible secret.

That was why he'd created the viruses. A grave and dangerous thing to do. Any Virtual caught creating a virus would be expelled from the net, possibly even executed.

Fuck his brother Virts was Getty's response to that. He had always styled himself after the brilliant pioneers of cyberspace: the knights of the network round-tables, who were poets, scientists, philosophers, and activists. It was a pity the Brainiacs were so wrong-headed, for Getty oftentimes felt he had more in common with them than with his own. Certainly, they seemed better suited to inherit the Virtuals' proud legacy. More so than the latest generation of Virts.

Solid State junkies, he was beginning to call them. Obsessed with the physical, excited by the tactile. And Hawthorne was feeding their addiction.

Getty knew, as no one else seemed to, that the Virtual world and way of life was in deadly danger—from Executive Hawthorne.

So Getty had done some research, and discovered the Executive's secret. He'd learned that no one had ever met Hawthorne face-to-face, and there was no indication of a residence, not even under assumed identities or pseudonyms. Hawthorne had no medical records, no lovers; all friends, workers, and acquaintances knew him by way of monitor.

Ordinarily, such reclusiveness would have been considered a MYOB program: a coded signal that the public face on the net treasured his Solid State privacy.

Getty knew that was bogus. Family Ksana controlled the Kings. If anyone could effect a *coup d'état,* it was Executive Hawthorne. And given the seductions and experiments occurring on the *Isle of Creation,* Getty felt his suspicions well justified.

"Executive Nagata?" The voice was in the room with him, Solid State. He did not recognize it, but that hardly worried him.

"A moment," he said, always odd hearing his speech coming in through the auricle instead of going directly to the ossicles. Equally odd to have limitations to his movements, to have to extend energy to move at all.

When he'd met with Hawthorne the other day, Getty had secretly planted viruses, subtle cockroaches able to trace Hawthorne back to his source while leaving trails to follow.

He'd created seven viruses; his present focus was on

all seven simultaneously. Four were flagged as having worked. One had fallen dead. Two had been stopped.

So Hawthorne had tried to follow the traces back to their source. And he had failed. Getty snickered. It felt good to turn the tables on that bastard. That "son of a Mainframe" as the groundlings liked to say.

Unfortunately, the trails of the successful four all ended in a cul-de-sac.

Clever Hawthorne, Getty had thought, gritting his teeth. He ought to have come up against a flashing point where the cricket entered the brain. Instead, there was raw data, evidence of more machine. Clearly, Hawthorne had suspected he might be followed and written up an enharmonic persona of himself, a form that could be traced right back into the computer while he slipped out another way.

Getty was determined to get past that barrier.

"Sir?"

Dropping back out of the computer, Getty stretched his back, cracking it. He was seated in a bowl chair, comfortably padded, a stable of every Virtual's home or work environment. He'd go hiking in the mountains this afternoon. Taste the air, feel the Solid State of things; it was a secret well kept from the groundlings that VR required the taste, touch, and smell of Solid State to lend the illusions their added dimension. The mind could elaborate where mathematics could not. And there was no getting around the body's need for exercise.

"Executive Nagata?"

"What?" he snapped, pushing to his feet. And then he froze.

"Who the hell are you?" He frowned. For one moment he was sure the petite woman with the coffee brown hair must be a VR construct, but he'd put a lock on all calls. Then he realized that the woman was here, in the flesh.

And then she was moving so fast Getty couldn't even think to step back. A hand slapped him at the back of the neck, and the Executive felt an alarming stab as two needles were plunged below his occipital bone. A crack of pain down his spine, and he tried to scream—

His mouth would not open. He made to reach for his neck, only to find that his hands would not move, either.

The woman, looking grim and almost ashamed of herself, stepped back. She was wearing biking shorts, a tank top, and sand encrusted high-tops, her hair tied back in a tail. There were, Getty noted, two chips at her right temple, one at the left. MSCs. One of which, he had to surmise, was a Sneezy, given the speed she had just shown.

"The clip's a nerve plug," she suddenly told him, again with that look of embarrassment. Getty stared back at her, humiliatingly afraid. He wondered which parts, beyond jaw and limbs, the plug had been programmed to paralyze.

From her Fanny bag, the girl removed a small box, all gold and black, and set it down before her captive. Getty flicked his eyes to watch. After a moment, small laser lights beamed up from the box, and there, in the center, was Hawthorne, complete from the waist up.

"Getty," Executive Ksana smiled.

And that is when Getty finally understood. He knew, without a shade of doubt, what Hawthorne was and why the tracers had found only more and more machine when they went looking for a brain.

He also knew that he was lost. He tried all the same, reaching out a tendril to the digital world of instant communication.

Nothing. He pushed and jabbed and searched until his skull ached; his mind fell back, an agonizing plunge that was almost physical, as if he'd been knocked to the ground.

He'd been flat-lined.

"I left everything else outside," the girl said to Hawthorne. "Shall I get it now?"

"Please."

She nodded once, glanced briefly, apologetically back at Getty, and then was gone.

How did she get in? Getty sent the sharp, bitter thought at Hawthorne. He knew the Executive had left the connection between them open. That would be like the son of a bitch.

Hawthorne turned back to Getty, hands behind his back, looking like a bizarre sort of djinn with his waist vanishing down into a smoky haze. "Climbed over the gate, of course. I cut off the alarms for her. It is amazingly simple to get to you Virtuals. You all live under the illusion that you're safe and invulnerable." The Executive's tone was mocking.

Getty flushed with impotent anger. *Does anyone know?* he demanded.

"About my less than Solid State, you mean? No. Of course not. Why spoil the illusion?"

No one even suspects?

The Executive cocked a brow. "Did you?" He shook his long head sadly. "That's what you get for denigrating the joys of Solid State, Getty. Sloppy job on the viruses, by the way," he added. "I don't know about your generation. You lack the passion to create a classically deterministic program. Then again, perhaps that is unfair. Those who can create such programs we have locked safely away in the Orange Kingdom, lest they threaten our mental playground."

We can unplug you!

Hawthorne tossed back his head and laughed once, loudly. "And shut down the library? Shut down instantaneous communications, instant intellectual gratification?"

If it means putting an end to you—

"Bosh!" Hawthorne was disdainful. "Even if you could get a quorum to agree with you, the vast majority of the computers are now running on solar. Over the years, I have seen to that."

Getty felt his stomach knot up; his heart was beating fit to burst. Never in his life had he felt so out of control, so terrified. *My God, my God, you're even worse than I feared! You're a—*

What? A Forbin Project? Don't be droll. I used to be as human as you. In some respects, I still am. I am, for example, human enough to want to speak with you before I get rid of you."

I'll be missed.

"Don't be ridiculous."

You can't replace me with an image! Getty felt the blood vessels in his temples throb with his need to scream. Sweat trickled delicately down from his hairline. This was not happening! He was sharp and brilliant, and he was a power. He was an Executive, a Virtual.

"No," Hawthorne agreed, "*you* I cannot replace with an image. Very ironic that. For all your posturing and sermons on the evils of the flesh, you have interacted with others in Solid State so frequently that I really can't replace you with a mere image."

In spite of himself, Getty felt a ridiculous drop of relief. It shamed and angered him. And then he replayed the words and the trapped fury he felt was almost unendurable. *Who have you replaced!?!?! You bastard—who!?*

"Only Executives Zworykin, Silkorsky, and Lise. Really, Getty, it amazes me, truly amazes me how little paranoia there is among the Virtuals. You should have suspected. Point of fact, it amazes me that only you have ever suspected anything. But then, that is likely due in part to our old Hack Mode state. Focus is *never* on reality."

I don't understand! What the fuck are you doing here?! If you only want to kill and replace me, why are you here?

"To do the job, Getty. Kelly"—he nodded to the girl, who had just stepped back through the door. She was carrying a square machine under her arm. It was encased in bone-painted metal and looked as heavy as it was compact—"will be acting as my hands. But I would not have a subordinate do it without my supervision. Beyond being a delicate operation, it must also be a supremely secret operation. And you know as well as I, if you want something secret, do it yourself. But I must confess"—Hawthorne's cold, distinctive smile pulled at his thin lips—"there is another reason. You see, I am of the old school, and I do mean old. I remember the days of networks, the days of bulletin boards and phone lines. In that sense, I have more in common with one of our Mainframers than with any Virtual now living. And like those poor trapped mice in Anaheim, I am obsessed with cheating, tricking, and ultimately winning the game. And like them, whenever I succeed, I feel a need to boast. Juvenile, I know, but there you are. Kelly," he said, "you may proceed."

"Yes, sir," she said, head bowed, and reached for the back of Getty's neck.

Chapter 21

One step Alexander had taken. One step in a barren landscape with a swirling sky. And with that one step, he had crossed back again into the world that had always existed outside his windows. Back to the city.

And right into the middle of Actor's Carnival.

There had been nights, in his sterile observation deck, when, with exquisite tenderness, Alexander had traced the ledges and archways of the city upon the windowpanes. He'd imagined the dust of old bricks under his fingertips, the polish of gold and silver walls.

Now, here he was, looking up at the moldings and sculptures, mullions and cornices, at the sun reflected in mirrored buildings. He could smell the sweat and perfume, hear the laughter, see the crackle of auras.

He could hardly believe it. Actor's Carnival. At last. He didn't want to be a gawking tourist, but there was no help for it. His mask was still in his pocket. He considered putting it back on, examining the landscape through the computer eye, but he wanted to see the circus as Christine had, all the colors and forms and movement, the patter of voices falling like rain all around him.

In a daze, he followed Cinder through the crowd, darting glances at the rings of performers, at the dancers and singers, the merchants hocking brightly colored poseurs and roasted cobs of corn.

At long, long last. Christine had conjured it all up in her bedtime stories to him, ending each one by pointing to the Ferris wheel in the distance. And he had drifted to sleep listening to the wheel's Doppler voices crying out with pleasure.

None of the stories could compare to this sizzling, pulsing truth.

"Want to go for a ride?" Cinder asked.

They were beneath the Ferris wheel, its poppy red gondolas swinging down and around, the spokes of the wheel neon blue and blazing white. Sander couldn't take his eyes off it.

"No."

"Are you sure?" She was, of course, back in human form, so real and tactile that he was ready to discredit what he'd seen in that other land. But there was that look in her eyes, that steady, inhuman stare with a red glow behind it. A deep bloodred glow.

He answered her question with a shake of the head. He'd never thought of the wheel as a ride; it was a goal to reach. And when he reached it, he wouldn't feel the need to break things ever again. The Webs would let him investigate, build, create. They would give him a home and a purpose.

He found it pathetic that all he could now do was stare at the Webs, Webs with painted faces and masks, Webs dancing, singing, performing. He couldn't bring himself to speak to any of them.

"This way—" Cinder said, breaking through his thoughts.

He caught the dizzying sight of the gondolas as they

came down over his head. And then they were under and past the Ferris wheel and headed in the direction of the new radio tower. Cinder was leading him toward a steeply plunging staircase. He balked, suddenly and uncontrollably paranoid.

She grinned a feral grin at him. "Keep using that imagination," she complimented even as her grip pinched and dragged him down the first step. "Watch your footing," she warned as they passed through a pair of shattered doors. Glass, already powdered from years and years of hard heels, ground underfoot. He heard piano music, out of tune and badly played.

Across the broken floor was a wide, tiled tunnel stretching out from a center platform. Flickering, pink and blue neon outlined a bar at one end. A chipped, graffitti statue standing guard before it. Smoke stung his eyes, and the stink of burning weed and bacon made him cough.

"What's here?" he demanded. "Cinder—" Alex blinked frantically, trying to adjust his eyes to the yellow light. He could make out dim forms, old furniture, a piano, people with matted hair nestled in corners like blind mice in a nest.

"He's here," Cinder answered, pointing right behind him.

"Alexander Julunggul Damaxion Kitatimate?" queried a voice as he turned. It came from the blood velvet couch near the edge of the platform. Lit by the glow of an old-fashioned laptop computer was a figure dressed in a dark green, dovetailed coat with matching pants, a silver épée mask hiding the face. "Jez-us! It *is* you! How the fuck," the voice was amazed, "did you ever escape?"

Alex felt his heart jump. "I had help," he said.

A shake of silver mesh. "I've been trying to get to you for over a year now." The limbs, long and thin, moved with a wild, almost nervous energy, like a star about to explode. "The Brainiacs said they'd encountered you, but I could hardly credit. . . ." The head shook again. "Where's the robot?"

"Captured," Sander answered with a twinge. Urban. How did this person know about Urban?

"Shit!" It came out as a hiss. "It's got to be now, then! We can't take the chance, can't wait for Hawthorne to catch us!"

"You're Noel," Alex realized.

The épée mask cocked to the side whimsically. And then a hand came up to drag off the mask. "That's what the Brainiacs call me." The bronze-skinned young man shook out a head of raggedy dreadlocks. "But you can call me Filo."

Hawthorne was certainly a genius, Filo had to admit that. "Sit down," he urged the Web, tossing aside the épée mask. There was no point in it anymore. The time was now. It had to be now! Hawthorne had control of the robot!

"You need anything?" he ventured to ask with a dismissive wave to the bar, broken and angled. "There isn't a whole hell of a lot, but they manage to keep the glasses clean."

"Why are you writing up a cryptographic decoding program?" the Web said with sudden suspicion; he'd edged close enough to peer at the computer screen.

"To disrupt the satellites. Do you know what you are??"

Alexander looked as if the floor had just dropped out from under him. The exposed side of his face went dead pale. Filo saw the jaw go hard and the eye grow bright. *Good!* he thought. The bastard had anger. That's what they needed.

"Why don't you tell me what you think—"

"Know," Filo corrected.

"Know that I am," Alex obliged softly, darkly.

"And why don't you tell me who you are and how you know it!"

Filo paused to examine the Web, the varnish-colored hair, and the eyes—hazel and very angry. He noted with interest that Alexander had discarded his signature white Web mask, and wondered why. Around them the piano music played on, the woman at the keys, like the forms sleeping in the smoky corners, seemed a mere phantasm.

"I know because I know Hawthorne, your creator. He's a Virtual, an Executive, one of the highest, one of the oldest. You are his goddamned pet project."

"And you are?"

"His CM. His second in command."

Alexander caught his breath. "I see."

"No, you don't see! But that doesn't matter. I'm against Hawthorne, that's all you need to know. That, and that Hawthorne has every contact lens worn by every Virtual scanning for your Web face!"

Alexander shrunk back, and Filo could smell the fear this time as well as see it in the dilation and shrinkage of the pupils. The Web looked for all the world like a cornered prisoner.

"And scanning for you, too?" the young man guessed.

"Not yet. But he will. He still thinks I'm loyal—"

"He doesn't know you want him dead," the Web interrupted, suddenly, almost impatiently, ". . . for what he did to Dresden."

Filo caught his breath. *God!* "How—? Oh. So you really can pick up dreams."

"I've an endoskeleton that picks up beta state, and electrodes to sync my brain to them. You bet I can."

Filo felt the blood drain out of his face. "Picked up on my fantasies, did you?" he asked with forced casualness.

"The ones where you fantasize about what you

ought to have done when Hawthorne started experimenting on your friend Dresden instead of what you did do? Yes."

"Damn brilliant of Hawthorne to be able to create something like you," Filo grated.

"Oh, yes," Alexander's voice sneered, "pure genius, I'm sure. You'll forgive me if I don't go into raptures!"

"Then, you'll agree that Hawthorne has to be stopped. Do you know what he is?"

Alexander snorted and glanced up and off. "A monster?" distantly said, almost wishful.

"He's more than that! Hawthorne's a Virtual Reality construct, part and parcel of the net!"

Alexander grew very still. "That's . . . he can't be!"

"Can't he?"

"He had to have been human once!"

"Once!" Filo agreed, bitterly, hatefully. "He transferred his consciousness years and years ago. He was afraid of dying before he could accomplish his goal."

"Which is?" the Web whispered.

"To make sure the hate wars never happen again. Never."

"I see." Alex's eyes were bright, and his lip was twitching as if to smile.

"He's going to do this by giving every soul in the city their own little fantasy world. Your job is to transmit human dreams and wishes into the computer. The computer uses the information to create mundane fantasies. These are then radioed out to the poseurs everyone's wearing."

"The towers are transmitters; the poseurs receivers," Alex murmured.

"Right in one. The Virtuals would stop Hawthorne in a second if he tried to give all the grounded crickets. So he instead builds transmitters disguised as radio towers. Then he disguises the receivers as a cheap fashion statement, getting a lot of them out to a lot of people with no one ever suspecting what he's really doing. But there's one hitch—or rather, there was."

"Urban," Alex said suddenly.

Filo nodded. "Virtual Reality constructs cannot be realistically experienced with cheap poseurs. You need lenses and crickets—unless, of course, you have the technology to bypass those requirements."

"And now he's got that technology, and the hitch is that he hasn't got me—" the Web muttered faintly. He shifted, looking disturbed. "He's also got a Jabberjaw, a . . . friend of mine. He wouldn't hurt the man, would he?"

Filo looked at the Web with pity. "You might say. He'll do to your friend what he does to most grounders who fall his way—implant a cricket in him and drive him mad."

Alex's eyes grew frighteningly cold and bright. "What are we going to do?"

"Hawthorne can't be stopped in Solid State."

A distant look crossed the young man's face. It was a very familiar expression. The Web was hyperfocusing. "Viruses."

"You think I haven't tried? No. The viruses we came up with—"

"We?"

"The Brainiacs and I. We failed miserably. Hawthorne's had too many years to create ways of detecting and destroying them. I'm afraid you're it."

The hazel eyes grew instantly hard and sharp; *right out of hyperfocus into real time,* Filo saw and was impressed. "I'm a human-computer interface," Alexander said; "I translate human thoughts into computer transmissions."

"Which means you can follow my thoughts right into the net," Filo agreed. He was glad he didn't have to explain. "Piggyback with me, you might say."

"And providing that you can do this without Hawthorne knowing, what am I supposed to do once I get there?"

"Live out your fantasies."

"Fuck you."

"Listen to me—"

"I think I've listened enough. Cinder?" he said, turning to look behind him, only to freeze and glance about confused. "Cinder??? Where is she??"

"Who?" Filo frowned; so far as he remembered, Alex had arrived alone, sent, he assumed, by the Brainiacs.

"The woman I came in with! Cinder."

"I didn't see anyone." *Was the Web right in the head?* Filo worried. *God, that would be it, if this bastard was fucked up in the head.*

"Cinder?" Alex shouted. The tunnel echoed his voice over and over again.

"Should I send some Brainiacs looking for her?" Filo ventured.

But Alex just shook his head. "I don't think so. Wherever she's gone—I don't think so." For a moment he just stood, breathing in slowly. And then, "It looks like I will be going into VR with you after all."

Chapter 22

Emerson started out of a deep sleep, a creeping fear covering him like a quilt. He shoved up from the couch. The lights were dimmed, making the room look as if it existed at the bottom of a well. The curtains rippled and flicked in their corners. With an upward glance he noted that someone had upped the speed on the ceiling fan.

Urban was gone.

The Jabberjaw rubbed at his grainy eyes and put on his glasses. He noted with a pang that the food and coffee were also gone.

Damn. He tugged the wrinkles from his turtleneck. He'd always been picky about his appearance; there'd even been a time when he'd worn a tie, but his peers had made a cruel game of dragging him about by it, so he'd switched to sweaters.

A glance at the door.

So, he thought striding toward it, *faint words never won fair lady,* or something like that. He reached for the knob.

"I wouldn't."

Emerson started and shot a look over his shoulder. Behind the couch, Ethelred scratched at a floppy ear. The back paw came down, and he eyed Emerson dolefully.

A heavy, puffy sigh. "No one listens to me since my ears went down."

Emerson felt his hand touching the cold metal of the handle; it fell open before he could understand what he was doing, how he got there.

On the other side of the door was a swollen moon in an indigo sky. To either side of the door were windows, tattered curtains snapping through the broken panes.

Emerson licked his lips. A gusty wind tore the ragged leaves of a dying tree, and the lazy buzz of a fly wafted near his ear. He heard the predawn crow of a rooster in the distance; the air smelled tinny with the stink of brackish water.

This was all wrong. He was in a skyscraper. Wasn't he?

"Ethelred—" He glanced behind. The door, barely hanging on its rotting hinges, was shut. He could not remember having crossed the threshold.

Moving with slow trepidation, as if through a moat, Emerson took hold of the rusted latch. It flaked in his palm as he dragged it back open and stepped through.

He was deep underwater, afraid to breathe. A sleepy green ocean weighted him down. Smoky twists of light peered through vast mushroom shapes. Slumbering forms swayed; snaking out from them were tendrils, sluggishly investigating, listlessly retreating.

And Emerson, feeling his lungs going, waved his arms against the heavy water, back out the door.

He stood on stone, gasping for air and wondering why he was not dripping saltwater.

God, God, oh, God, what was happening??

"Try standing on your head."

A look over his shoulder, timid this time. Gray bricks walled him, gray flagstones were underfoot, and gray beams formed an aperture over his head. Against one wall stood a vast mercury gray mirror nestled in wine red silk. Held within a gilt frame, it reflected mountains laced with ribbons of cobbled road, a sheer blue sky, fields of pale grain . . . and Ethelred.

The creature was munching on a stalk of wheat.

"Try standing on your head."

Emerson swallowed. And then he heard the sound of tiny bells and felt a line of thread across his hands. And that is when he understood.

"Ah, Christ—" he whispered. "What have they done to me?" But he already knew what his mind was doing. It was weaving poetry about him like a winding sheet. "Locked me away with fucking Tennyson!" he breathed; his knees felt weak and his hands were sweating. "God, why Tennyson!?"

"Don't complain. It could have been Charles Bukowski," Ethelred observed.

"I don't want to be stuck in Tennyson!" Emerson snapped, and wondered nervously if Nature, red in tooth and claw, were waiting for him on the other side of the door. Which would he find if he stepped back through? Lotus Land or Locksley Hall?

"Ethelred!" *This is a mistake,* his head told him even as the name left his lips. *He's going to feed you nonsense. On the other hand,* he reasoned, *what here (wherever here is) is not nonsense?* "Ethelred, will this keep going on—I mean, if I go through the door again? Will I end up in another poem?"

"Huh? Oh, oh, yes. Yes, of course. Virtual Reality's programmed that way, you know. Encourages fractal association."

"How can I stop it? Ethelred??" He heard the edge of desperation in his voice and hated himself for it. Hated this creature for being the only tether in the maze. Threads were floated down over him, silken and rainbow-colored; they dangled and wrapped around his fingers.

"Cinder probably knows."

Cinder!

"Where is she??"

"Gosh—" Ethelred twisted his nobby head one way and the next. "Isn't she on your side? Oh. No, wait. All sides are the same. She ought to be here somewhere." A shake of the floppy ears. "Can't *you* see her?"

"If I could, you stupid animal, would I be asking—" *Wait.* Emerson stopped himself. That was it. If he could envision Cinder in the right way, perhaps he could break the recursion.

He knelt; the threads were knotting about his arms now, green and harvest gold, purple and sky blue, and he felt a surge of panic; the strands were sticking to him, trapping him. He looked into the mirror.

A shadow crossed the reflection, like a cloud, ruffling Ethelred's thick mousy fur. The shadow became a form, standing by the creature. Emerson imagined Cinder's oddly long nose, the line of her jaw. The shadow began to fold and melt.

And then it moved.

Ethelred's form distorted as Cinder's image, silvery and reflective, pushed its way through the liquid mirror. And then a mirrored statue of Cinder was standing before Emerson, a gleaming replica from the cap and goggles, heavy jacket and jodhpurs, down to the boots on her feet. Upon her reflective surface, Ethelred and the grain and the mountains remained, moving, staring.

Eyes, Emerson thought, even as golden threads wound about his throat. And the mirrored lids popped open revealing eyes dark and hard and alien, the haze of red stars gleamed from their depths, the fire in deep caverns.

"Very creative, Emerson," she said, and shattered, top to bottom.

He tumbled back as glass shivered to the floor in a spiderweb formation. Cinder shook off the splinters and stepped out.

Emerson caught his breath. The gray world had gone dark, the threads were gone, and his mind was suddenly, wonderfully clear.

"I was in a room with Urban," he said aloud, getting shakily to his feet, "and there was this Virtual—"

"D-base," Cinder supplied, settling into a chair. They were, he saw, back home. His home. There was the checkered floor, the glass doors, the chrome counter, and the polished Jewel Box framed between sheer curtains. The two of them were at the favored gray and red marble table in the corner.

He settled across from Cinder in the chair of honor, a chair on which he'd never sat upon in his life. It was surprisingly stiff and uncomfortable.

But how did they get to the coffeehouse? And why was it empty?

"Were we—that is, Ethelred said something about Virtual Reality."

"That's where you were," Cinder agreed.

"But not anymore?" he ventured nervously, and took a sip at a waiting, bitter cup of espresso. Where it had come from or when it had appeared on the table he had no clue. Real espresso as he'd only been allowed to taste on his birthday; real and with a curl of lemon peel.

"What do you think?"

"Don't fuck with me, Cinder! Just tell me what's happening!"

"You were in the net, Emerson," she said, penny brown face watching him sympathetically, "in a computer-generated program. It played upon your fears. Tennyson's poetry scared you, did it?"

Emerson felt a flush creep up from his throat. "We had to have all the classics memorized, we kids. And if an adult asked, we had to recite, and if we got even a line wrong, it was extra chores. I did all right most of the time, but never with Tennyson. I don't know why, I just got scared stupid when asked to recite one of his poems. I ended up cleaning the toilet a lot ... What was I doing in VR, Cinder? I'm not a Virtual!" The delicate china of his demitasse coffee cup clinked lightly upon the saucer.

"You're an experiment," she agreed, chillingly.

In what? he wanted to ask, and dared not. He felt he already knew.

"Have I—have I got—I mean—are there implants—?"

"Of course."

He felt cruelly violated, as if someone had sliced him open so they could laugh at what they saw inside.

"Are you—" he ventured, "are you just another figment of my imagination?"

She smirked at that. "What else could I be?"

He shook his head, numb.

"What did you think I was?"

He felt himself staring at her, magnified by the lenses of his glasses, although he knew he hardly needed lenses here. "I thought you were real."

"Are you also obsessed with reality? How cliché. But you won't understand, will you? I'm not what you would name 'real,' Emerson. I never was."

"Never?" he echoed slowly.

"You're the door, Emerson." Her eyes were bright. "You and you alone. Urban is not organic, and Alexander's fantasies have been locked out of his head. I had to have someone who could imagine me."

He stood up, felt the chair scraping backward across the sleek, waxed tile. "You're just a myth, like—"

"Like Ethelred, yes."

"So, when I thought—"

"Imagined."

"Imagined you, you were able to step through me and into this," he said dazed. "That was it all along. That's all you wanted me for, wasn't it? You gave me a lift, helped me to leave the coffeehouse not because you gave a damn, but because you wanted someone you could throw to the Virtuals. You just wanted a way into the damn network! Is that it?? Well, all right! You're in the Virtual Net! Now, get us out!"

"We're not in the Virtual Net, Emerson. I told you, you *were* in the net. But then you called on me, and that broke you out of it."

"What the fuck do you mean?? What's all this, then?" He waved at the coffeehouse, at the coffee cups that were still full despite the drinks he'd taken. "If this isn't the Virtual Net, what is it?"

Her eyes grew very bright. "This is all in your head, Emerson. That's where we are. Deep inside. You're right. I want to get onto the net, but only Alexander can help me do that. You'd better pray he comes, Emerson; only he can interface between computer chips and the brain—which makes him the only one who can lead us out of your skull. But don't worry. I have hopes that he'll be here soon."

"We're . . . inside my head?" Emerson repeated blankly.

"Didn't you know? You're a paranoid schizophrenic."

He had no heartbeat. Where had it gone? And he needed to swallow, but that, too, was impossible. Cinder was sitting mockingly modest at the table, hands folded upon its shiny surface.

"S-s-schiz—"

"Schizophrenic. That's what they usually call someone who converses with large rabbit-eared monsters." Her smile was bright and cold. "You've been one for about three months now. We, who exist on the other side of Twilight Bridge, walk with nuts like you. And when the need is particularly great, as it is in this case, you become the doors we step through. The stronger your imagination, the easier it is for us to use you." A Cheshire grin suddenly split her face. "And you have a wonderful imagination, Emerson. Simply marvelous."

Chapter 23

"Tunnel's cleared," a huffing voice announced, and the conductor of the line, as she was called, appeared from out of the misty shadows. She was a mountainous mother of a woman, olive-skinned with hair bleached the color of ginger ale. Her black eyes were all but lost in the folds hanging down from brows plucked clean and penciled in. A cat, patched tar and rust, rested in her mutton arms; its eyes, tarnished gold, blinking once and then shutting tight. "Now, pay up."

"Half now, half later," Filo dickered from where he stood, leaning against the gaudy bar right next to the statue of Plato.

Alexander shifted from bad leg to good. He did not like Filo, with his ragged hair and vengeful fantasies. But alone in this dark and sinister underground, without the constant of either Urban or Cinder, there was only Filo and the statue.

The woman sniffed, shifted the cat in her arms. "Three quarters now—that is, if you want the doors not only locked but guarded. Else, who knows who might find out you're down here doing whatever it is you're doing?"

"It would be most unfortunate for you if they did," Filo countered, "or don't you recall who my friends are?"

The conductor looked decidedly unsettled. "Yes, well," she hemmed.

"Pay's over there," Filo said shortly, with a jerk of his head toward the opposite end of the bar. The woman swayed over and snatched up the box in a fleshy hand.

"Pure?" she asked skeptically.

"As pure as Blues get," Filo sneered. "You'll get a second box if the door is kept locked and guarded and if you trip yourself out for an hour or two."

The woman seemed to consider that, biting at her upper lip, eyes shifting. "Sounds fair," she agreed, shoving the box into a pocket somewhere in the tent of her dress. She shuffled toward the stairs, cat under one massive arm. Alex heard her heaving herself up step after step, and, for just a moment, he felt himself lost in her daydream of being light and young.

"Charming woman," Filo muttered, then threw a doubtful glance at Sander. "Hawthorne's part of the net. That means he's everywhere. There's no way to stop him, short of shutting down every computer in the city and in orbit."

"There are other ways to stop a computer," Alex lobbed back; he was getting tired of arguing. He picked up and examined a cup someone had left on one of the tables. It was quite disappointingly made of plastic.

"Hawthorne's not a computer. He's the sum of a human mind in a computer. You'd best know the difference before you face off with him."

"Whatever else he was, he's now a computer. Logical thought, problem-solving focus, ordered reasoning.

And unlike a living being, with its peripheral vision and other warning senses, you can get a computer to concentrate all its computing abilities toward one single problem."

"And how will you do that? Give him something irrational? Unsolvable? This isn't a crude calculating machine; Hawthorne can option out of solving whatever takes too much memory!"

"If you don't care for my solution," Alex snapped, "you can go in without me!"

"So it's your way or nothing??" The Virtual thumped a hand on his chest. "I've been working this out for years—"

"And you haven't succeeded yet."

Filo looked away, disturbed. After a moment he shoved a hand into his pocket and brought out a couple of pieces of wax-wrapped globs. "Candy?"

Alexander searched the other man's brandy brown face, then accepted the candy. He unwrapped it and popped it in his mouth. It tasted pleasantly and smoothly of licorice, though he did not like how it stuck and gummed between his teeth.

In what seemed to be a salutary gesture, Filo unwrapped the other. He chewed on it while his hand nervously rubbed the wax covering into a ball. "Let's get started."

The Virtual crossed to the couch and gestured for Alexander to take the armchair next to him. Seriously beginning to doubt his cocksure idea, Alexander settled onto the creaking, uncomfortable springs.

"When I put in the lenses, I won't be able to look at you. If I do, Hawthorne will see you, too. So be sure to keep out of my line of sight. I'll shut my eyes as fast as I can. That'll be the signal for you to grab me. I sure hope this works."

"It'll work," Alexander said automatically.

Filo brought out a lens case from his pocket and

opened both halves. In their pockets of solution
floated thick black lenses. The Virtual kept his head
turned from Alexander as he quickly and neatly
scooped out each lens and touched them to his eyes.

A heartbeat passed as Filo stared at the statue of
Plato, and then he turned, eyes shut, back to
Alexander.

The Web licked his dry lips, and reached out to
take Filo's dry hand. He shut his own eyes as he did
so, instantly seeing, on the black of his eyelids, the
electricity that was Filo, and just beyond that, a circle
of light that flashed and pulsed invitingly.

Alexander caught fragments of thoughts, beta state,
Dresden's face, twisting "what ifs," beginnings altered,
ends changed, the eyes of Plato watching.

Deliberately, determinedly, Alex ignored the images
and aimed himself at the circle of light. It brightened,
and suddenly he felt himself sucked toward it. Instinctively, he kicked back from the pull, but it was too late.

The solidity of his body slipped out from under him;
a mental cry of panic filled him, and he felt himself
turned upside down, felt his stomach drop and his
head spin.

And suddenly, he was walking down tunnels that
reeked of smoke and oil.

Alex caught his breath. *What the hell!?* Where was
he? Not in Filo's mind, surely! The net, then? He was
aware of a profound, almost irate sense of disappointment at the thought. He'd expected far better of the
Virtuals, aesthetically at least. The tunnels were dark
and dank, and they reeked of mildew. Little pits in
the walls flared with a lime yellow light, leading him
on, and the faint coppery gleam of railroad tracks glistened beneath his feet.

He kept walking, his footsteps sounding hollow and
uneven on the tracks. He was beginning to wonder if
he ought to go back, if he'd somehow trapped himself

in an odd part of the computer or the cricket. And then he heard Cinder's distinctive voice.

"Solipsism," she said. "There is no such thing as true objectivity."

"Meaning that I'm a Halfway wandering about the streets talking to myself." That was Emerson. No mistaking the bitter, frightened edge. He could almost see the Jabberjaw shoving at his glasses.

Oh, sweet Jesus, Alex thought.

"Reality is like an artichoke. From the heart out it is simply leaves; they seem to be greater than the center, but they are just large, paper-thin illusions."

They were at the end of the tunnel. A great, vast, crackling fire dissipated the chill and caused him to squint. It threw tall, thin shadows up across the curving, craggy walls. Cinder and Emerson were before this fire, Cinder calmly seated, Emerson on his feet and fretting. The Jabberjaw glanced up at Alex, then away, hands twitching nervously.

"Good to see you again, Alexy," said Cinder with a smile. The shadows stretched up behind her, flickering tall and short with the light.

"Where the hell am I???"

"Emerson's head. I knew you wouldn't let me down."

"Where the fuck did you go? And how did you get here? How did *I* get here??"

"She's fantasy incarnate!" Emerson snarled, as if the question annoyed him. "Your magnetic center, fucking doorway into my head, and I can't close it!!"

Sander blinked at Emerson, then threw a look of inquiry at Cinder, who just shrugged and gestured for him to sit. The Web remained for a moment stubbornly on his feet.

"Please," she urged, "we have a great deal to talk about."

"Yeah, we do."

"She's a muse," Emerson blurted, arms wrapped around him. "A poet needs a muse, so I asked for a muse and Cinder's that muse. Only I can't write the poetry. Shadow ink on mirrors—can't be done."

Alexander scowled. "What?"

"There is the muse, and there is the monster." The Jabberjaw turned on Alexander; the eyes behind the glasses were hard as stone. "But I'm locked out. No daydreams, no nightmares, just dead sleep. And Krakens like you. The mocking light of day, toilets, and Lotus Eaters."

"What's the matter with him?" Alex asked, shaken.

"Nothing," Cinder said.

"Nothing? Then why the hell is he—"

"Because I'm back where I belong, here in his head." She smiled at his surprise, and strange shadows flickered behind her. "So he's back to acting like himself again."

Sander licked his lips.

"She says I'm schizophrenic," Emerson muttered, half, it seemed, to himself, half with a crazed plea to Alexander. "She's inspiration, invention, she must be right. But they poisoned my coffee. It infected my ears. It makes the meter all wrong. She keeps the claws away, and the blood."

"God," Alex whispered.

"But why should I tell you?? You're just a shadow!" Emerson suddenly turned on him. "A shadow, a reflection, a dream! That's all you are, that's all you've ever been! *Get out! Get out of my head!*" he screamed, his shadow rising behind him until it filled the back wall of the cave. Alexander shrunk back. *"Now!"*

"It won't work, Emerson," Cinder said, cutting through. Her smile was cruel. The shadows behind her altered subtly, as if painted in very wet ink. They had been human-shaped; now they bore the heads of animals, laughing animals.

Emerson seemed to sink within his skin, and his shadow fractured and fell off the wall. His Adam's apple bobbed. "Do you know what she wants you to do?" he asked of Alexander; the words were filled with sadness and despair.

"She wants me to turn back the clock," Sander heard himself answer roughly. "Overthrow the Virtuals, erase my 'uncle' from the computers, and give the technology back to the people."

"It's what you want as well, don't you Alexander?" Cinder asked sweetly.

"You don't know what I want."

"Why don't you tell me, then?" She shimmered in the firelight, her dark skin and earthy clothing blending gently. It was dangerously seductive, that ancient feel of magic. Sander had felt it when they were together on the other side of reality, with Cinder in her true form: a primordial power that made him want to explode like fission.

Behind her, one of the shadows raised clawed hands and swiped.

Blood seeped out of the cavern walls and dribbled down.

Alexander blinked. "What's casting the shadows?" he ventured.

"Whatever is denser than the light," Cinder responded.

"Fuck you, Cinder."

"It is the only empirical truth there is, Alexy." Her eyes were deep and black. The faint glow of blood expanded and seeped across the dark, like natal fluid flowing from mother to child. "I am chaos, I am the river that flows to the sea, and the silt that stirs at the bottom of the ocean."

"You're a pain in the ass."

"You are the mind, Alexander. New, fresh, complex. You can rid reality of Hawthorne—if you just make use of me."

"No!" Emerson was looking frantic now, disheveled. "You can't do it!"

"Why not?" Sander demanded; God he wanted to throw something, something large and breakable! "Hawthorne's going to try to impose *his* reality if I don't stop him, and make use of me doing it. Why shouldn't I put an end to him and take the power for myself?"

"You don't understand!" Emerson shouted. "Don't you see? It caused the wars—"

"I know—"

"No, you don't!" He swiped at the fire. "Out of shame for its failure in the world market, Japan nuked itself and the Pacific rim out of existence! Doesn't that tell you anything?? Consider the computer wizard caste that destroyed India—"

"Emerson—"

"Don't you see??? Two thirds were the technology, the plagues, the chaos of too many rats in too small a cage! But the other third—think about the disappearance of Australia! They say the Sydney Opera remains, defying all rationality, floating on the waves like a sailboat!"

"That's a crazy, unsubstantiated myth!"

"Myth??" Another swipe at the fire, this time Emerson's hands went up, and the fire flared at the ceiling. "You've seen Ethelred! You've stepped on his damn ears!"

The Web swallowed, suddenly chilled.

"Do you understand now?" He pointed at Cinder. "They seeped in, by way of Virtual Reality, they slipped through the doors we opened, and they drove the world mad. One third of the wars that destroyed the world were caused by her kind. By the myths and the imagination!"

"Is this true?" Alex asked of Cinder.

She shrugged, not in the least chagrined or ashamed. "It's always been true. Genius and madness share the same coin. You don't get one without the other—sacrifices must be made. The only other alternative is Hawthorne's."

"How about neither?"

She shook her head, amused. "You can't defeat Hawthorne without my help, Alexy. You know that. And my help does not come free. I gave you what none of your companions could ever give you: I let you out of your cage. In exchange, I ask that you choose the one who released you over your jailer, the fantastic over the mundane, the dreams that let you soar over the reality that held you down. Is that so difficult a price to pay?"

"What? Those are the only choices I get? No third eye? I can create another answer, an answer to both you *and* Hawthorne! You don't know what I want, Cinder, but I do. And I have every intention of getting it!"

"We'll see about that, won't we?" said Cinder. A log fell, and sparks puffed up from the fire. Sander saw that the shadows on the wall had merged. They formed a black compass of arrows, up, down, side to side, and the four points in between.

"Come back when you need me," Cinder said.

Sander stared at the circle and its arrows, recognizing it, as he might a diagram he'd drawn. He'd created this, made a door out of a human mind and into a computer reality.

But which direction was the way out?

The only way not pointed to, of course. He stepped toward the shadow compass and walked through it.

* * *

There was no curvature to the Earth he stood upon. A vast, flat, dusty landscape stretched out forever in each direction. Directly under his feet, in the place of his shadow, was the compass: a circle of arrows pointing north and south, east and west, and all directions in between.

This was the interface. Next step was to enter the network itself.

Once again, there was one direction not designated. Sander looked up. The sky vaulted overhead, azure to sapphire and into black, stars flickering like sparks.

The compass below his feet rose up, a platform carrying him toward those stars. Vertigo rocked him, and he had to force himself to remember it was all an illusion, all VR manifestations. Skyscrapers broke through the crusty plain, rising with him, until finally he stood atop the highest point, gazing down at a vast city.

And then he realized that it was not a city at all. What he was seeing was microcircuitry, labyrinths of hardware with sparkles flashing through, quick and light as fairy dust.

It was vast, vast as the heavens. He felt profound astonishment as he realized how colossal the memory of this machine was, how little of it was being used. Deep in his gut he felt an ache for it, a hunger. He could see the flash of photons, forks of energy.

Information as energy, and he could dip his hands into it and drink his fill.

Made by species human, like the city, he knew the music of this place. None of his companions, one after the other coming and deserting, dropping him as fast as old bones for freedom, had ever heard the beat, the pulse of the city. They never noticed how the fires along the broken highways curved and melted into information. How easy it was to twist and soar over those smooth, powerful roads, counting off the lamps that faithfully illuminated them.

This miniature was a mirror for that vast exterior, an internal empire.

And he was its long awaited King. He had only to reach forth his mind, and he could take control of it all.

Fuzz, flash. White noise. The gray of power shortage, blinding him, startling him. A loud sizzling buzz, an arch of light.

Sudden darkness.

"Alex, honey, what happened?" Christine came up behind him, leaning on the back of his chair. He could see her reflected in the dead dark monitor, a willowy ghost. And then he felt her hand upon his shoulder, her warm bird-bone hand.

"Oh, my," she said, smiling at him there in the monitor. "Power's gone out again. Too bad. Now you'll have to come back to reality."

Chapter 24

Getty felt wired, an electrified, highly focused state that he identified as pure intellect running clean. Thoughts and ideas sung at a perfect pitch, all correct, all connecting. It was the ideal condition for a *Per Tout Virt* who held the universe neatly composed in his head. It happened occasionally when he was in Solid State, making him all the more aware of the eroticism linked to being separate and outside the Mainframe.

Singhutha was feeling the same, or so the gooseflesh on her long, exposed arms proclaimed. The others just shifted unhappily, eyeing him suspiciously. It was a rare Virt who felt unafraid in Solid State.

There were six of them, representing five families: six Virts, three of them full Executives, each paranoid enough to meet face-to-face instead of on the net. All here at his beach house, in the comfort of his living room.

"Can you get a two-thirds vote?" Obando had seated himself, like the kingly bastard he thought he was, in Getty's favorite armchair. The Executive's tar black features were scrunched in an unattractive scowl. "If not, then, what the fuck is this all about?" He was a thin man with a large triangular head and nostrils that quivered and puffed like those of a dragon.

"Julian, the apostate," Singhutha silkily answered from where she sat curled on the couch, but she seemed worried.

"Don't you mean Judas?" Getty retorted, and was gratified by the startled shifts that received. Singhutha tugged at the white dress she was wearing, as if it had gotten too tight. She'd once told him that she despised Solid State because it made her feel fat.

"Wrong hair," Executive Djojeo Caesar observed with a grin. Settled cross-legged on the floor, CM Djojeo was a clownish man who liked to think of himself as wicked. He gave his own red mane a stroke, a gesture that, in VR, would have seemed smooth and sly; here it just sent dandruff flakes falling to his shoulders.

"Guzzling the Tokay before the cake." That was $E_a=E_i$ with her round spectacles and frizzy black hair. She sat stiffly on the other end of the couch, her drumming fingers a clear indication of her wish to get back to VR. "We were talking opportunity costs—"

"Thirty pieces of opportunity," Getty interjected.

Min looked uncomfortable, more so than he ever did in VR. There were always more lines in his face in Solid State, and he always insisted on wearing a suit, never mind that the tie seemed to be choking him. A man of delicate sensibilities was Min.

"I've better uses for my time than to listen to you accuse," Obando said tightly, the leather of the chair squeaking as he shifted. "Have you evidence that Hawthorne has finally gone over the top or no?!"

"Would an attempt on my life be *fin des haricots*?"

They stilled, one and all. Singhutha mouthed a "What??" and Min paled under his tan. Getty felt his

own anger, like clear cold water running down his
throat. This generation and their younger siblings did
not get angry enough, he thought. They forgave the
stupidity of the lower castes and felt no righteous
anger at the misuse of computer time and programs
by their own supposedly superior class. Well, that was
about to end.

"Finally interested. At last." Getty pushed up, too
agitated to remain seated. That was a major difference
between VR and Solid State: he was able to keep his
image still in VR. "Hawthorne tried to murder me."

"When??" Min asked.

"Yesterday. Fortunately, he made the mistake of
placing my execution in the hands of a young opera-
tive named Kelly. Kelly decided not to follow through.
She's having doubts about Hawthorne's sanity, you
see."

"*O tempora! O mores!*" Singhutha muttered sardonically, but her face was peaked and she seemed short
of breath.

Obando's wide nostrils flared, as if smelling a very
bad stink. "Would Kelly be willing to testify?"

"If she was wearing lenses," $E_a=E_i$ said, fingers
twitching, breath coming faster, "the record of the attempt might be retrievable, even if Hawthorne tried
to erase it."

"A fabrication," Singhutha snorted, "unless Kelly
backs it."

"My God," Djojeo no longer looked wicked. He
looked decidedly frightened, perspiring.

"Getty, why"—Obando rubbed at his eyes—"why
didn't you call a council? Why haven't you??"

Why hadn't he? Getty took in a breath.
"Because . . . because of what Hawthorne is—"

"Getty?" Singhutha's voice had a tremor to it.

He met her eyes, not the usual pothole stare, since
none of them dared to wear their lenses when meeting

in Solid State. The pupils were dilated. She pushed up from the couch, took one step forward, and collapsed at his feet.

"Sing—" Min cried even as he slid from his chair. The others were fading, their eyelids fluttering, heads lolling. A sheen of sweat glistened in the hollow of Obando's bony throat; the white of his eyes glowed alabaster. He stared at Getty, betrayed, and then he, too, the last of them, crumbled dead.

Getty stared at the bodies, at little $E_a=E_i$ and dark Obando. Djojeo was already looking waxy and stinking from loosened bowels. Last, Getty looked at Singhutha, his sharp-tongued partner, and Min, his CM and oldest friend, breathless and cold.

And then the image of Getty fell away and the robot beneath tilted its white head, hot red firefly sparks drifting through the black blindfold of its eye. It stared out beyond, as well as within. It looked down at the world from its satellite soul. And it saw afresh the bodies, dead from the poison gas it had breathed out with every word.

And it felt—

Satisfaction. Swift, easy, painless, and they had never suspected.

But beneath the satisfaction was uneasiness. The immediate assignment had been perfectly executed, but its primary function had been . . .

Corrupted.

And a very small, distant part of its programming ached, and screamed, and pounded on the glass of that windowed eye, trying to escape.

"Sander . . ." it cried out, *"Sander where are you??"*

He turned, hardly daring. Christine was waiting, patiently and attentively for a response.

"Christine?"

"You all right, sweetheart? Not going to break anything, are you?"

"I—" He glanced about, at the waxed blond wood floors, the plants he painstakingly tended, the kitchen filled with the fragrance of fresh-baked bread. Web music waltzed through the loft.

Christine reached out and placed a featherlight hand on his forehead. "Alex, what is it?"

Had it all been an illusion? Cinder and Emerson and Urban, and the whole of his life after Christine's death? Or was this here and now an illusion?

"Fantasy flash?" She stoked back his hair. "Or just hyperfocusing."

He caught his breath; his heart ached. It was too much, too much if it wasn't real.

"Come on." Christine pulled at him, her wonderful brown face glowing as only hers could. "Let's dance."

"My leg—" he heard himself protest. It shamed him to dance with her. She was so graceful. Webs like her were dancers.

"Now, don't you be a fool. There's no one I'd rather waltz with."

He felt her arms slip about his neck, and he placed his hands hesitantly on her waist. It was terrible, he couldn't do this. Her cheek felt so soft next to his.

But there he was gazing into Christine's eyes, at the yin and yang of her half-masked face. And they were dancing on star-flickering music. She was wearing a dress of sapphire blue, the skirt full and satin soft, his favorite. It draped and swirled, and they waltzed one way, then the next.

She was young and alive and hot as the sun on his face.

And then he saw the skyline.

The shiver ran down his body, and he broke away to stare out the window.

He should have known, he realized, for there were

no sounds trickling through the slats, no drunken shouts, no thrum of helicopters or scrape of King player skates. There was silence. No wonder, since the city outside wasn't his city. Just as the woman breathing behind him was not Christine.

His city, the city he had sketched over and over again, varied wildly: a crazy quilt of liquid monoliths, glassy cylinders, curving stone with punch-hole windows. This city was a latticework of sleek knife-edged pinnacles and wide straight highways.

Hardware, he remembered. Microcircuitry.

"Disappointing."

The word was spoken by a gaunt gentleman with slicked-black hair and piercing black eyes. Christine was gone.

"I'd thought," the man continued, "that you would smell this trap faster than you did. But then, sentimentality is a forgivable weakness. I indulge in it myself."

As Alex spun all the way around, the man vanished.

"Bastard!" he shouted, racing forward. Nothing!

Damn! He'd entered the computer, and had been discovered quick and easy as that!?

Damn it! Damn it! Damn it!

And then he saw that the trapdoor to the storage area below the loft was open. Emanating from it was a soft, inviting light. And he knew, without a doubt, that the light was from the elevator. If he went down, he would find the doors of the lift open and waiting. Likely, they would take him to Hawthorne.

No! he thought. He was not going to meet Hawthorne on those terms! The man had fucked with him long enough! He spun back to the window. His heart was pounding, fury narrowing his concentration; he could feel it sizzling off his skin and burning his eyes.

He glared out the window, at the city. Inside, with the city outside, once again. *No! Not again! Never again!*

He ran at the window.

There was a shattering crash, images of shattered glass floating, and he was plunging toward tunnels black and dark that burrowed beneath vast highways. Hawthorne would not stop him; nothing would stop him!

He shot into the tunnel. *Lock-out code.* His mind clamped on that. He could see it, almost smell it. Bitter amusement quieted the fury as he swept through the darkness. His bones, he realized, were working. They were interfacing with the computer. Deciphering it.

Hot beams of light and a kaleidoscope of colors, and he burst out of the tunnel. There it was. He had demanded of the computer that it show him its center, its most important program. And there it was, at the vanishing point of the highways, the most elegant monster in this incredible metropolis: a dome crowned with huge triangular landing pads, and wide olive green windows.

A cool wind tousled his hair. And he sensed the difference of this program. Meticulous—whoever wrote it—and demanding. It was the heart of the VR programming, and it was going to be his. He did not care what he had to do, he was going to take it for himself and use it to destroy Hawthorne. And then . . .

And then maybe he'd re-create Christine or cut off his world from Cinder's madness forever. Maybe he would, for once, do what he goddamned liked!

The green windows seemed to rush forward, growing larger and larger.

Break! He wished and willed, *Break!*

He struck one—but the window did not break. Instead, he felt himself seeping through, like oil through a sieve. Slower, slowly, and the window stretching elastically out, farther and farther.

For one heart-stopping moment, he feared he was never going to penetrate.

And then he was standing upon a checkered floor of concentric diamonds that swirled into a vast black center.

"What the—?" He took a moment to catch his breath. Surprised, scared, trying to work it out. The fury was gone, leached out of him by the green barrier. Now he was startled to feel cold, as if he'd been slapped.

Brilliant. It occurred to him, his mind tumbling and calculating. The program had filtered him through, screening him like data, checking for viruses and intent. And somewhere during the entry, it had cut off the rush of endorphins carrying him recklessly, likely dangerously, toward its nerve center.

Alexander smiled; he couldn't help it. The program was a masterpiece of encoding. Of course, all it had done was cool the hot anger. The cold anger remained, along with his very focused intention.

He made his way carefully across the squares to the center. It was so glossy, it shimmered as if wet. And, indeed, when his boot touched it, the floor rippled. Warning system, he thought, admiration growing. He hoped to hell that Hawthorne had nothing to do with this operatic work of art. He did not want to have to like anything created by Hawthorne. And that included himself.

On the other side, nestled within gold-papered walls, was a series of chrome arches. Only one had its vast, brass doors open. He took a breath.

This was it. A step through.

Before him was a narrow wooden staircase. He heard a whisking sound behind him, and he turned to see the chrome doors shut and then vanish, trapping him in the dark, with the rough wooden stairs.

He turned back, and only then felt something in his

hand. To his surprise he was holding a little silver and gold butane lighter, clicked open and burning bright.

How blind can you be in Virtual Reality? he wondered.

A lift of the lighter. He took in a breath, and started up the stairs. There was no rail, and they creaked under his feet.

Three, four, five. The top: he could feel the program opening before him, letting him enter a wide, musty room. He felt annoyance that his mouth should suddenly be dry with fear when none of this, after all, was real.

He lifted the light to see.

Books. Old books. And shadows that darted across a dusty floor, and spiderwebs with odd patterns in the corners. And a pair of bay windows looked out, as if from some rickety old tower, on a fantastic city that stretched to infinity.

"Thank God," a voice said.

He fought startlement, eyes widening as he turned and saw Urban Myth, standing forlorn and lost in a corner.

"Alex," he said hoarsely, "you've got to help me!"

"Yes," another voice agreed, this one from a figure standing before the window. "You must help us," she insisted, more command than request.

She was a dowdy sort, hair hennaed, eyes hazel, face sad and plain. It took him a moment to recognize her.

His mother.

Chapter 25

Kelly couched in the rubble and rat-infested garbage of the rail tunnel, feeling a dull sickness inside. She was conservatively dressed in a black tee and olive jeans well broken in. Light black running shoes insured good traction.

Doc kindly adjusted the infrared of her lenses to accommodate the candlelight issuing from the station area, and she took note of the platform height, tensing her muscles accordingly. Usually, she would have grinned at this point; this, after all, was it: the capture. All she had to do was nab these two and shepherd them out to the waiting helicopter. And then . . .

And then it would no longer be her problem. Whatever the Executive had in mind for these captives, it wouldn't be any of her concern. But if that were so, then why did she feel so queasy, as if she were about to do something terribly wrong?

The woman, the station manager, as she'd huffily called herself, had eagerly betrayed the duo she'd trapped in her underground. "Locked them in, though they think the door's barred on their side!" she'd gleefully informed Kelly. And for this Kelly had handed her a bottle of Valium.

Clever, ambitious woman. She'd go far, knowing so cannily when to squeal to the Virts.

The routine exchange stuck in Kelly's craw. They always did. She despised treachery.

"Mama?" she had said, wandering down the hill at last, "Mama?" Not loudly, quietly. Because her mama had to be out there. Had to hear her calling quietly, like a good girl.

Impatiently, she dismissed the memory, and trained her eyes on the light coming from a small computer screen.

There were two men in that dim light, one brown, one white. The brown one was wearing a fancy jacket and silver shoes. He was up and pacing. She scanned him; his movements were smooth, but she knew she could take him easily.

The other, seated on the couch, was Alexander.

Alexander: pale face exposed, tarnished blond hair, *dangerous.* But the face she saw reminded her of a little boy staring off into space. A scared little boy.

Piece of cake. Almost too easy. She scanned the dark for others. As the station manager had promised, there were none. She readied her gun. It had a tiny, targeting monitor on it; although a little ungainly, the monitor eliminated the need for a telltale—and in this smoky, dim-lit place, easily seen laser light. She hoped she wouldn't need to fire it.

She sprang, felt her knees crack a little with the push; a quick tumble and she was up in a crouch. The man in the fancy jacket saw her, cried out, and fumbled for his coat pocket. Kelly got to him before he could pull out the handgun the Cookbook had told her was there.

With an openhanded punch, she sent him toppling. A kick to the stomach and her adversary was on his

knees, doubled over. She bent, shoved her free hand
into his pocket, and snatched out the gun. With disdain she tossed it into the dark and trash of the rails.
Then she brought out her cuffs.

"Wait!" the brown man cried. "Kelly, wait! Don't
you know who I am??"

Doc was already doing a secondary scan of the fellow for additional weapons. *Nothing,* her MSC assured
her. He was, however, wired. She recognized the glint
of a diamond, and lost her bearings for a moment.
Who—?

Filo, her Doc identified the features for her. *Executive Hawthorne's MC.*

Damn. She thought, shocked. *Damn.*

Alexander's mother examined him, up and down.
She was plain and thin-faced; hennaed bangs held
back from her forehead in a hair clip. Her eyes, familiar and jaded, stripped him down to his bioengineered
bones, then met his gaze with rank disappointment.

"Took you long enough!" She sneered. "Do you
know how long I've been waiting for you to show
up? No, of course you don't! do you know how long
Hawthorne kept my fertilized eggs on ice before he
finally let one of them grow into you? And that was
twenty years ago! That's how long I've been waiting!"
The woman spun on her heel, crossing before the windows. Her flat shoes flopped off and then back onto
her heels with each step.

Remarkable detail, Alex couldn't help thinking. The
illusion even had a smell, used and comfortable, like
maple syrup or hot buttered toast. He could feel the
intricacies of the program, its flashes and stops. Delicate, *complex,* as refined as French lace. There was a
signature to it, a very different feeling from the heavy,
more aggressive program that he had just passed
through.

"Jo," Urban said with an odd combination of reverence and impatience, "this is no time to bitch."

The robot's VR image, Sander noted with some anger, was as precise as ever: the usual tangle of curling brown hair, the intense gray eyes, and a muscled body rakishly dressed in a billowy white shirt and black vest. The gray slacks had their mandatory stripe down either side and the boots were properly scuffed. The sight infuriated Alexander, tightening his throat till he could barely breathe. He swallowed and looked away.

The woman threw the robot a sidelong look. "You'll have to forgive Tink," she coolly informed Alexander. "He's in a bit of an uproar because Hawthorne's figured out his password."

"I'm in a bit of an uproar because he just used me to kill five Virtuals!" Urban angrily corrected her. "And he's going to take over my body, use it as a Solid State form. . . ."

"Not if I have anything to say about it," the woman growled, "and I do."

"And you are?" Sander demanded.

"You don't know?" The woman cocked her head at him. She was wearing a black sweater and skirt, same as in the photo. It shook Alex to look at her, to hear her speak, even though he knew, he *knew* she was just a computer construct.

"Not by name, no."

"Joycelyn Kasana," she responded curtly. "Like that means anything to you."

"You're my mother." He instantly regretted making the accusation; it sounded stupid. She paused to meet his eyes.

And then she laughed at him.

"Mother??? Hah! Yea and nay on that, kiddo! I'm what's left of your mother, that's what I am! A computer construct of your mother. Biological mother only, mind you. Took the eggs out of me, right before they botched that job of freezing me and killed me. Didn't ask for my consent."

"God."

"My uncle did it to me. Hawthorne. You know about him by now, don't you?"

Sander felt himself paling. It suddenly occurred to him, facing this woman who provided half his genetic template, to wonder who had provided the other half. He suspected he knew the answer, and he also knew that he did not want that answer confirmed. "I'm beginning to," he said softly, sickly.

"Good. Then, maybe we *can* fuck him over." She grinned a nasty grin. "Welcome, kid, to the apocrypha." Her arm rose with a flourish to encompass the vast dark space. "We're in the attic of the Library of Alexandria. You know what the Library of Alexandria is? It's a VR program that *I* constructed. And once I'd created it, Hawthorne took it from me!" She was pacing again, only this time she seemed to vanish and reappear with every other step, as if the program that generated her had a glitch. "Do you know what else he took from me?"

"Eggs," Sander deadpanned. It worked, she froze, paused, and turned to look at him with eyes as bright and crazy as Cinder's.

Damn, he thought, suddenly sweating, *should have kept my mouth closed.*

"Yes," she hissed softly. "He took my eggs—all that I'd ever created!" She touched off her fingers, counting, "I invented the lenses, the MSC implants, crickets, and brain modifiers! Goddamn it! And I invented him"—an imperious finger at Urban, who cringed—"Tinkerbell!"

"Don't call me that!" the robot pleaded.

"The satellite, the robot—they were mine!"

"I belonged to the military," Urban reminded her.

"Like shit you did!" she snapped back. "You were on loan! That's all! What I create is mine." She was back in front of Alexander again, zipping forward as if on ice. "They couldn't understand what I did. No one was smart enough to duplicate it, not without my help! And I liked it that way, and I kept it that way! And then Hawthorne, that fuck, killed me off! By accident, you understand, but he did it all the same! If I hadn't been wearing the cricket before he put me under, if I hadn't translated myself—"

"You had fail-safes," Alexander observed; his emotions were cooling, and he felt his mind calculating, drawing conclusions.

"Damn right I did!" Her feet were no longer moving, rather she was floating over the sleek floors. "What do you think this place is? I guessed someone was going to try and take the library from me. So I created the attic for myself. Look, you see those?" She pointed to the shadows where a small, multi-legged thing paused in its scuttling, then resumed. "Colophons. Viral protection. And there." A gesture to a nook where a round form pulsed like a sea anemone. "And there, on that book." A ladybug creature clung to the foxed pages of a huge open volume. "They trick the computer into thinking we're an entirely different program. Heck, the computer running this program doesn't even recognize what it's doing!"

Yes, Alexander thought. He could see it now, feel it in his bones: the intricacies of the program. He was amazed; it was beyond his ability to manipulate. It was that brilliant.

"All right," he conceded, "so that's what you are. What about Urban?" The robot, who'd been leaning against a table, came up, as if to attention. "What part of him is here?"

"Fail-safe," Jo said simply. "They took Tinkerbell from me, but I programmed it to hide part of itself here, behind this encryption, should anyone ever attempt a total takeover. When Hawthorne did, a key part of Tink turned up here, safe and sound and still all mine!"

"And now you want the rest. All right. There must be another code to retrieve the satellite from Hawthorne's control, otherwise this would all be moot. Why not use it? What do you need me for?"

"Idiot!" Joycelyn wrinkled her nose, scornful. "If I did that, Hawthorne would discover me in a minute! But thanks to those antenna bones of yours, you can send the password directly into Tinkerbell, with Hawthorne never the wiser!"

"You've got to, Alex," Urban said. "You need me! Both here and in Solid State! The robot can guard you—"

"I don't *got* to do anything! I especially don't got to do anything for you!"

"But—"

"What does it matter to you who's pulling the strings?" Alex cut him off. "You're the Golem, a mindless machine. What does it matter if Hawthorne is the lucky one who gained control of you with the written name of God?"

"It matters!" There was a desperate edge to the denial. "Can't you see that I'm not—I'm no longer—"

"Don't try to convince me that you really give a shit about those Virts you murdered. I *know* what you can do, I've seen you in action!"

"I care—" Urban moaned, "I didn't want to do it, Alex, I swear! It felt wrong! It felt—"

"Stop it! You can't feel! Mathematics, Urban, that's all you are. Encryptions, programs. Oh, yes, you want to be free of Hawthorne, but only because you know that as soon as he's finished using you to take out his enemies, he's going to take you over. And your primary programming can't let that happen, can it?"

"Nope," Joycelyn agreed, vanishing and reappearing in a different spot.

"And you"—he turned on her—"I don't know why I'm listening to you! You're just a computer construct like Hawthorne!"

"Not!" Joycelyn retorted. "I'm a ghost with access to a great deal of information. Hawthorne's a computer linked to a very troubled, very obsessed ghost. There is a difference!" Her chin lifted, a mockingly arrogant gleam in her eyes. It was doubly irritating to recognize the look as one of his own. *Goddamn it!*

"You mean the difference between a lie, a fabrication, a myth?"

Urban captured an outraged breath—*lie!* Alexander thought, remembering the machine that did not breathe. And then Urban was coming at him, backing him into the books. "I should have beaten the shit out of you the first day I met you!"

"If you'd been human," Alex sneered back, "you would have!"

A wince around the eyes. "All right, so I'm not human, so Joycelyn's not human, so you feel betrayed. Well, get over it, you self-centered bastard! I'm a machine! You want me to acknowledge it, fine. *I'm a machine!* I'm also one of the best companions you ever had! I can't abuse you, I have to protect you, I'll be forever loyal—"

"—If I have your code!"

"—If you have my code," Urban agreed, "and I won't die on you. What more do you want?"

But you're not real! Sander thought. *Nothing's real, none of it!*

"Well?" Urban demanded.

Sander swayed, heart pounding in his ears. *What do I want from him, from it? What have I ever wanted?*

"I want—" he said slowly, "to know you're doing this of your own free will." He sucked in a breath, felt his shoulders hunch. "I want to know that you *want* to stay with me. That you choose to be with me."

Urban stared at him for a long time.

And then the robot hauled off and put a fist right into the wall. It broke and splintered with a *crack!* real enough to make Alexander start.

"Damn it!" Urban shouted, jerking back his fist, "you know and I know, Sander, that I can protest and swear till I rust that I'm doing this on my own free will, and you won't believe a word of it! What kind of catch-22 is this? Do you really need a reason to say *no*?"

"I really need a reason to say yes!" Sander snapped, "so, give me one!"

"I can't! I don't know if my responses are feelings as you have them. All I can tell you is that whatever they are, inferenced or genuine, I have them. And if I were free to go anywhere, do anything, I believe I would choose to stay with you."

"Why?"

"Because you need me and because, damn it, I care about what happens to you!"

Alexander licked his lips. He wanted to believe it, yet dared not. That something in this universe genuinely cared about him—

"Is he telling the truth?" he demanded of Joycelyn. "You created him, you should know. Is he able to think autonomously, or is it just the programming?"

Urban grew very still; his eyes shut as if in deep pain. Clearly, he anticipated no mercy from the ghost of his creator.

A blink of hazel eyes, and Sander could almost feel Joycelyn, the computer program, searching out the answer.

"He is not what I created," she said at last.

"Meaning?" Sander growled impatiently.

"Meaning he's changed and grown and adapted."

"But are his responses just part of the program??
Does he think? Does he feel!?"

A shrug. "There is a point where an organism, organic or otherwise, takes on such complexity, or alters
so radically from its origins, that it becomes something
different. He is something different. I can't say if that
something has free will. But then, I can't say that humans have free will, either."

Sander brooded on that. There was, he reflected,
only one answer. There had been only one answer
since he arrived here. "So what's the password?"

Joycelyn smiled. "First, you swear to me that once
you've defeated Hawthorne, you'll give Tinkerbell
back to me. Tinkerbell and everything else that is
mine!"

Alexander stared at her for a heartbeat. *All right,*
he thought at last. *If that's what this fucked-up program wants, why not?* "Fine," he said tightly.

She grinned at that, looking positively radiant with
triumph. A hand, knobby and with a surprisingly real
grip, warmly pressed his shoulder. "That's m'boy!
You'll like the password."

"Just give it to me!"

Her grin broadened. "It's: *Come to Mother.*"

Chapter 26

She'd only seen Filo a bare two times in her life, both times called up on a screen in Blake's office. He was, she remembered, the leader of Hawthorne's L.A. Weeklies, the only Virtuals she knew to wander about the city sightseeing. She had to confess to herself a healthy skepticism for the practice. Virtuals were to be coddled and kept safe, like Mainframers.

What was Hawthorne's CM doing with Alex?

"Are you hurt?" she asked, but she kept the gun trained on him. She had to fight the urge to put it down and offer him a hand.

He nodded a little shakily, and pushed up onto a knee. He brushed at his trousers, licked his lips.

"What are you doing here?" she asked. She noticed that his eyes were clear, a beautiful shade of pecan brown. To see a Virtual's irises, naked of lenses, disturbed her more than if she'd seen one naked.

Clearly, Hawthorne's CM did not want his Executive using him as a spy.

"I'm helping him," Filo said with a nod to Alexander.

"Helping him do what? Why isn't he moving?"

"He's in the net—I think."

She gaped at him. "You're lying!"

"I'm not!"

"He hasn't a cricket or lenses!"

"He doesn't need them! Listen to me!" He took a step forward. She brought up her gun, stopping him.

"Don't make any sudden moves. Please. I really don't want to hurt you."

"But you still work for Hawthorne," he observed, and seemed satisfied when she winced. Shall I tell you how many deaths he's responsible for? How many brain-damaged Halfways are traceable right back to him? How many of them were Virtuals, since you don't seem to care what he does to Grinders—"

"Shut up!"

"He's a computer! You must know that by now!"

"Yes, and I don't care! It makes no difference to me whether the sparks are moving through brains or wire!" Her vehement insistence sounded hollow even to her ears.

"It *does* matter!" he insisted back. "An organic mind can grow and change. All the computer can do is gain more knowledge. Listen to me! I've been his CM! I know him!! I spent years recruiting my friends for his damn Weekly network! And I watched the best of those friends die because of him, and for no good reason! Right here, Kelly. My friend died right here in this damn station!" The young Virt was shaking with remembered outrage, trembling in a fashion that was almost delicate. And Kelly found herself watching in a detached, almost fascinated way.

How our myths betray us, she thought. Then snorted at herself for being so hackneyed.

"Grow up," she said.

The Virtual stiffened, and his eyes dilated with

anger. "I did. You're the one who's blindly doing his bidding like a good little girl."

"That's enough," Kelly snapped, heart thumping. She was miffed to realize that she had allowed him to distract her. *Damn it!* She was forgetting all her hard-earned training.

"It most certainly is," a voice from her gun said.

And then the gun fired.

It jerked Kelly's hand so unexpectedly that it went flying and skidding across the platform. The report rang through the tunnels, and Filo went spinning back, tumbling over the arm of the couch.

The Virtual lay gasping upon the floor, blinking up at her in surprise, even as his muscles gave way and his head fell.

"Madre." Kelly ran to him. She started to pull off his shirt. She had to staunch the bleeding—right in the solar plexus, damn it! She tried to catch a breath, found she couldn't. *I didn't pull the trigger!* she thought, and, aloud, "I didn't pull the trigger!"

"You have my apologies, Kelly." The little monitor on the gun had a face on it. *Hawthorne's.*

And for the first time in her life, Kelly felt a fear of him that had nothing to do with reverence. As she worked, she felt Hawthorne watching her from the monitor.

"I've long suspected that Filo wasn't being entirely honest with me, but I never suspected this. You might say that I acted on impulse, rashly even."

"Yes, sir," she whispered mechanically, wadding up the shirt and pressing it to the wound. Under her fingers, Filo's skin felt cold and clammy. He was going into shock. The blood seeped through the shirt, contrastingly warm.

"The King players will be on their way. You can try to keep Filo alive if you wish, but remember that Alexander is your first and only priority. See that you get him back here promptly." The face continued, "It's long past time we ended this farce."

"Yes, sir," she swallowed, finally glancing back at the gun. On it she saw the Executive's face, smiling thinly.

And then something came down on the gun, flattening the tiny monitor with a metallic crunch.

The something was a black boot; it belonged to what looked like a man. But the Sierra with the saucy gray eyes and curly brown hair was not a man.

The false face threw a look at Filo. "Ah, Christ!" he said, voice painfully contrite. "I'm sorry."

And then the monster looked at her.

"Your call, Sander. Do I kill her?"

Hawthorne tracked the two dozen programs on his *Isle of Creation* and the progress of the Virtuals indulging in them. He measured the power surges along electrical lines, looked through the lenses of wandering Weeklies, and simultaneously, stood within the dome of the library, his most favored spot in his vast cyber kingdom. Satellite images, globes of the Earth and of the nine planets, swirled around him complementing the music of Debussy.

It intrigued him that, even here, even as he was now, that damned composer continued to fascinate him.

From this nexus point, Hawthorne explained to Kelly his reasons for shooting Filo, and gave her explicit orders, all of which she accepted with stunned obedience. That troubled him. Her failure overall troubled him deeply.

He'd not expected it of her, to have come so very close to betraying him, as he was sure she had. He had not expected her to wear out so fast; he had relied on the false calculation of her enduring at least as long as Blake. An incorrect assumption.

And Filo. No real surprise there, but it was disappointing.

"You shouldn't have shot him," someone said. And Hawthorne, startled for the first time since he was flesh and blood, looked up to see Alexander standing before him.

Hawthorne frowned. "How did you enter without my knowing?" he asked, even as another part of him continued to speak with Kelly.

Alexander grinned, and that is when Hawthorne realized that the youth's face was unmasked. The boy looked remarkably like Joycelyn, in the hazel eyes, almond-shaped and infused with green in the brow. The nose, too, and chin, both small but strong—those were Joycelyn's. But not the mouth, not that thin, pouty mouth.

Interesting.

"Figure it out yourself," Alexander challenged; he had placed himself so that he stood on one of the Earths. It spun slowly beneath his feet.

"Hmm. And so I will. He isn't dead you know."

"Filo? Yes, I know. But he will be if he doesn't get medical attention soon. Why did you shoot him?"

"Because Kelly was listening to him. Welcome to the Library of Alexandria, by the way," Hawthorne invited belatedly. "Make yourself comfortable." With a casual wave, he created a pair of floating black deco armchairs. He noted, as an unexplained fact, that the connection with Kelly had been suddenly and inexplicably severed. That did not worry him; the King players would be able to tell him what had happened soon enough.

His nephew watched him, and then suddenly smirked. "Was I named for library or was it named for me?"

Hawthorne rearranged his lips into a twitch of a smile. Simultaneously, he watched a pressure change

over the Arabian sea permit storm clouds to flow in
across Bombay, gave instructions to the Kings, re-
corded Emerson's heartbeat, a steady ninety-two, and
realized that Urban was missing.

And he noted that a part of his mind was still
searching for an answer as to where Alexander had
been and how he had got here. And that part of his
mind was still coming up empty.

"Where have you been for the last hour?"

"You don't know? How comforting."

Hawthorne's face rearranged itself into a frown of
consideration. His long hands laced together but for
the forefingers, which he steepled at his mouth. The
computer calculated options, each and every one in
a microsecond.

"There is only one answer. I must be blind to a part
of myself." He smiled a little, and sat himself down.
"That is something a computer can do with frightening
ease. A program running without my knowledge, my
right hand not knowing what my left hand is doing.
Where is this program, I wonder?"

Alexander eyed him with what might have been
respect, or perhaps it was mockery. Defiantly, the
youth settled into the other chair. As he did so, it
changed into a rococo throne of elaborate swirls
and curves.

Hawthorne was impressed. "You've discovered how
to hack into and alter my programs in so short a
time?"

"I'd say it was because I was your son," Alex responded bitterly. "But I've concluded that the only
real parent I ever had was Christine." The young man
cocked his head, and the music of Debussy altered,
smooth as a clearing of clouds, into a montage of Web
music. "Why did you murder her?"

"Don't you like Debussy?" Hawthorne leaned back
and casually crossed his legs.

"Why did you kill her!?"

"Your love for her was such that you were beginning not to care about the outside world."

The hazel eyes flickered. *What was that?* Hawthorne wondered, *anger? consideration?*

The planets changed orbit. It was a subtle change at first, but for Hawthorne it was monumental, as he had not ordered it and could not stop it.

And then they were all orbiting around Alexander.

Hawthorne frowned, and flicked a finger. The planets refused to go back, locked now in their movements. That irritated Hawthorne as much as he could be irritated.

"I've learned a lot since I got out, Uncle."

"So I see. Where is Urban?"

"You don't know that, either?" Alexander mockingly mimicked shock.

"You retrieved him, didn't you?" Hawthorne shifted more memory into the problem. "But how— ah. He must have had a second password."

"Which I've already changed."

"Which I will figure out," Hawthorne retorted smoothly, and immediately gave over another portion of his vast memory to calculating what that word might be. Urban was essential to the plan, not only the valuable satellite with its VR capabilities, but the robot itself, a body Hawthorne could enter and use to walk the world again.

"Do you know why?" Hawthorne absently asked.

"Why?" Alexander repeated. "Which why? Why you imprisoned me? No. Why you engendered me and what you did to me and for what purpose? Yes."

Hawthorne turned that over. Filo or Urban or both must have hacked out the secret. He was going to have to put better wards on that information.

"I see," he said. "Well then, do you know why I

want to give each soul on Earth their own, individual reality?"

"To avoid a repeat of the hate wars." Alexander's tone was decidedly jaded.

"To avoid *all* quibbling."

A frown. "All right. I'll bite. What quibbling?"

"The quibbling of little minds. The ones that waste great minds. Brilliant minds." He felt the anger now, hard and brittle, precisely as he had felt it in the flesh, never greater, never lesser.

Alexander shifted in his chair, eyes flickering, concentrating in that familiar way Hawthorne had seen not only in this Alexander, but with his niece, many times. "And what of the great minds," the Web asked, "do they get a reality?"

Hawthorne opened wide his hands. "What greater, richer reality, what greater store of learning than the kingdom of the Virtuals."

"The Virtuals might object."

"They won't be around to object."

Alexander stared at him, and Hawthorne wished he could feel something for the youth. But he'd melded his mind with the computer before he ever got around to creating Alexander. He had never bonded with the child, never had an emotional attachment to little Alex other than his plan, his grand, all-consuming plan.

And given what he'd had to do to all the previous Alexanders, perhaps such indifference was all for the best.

"And do you really think," Alexander said at last, "that your great minds will be devoid of their own petty bigotries?"

"I isolate great minds, Alexander. Don't you remember?"

The young man shivered, as honest and spontaneous

a reaction as Hawthorne had yet seen. It thrilled him to see it, to feel that he had elicited it.

Alexander looked away. "Why *did* you do that to me, *Uncle*?"

"Because I figured that you'd be an introvert. Allowed to interact with people, you'd likely shut them out. If, on the other hand, you were isolated, you'd yearn to know all about them, making you open to their fantasies. I fear, however, that your adventures outside have ruined you."

"I sincerely hope so, Uncle," Alexander said, rising to his feet.

"Going back to your little corner of the computer? Now that I know it exists, I'll easily be able to trace and find you."

"Will you?" Alexander asked softly.

"I have your Solid State form, Alex. Why even bother?"

"You don't have it yet," he said with a enigmatic smile. "And my name's not Alex, it's Sander. Goodbye, Uncle."

A turn, and Alexander was suddenly on a motorcycle, goggles shading his eyes. The dome was gone.

Incredible! Hawthorne thought, though he could not feel amazement. They were out of the program without having exited it. Even he could not do that! How had Alexander?

Hawthorne hastily dropped all other programs, focusing himself on the mystery. Something was not right here! Something was most decidedly wrong!

There was a roar from the motorcycle as Alexander kicked it to life. Hawthorne saw old highways suddenly appear. The rising sun rolled its colors over the winding roads and rolling hills. A wind combed through Hawthorne's hair with long fond fingers, and he smelled the green of summer upon the air.

Alexander revved the motor again, and, with a wave and a laugh, sped off, leaving Hawthorne standing on the highway, feeling something very akin to astonishment.

Alexander was getting away. And that—in a world where everywhere, to Hawthorne, was here—was impossible.

Chapter 27

He felt the power of the cycle under his hands, its speed, the wheels carrying him around curves and through the tunnels. There was the wind in his face and tugging his hair and the chill of morning giving way to the orange and gold of a summer sun. He could even feel the snow he saw on the distant mountaintops.

And he could sense Hawthorne, focused dead on him, trailing with a speed that was faster than thought.

That was all right. He could keep ahead of the Virt, just. He'd tricked Hawthorne into focusing on him. Now he had to make sure the computer honed in on him and only him, to the very end.

There!

Up ahead was a bright starry blaze, white with spectral shards of light. He braked the bike, and let it vanish from beneath him. Then he grinned and turned to stand before the gateway. A nanosecond later Hawthorne strode up to him, his expression not quite angry, not quite amused, but certainly surprised and intrigued.

"My God, who would have thought?" the Virtual said, stopping before him. "You're not Alex, are you?"

Alexander smiled at him, then let his face and form blur into tiny squares; he shifted the colors and altered his outline like a jigsaw.

"What do *you* think?" Urban asked, finalizing his form and grinning roguishly.

"I don't understand." Hawthorne looked sincerely perplexed. "Where did he go?"

"Here, Uncle!" the voice came from behind; and suddenly a pair of arms wrapped around the Executive and jerked him back.

And then, quite unexpectedly, there was the brilliant flare of the gateway, white as a star, and a falling sensation that captured Urban, dragging him inexorably into the heart of it all.

Jesus. Sweet Jesus, Kelly thought, shooting to her feet and backing from the robot. She had whipped out her little hand laser, but she feared it would have no effect on the creature. Or that the thing would move too fast for her to stop it.

What was she going to do?

The robot knelt by Filo. The shirt pressed to the Virtual's chest was almost completely bloodstained, and Filo's breathing was growing shallow.

"Damn!"

"King players are on their way," Kelly heard herself say.

"Not anymore they're not," the robot said with frightening authority. It—she could not think of it as "he"—checked on the wound. Even after watching it from Hawthorne's "office," she could not believe the accuracy, the reality of the vision! The wrinkles crisscrossing the back of the vest, the stains under the arms. And she knew that even though it seemed to have its head turned away from her, it was watching her.

"I'll send help for Filo quick as I can," he promised.

"We know what you look like and how to stop you," she tried.

"Just what I like." The robot smiled back at her. "A challenge. Tell me, do you think anyone would recognize me if I looked like this . . . ?" It rose, and she caught her breath.

It was Hawthorne. The slicked ebony hair, the dapper wool suit, the hawk nose and thin mouth. Those chilling pothole eyes. Even the expression. Ironic, kind and cold at the same time.

"You're not him. I know you're not him."

"Are you sure of that, Kelly?" the face and voice mocked her.

"You're not him!" she insisted, shaken. But in her heart she knew doubt. Hawthorne was a computer image, as were the face and form of Urban. That the Executive could place his image and mind into the robot was a possibility obvious even to one as tech illiterate as she.

And that was a truly horrifying thought; because it meant that there was not as much difference between the two as she'd previously supposed.

"Come now, Kelly." Hawthorne tsked. "That little laser is a threat only to flesh, and I am not a creature of flesh."

He took a step toward her, and she, uncertain, took a step back.

And then Hawthorne came to a dead stop. The image faltered, wavering about the edges, and abruptly vanished, leaving behind the stark white plastic of the robot.

Kelly caught her breath and raised her weapon.

And then reality ripped away.

*　　*　　*

Alexander was in the cave of Emerson's mind, the rock vaulting up and overhead, and fire blazing and crackling at his back, the shadows weaving and changing.

There was something struggling in his arms.

Sander released it, stepping back; and there before him stood Hawthorne, tall and lean, with a sharp nose and a thin mouth, electricity sizzling through him in circuit patterns.

The avian face gawked with amazement.

"Clever," jibed Cinder's soft contralto, "but how are you going to get rid of him? And did you mean to bring the robot along as well?"

Alexander stiffened, as just behind Hawthorne he recognized Urban, on one knee as if he'd fallen. The Sierra was staring up at the cave wide-eyed and fearful.

"Urban!" Alex caught his breath. *No! Urban wasn't supposed to be here.* "You idiot! Why aren't you—?"

"You drew me in with Hawthorne!" the robot snorted, pushing up. "Don't you know your own strength?"

"No," Sander replied blankly.

"Of course he doesn't." Hawthorne, transparent and surrounded by a sizzle of forked lightning, brushed at his clothing, straightening out wrinkles. "His whole life as an interface has been from human subconscious to machine, never the opposite. I'm amazed he was able to do it at all. Seems I wrought better than I knew." Electricity flashed faster and faster through Hawthorne's ghostly form.

The Executive took a step past Alexander, who shied back from the energy and stopped just short of the fire. "Cinder, I presume?" The Virtual studied the brown woman in her brown clothing, frowning with what looked to be honest confusion. "Whatever are you??"

"She's mine," Emerson confessed from where he sat huddled against the shadowy wall under the sketch of a bison all ocher and black ash. "Doorways and birth canals. We give birth to creations we can't control. You and Urban, and Alexander as well. Nothing we create is ever under our control. It does not serve us, we serve it."

"Such a wonderful mind," Cinder smiled.

"You're not a VR construct"—Hawthorne was frowning—"not organic, not machine—"

"She's an eidolon, Uncle," Alex interjected. "Can't you see that? An idol, a reflection!"

"But where did she come from???"

Cinder stood, brushing at her jodhpurs; she turned and put a hand to the jagged rock of one wall. "Here," she said as her fingers sunk in. With a jerk, she pulled aside the rock like a curtain. On the other side stretched a swirling, rocky landscape of lava colors. And right at the threshold, beneath a bare white tree, was a grave. In it, sleeping, sat five old men and five old women, the wind whipping their hoary hair.

Hawthorne blinked, seemingly confused. "This makes no sense."

"Exactly!" Cinder crowed, and then to Sander, "Time to reopen your stargate, Alexy. Time to let us into the computer."

"And exchange one tyrant for another?" he said. "I don't think so."

"Legends and myths are dreams, not dictators." Her face was unexpectedly soft, almost wistful. "Or have you forgotten how we infused your dreary, frightened, imprisoned little life with strength and will and grandeur and freedom?"

Alex winced. That cut too close to the bone.

"Give your world what you got from us," Cinder asked. "Give me access to your Virtual universe, before creatures like Hawthorne lock us all away."

"I'm not sure what this is all about," Hawthorne cut in, "but she does have a point. It's time for you to reopen the interface. Or do you really plan to keep me and Urban trapped here forever in your friend's head?"

"Quid pro quo, Uncle," Sander retorted. "You had every intention of keeping me imprisoned forever; maybe I don't care what it takes to do the same to you."

"How very cold and unfeeling of you. Perhaps this will change your mind—" Hawthorne's hand shot out and, startlingly, went right into Urban. For a second Alexander caught his breath; then he remembered that his uncle was only an image. They all were. Imagination, not flesh. Souls, not substance.

And then Urban cried out as Hawthorne, a cool smile on his face, jerked out a crackling strip of color.

"What are you doing!?" Sander cried as the Executive tossed the sizzling blue strip into the fire and reached in again.

"I'm deprogramming him."

"No!"

"Do you want me to stop him?" Cinder offered congenially. "I can. Just open the gate. I won't let Hawthorne get out, I promise."

"You will both stay right where you are!" Hawthorne warned, his hand deep inside Urban's chest. He seemed to be holding the Sierra's heart for ransom. And Sander, dread in his soul, kept very still. *No,* he thought, *no, don't let him murder another one.*

"You care for this bit of software, don't you, Alexander," Hawthorne said, his voice both curious and sympathetic; Urban remained where he was, sweat glistening on his brow, fear in his gray eyes. "Of course you do. You've cared for all your companions, deeply, hopelessly, even the one who beat you, even the one who drugged herself to death. You've loved them all, even this one, who isn't even human and never will be."

The Virtual's hand jerked out, ripping free a screeching, scarlet-tinted rag. Alexander cried out. Urban staggered, eyes glazing.

Sander felt his throat tighten in panic. He had to do something! Break the window, connect with Urban, break the window, and snatch him free, break—

There was a shattering, cracking sound. Sander turned in time to see the stone wall behind him crumble and fall tinkling into splinters. And then he was looking out at the Red Line amusement complex, at the very couch on which he was still sitting! And there was Filo, sprawled out on the floor and bleeding, and there was Urban's white plastic body, still as stone.

And there was the woman who'd been chasing them, the petite woman with coffee-colored hair, the one who'd captured Emerson and Urban.

Her arm dropped, and whatever she'd been holding slipped out of her hand to crash to the floor. Mouth agape, she took a careful step. Then another, and another. And finally, one across that threshold of splintered stone to stand within the cave.

"Stop it!" someone shrieked—Emerson—and Alex looked back to see Hawthorne's hand sink back into Urban's human image.

And, suddenly, despite his captivity, Urban began to sizzle with energy. Hawthorne cried out in pain, tumbling away. Aghast, he stared at his hand.

"I felt that."

"Urban," Alexander took a step at the same time, reaching, then froze, as he saw that his hand was now white plastic. His sight took in everything, three hundred and sixty degrees. God! How—

And then his hand went up in a crackle of electricity, and he felt himself vanish, neither flesh nor plastic but energy. And now Hawthorne was the robot, its body turning smoothly on the gyroscopes, and Urban—

"I'm—" The Sierra gulped, rubbing palm against flesh palm with disbelief.

Flash!

Chapter 28

Madre de Dios! Kelly felt the laser leave her nerveless fingers, and crossed herself. She was still in the bar, where the robot and Alexander seemed frozen in time, where Filo lay on the dirty floor dying; and yet the bar opened into a cavern, a crazed dream occupied by Hawthorne, Alexander, the robot, and a brown-skinned woman in goggles and a leather jacket.

Where the fuck was she!?

And what was happening? Even as she watched, Alexander went ghostly and bright about the edges while Hawthorne became a plastic robot and Urban touched the flesh of his face with awe. Blink—no, it was Hawthorne who was flesh, licking lips, and Alexander moved a robotic arm and Urban sizzled with light.

Flash! And again they changed, round and round and round.

"I did it."

It took a moment for her to see Emerson. He was huddled up against the wall, watching in an agony of confusion. "Sander was going to ask Cinder to stop

Hawthorne," he explained painfully to her. "I couldn't let that happen!"

"No," Kelly agreed, no point in arguing, no point at all.

Come out of it, Kelly! Cut through! Where are you? She demanded of herself, sharply, as her old trainer might have. *Can you take it? Defend it?*

A cave. She realized. She was in a cave, with a fire, a shimmer of starlight to her right and to her left. . . .

To her left was a door that looked out on hell. Seated in a grave just outside that door were five old men and five old women. As Kelly stared at them, the oldest, an old, old great hag of a woman, broad features with white swirled graffiti, lifted her heavy head and blinked open turtle eyes at her, eyes a startlingly hazel-gray in that broad black wrinkled face.

Wrinkled lips quirked. *"Donde esta tu madre?"* the old woman said, and despite the crackle and cries and shouts around Kelly, she heard the hag, heard her as if the old woman had whispered the words into her ear.

Kelly felt faint, her throat went dry and her sight blurred. *Mary, Mother of God, protect her.*

Where was she?

Emerson had thought his answer simple: if the robot could not be abused, if Hawthorne wasn't what he was, then Alexander could not be blackmailed into opening the stargate for Cinder.

But now . . . now Emerson didn't know which was which. One was robot, one was data, one was a human-computer interface. Which?

"Very creative, Emerson," Cinder said, leaning against the gateway door. "They all forgot it was your mind, your reality. This is a very good reminder."

Emerson winced. He felt the eyes watching him, the ears listening. He had thought there was no shelter from the curiosity of the world except here, where only the mind's own horrors existed, but now, here they were—three outsiders, three invaders—no, four. There was that girl, the one that had hunted them up to the observatory.

Stupid girl was just standing there, staring, lips muttering prayers.

And he could not get rid of any of them!

Machine, human being, electricity, madness, sanity. *Flash!*

Alexander was flesh again. Alexander, who should have been as mad, too, but was stable as a rock. Alexander, the living interface between mind and machine. The Web's face, Emerson suddenly realized, was exposed, the mask completely gone. When, the Jabberjaw wondered, had Alexander given up the mask? When had he stopped being a Web?

Why?

The chalk and paint bison on the wall turned and looked at Emerson.

"Do you think I'm the wrong color?" it asked in Ethelred's voice.

"Yes," he answered. "You should be grayish."

"Oh." It rippled, and then, from out of the wall, grayish fur began to grow. "There," it said, when it looked like Ethelred. "Hey, my ears are down!"

"They always are," Emerson gravely informed the monster.

"Oh. Say, what's going on over there? What are you trying to do?"

"I'm trying to keep Cinder from getting into the computer," Emerson explained.

"But if you don't let her into the computer, everyone in dreamtime's gonna be in your head."

Emerson glanced toward the gate, feeling suddenly cold and apprehensive. One of the old women was awake, the swirls of white upon her broad brown cheeks spinning. She was staring at the girl. And then her lips quirked, and she said something. Only Emerson could not hear it.

"The old woman's talking to Kelly," Ethelred informed him. "That's why you can't hear her."

Emerson frowned. "Why should the old lady talk to her?"

"Well," the creature huffed, "Kelly's the only sane and completely human descendant here, isn't she?"

"There is that."

"Cinder never understood. You and Alex are real creative, but you don't dream any new dreams, not from the heart. Kelly does. She's had a real human life, not like you and Alex, all locked away. That's why the old lady likes her. Maybe she's the one."

"Yes," Emerson said, not understanding. Lava colors from the mythic world were beginning to seep over the threshold and into the cave. "Is there anyway to keep them out?"

Ethelred shrugged, "Push 'em back."

"That is the stupidest—" Emerson froze. Wait. Could he?

"Of course," the creature huffed, "if you do that, you'll lose the poetry."

That hurt, right to the bone. "Can I lose what has always been mine?" he wondered.

Ethelred seemed to shrug. "Can lose access to it."

The Jabberjaw looked to Cinder, his dark and terrible muse. She met his eyes full on. *Can you live without me?* her look asked him. *Have you enough imagination for that?*

And then he heard a cackle, a little laugh, and glanced past Cinder to the open gateway; the old woman was on her feet now, starting to climb out of the pit. Her hand was reaching through, reaching for Kelly—

"*Stop!*" he cried for a second time, and the three

intruders suddenly broke apart, falling away, Urban now a white plastic and steel robot, Hawthorne a phantom, and Alexander—

"Sander—" Emerson shouted. "Open the interface now, before Hawthorne can get his bearings—"

"Are you nuts!"

"Of course! Goddamn it, Sander! Keys can lock doors, too! Trust me, before it's too late!"

Alexander blinked. *Keys can lock doors, too!* And Emerson was the key; this was *his* reality.

And the girl, Kelly! He caught sight of her, his endoskeleton reading the dreams that crackled steadily around her, and suddenly knew what would happen. What *must* happen.

"Cinder!" He yelled, pushing to his feet and slamming a fist at the wall beside him. It splintered like crystal. The breach went white and blazed like a star.

"Sander! No!" Urban's voice shouted from the robot face, "You can't!"

"Indeed he can!" Hawthorne laughed, leaping for the exit.

Only to be snatched up and into the great white hand of a cloudy creature with a red aura, eyes the color of old pennies.

Hawthorne screamed as the monster's face split, and it swallowed him whole.

There was an odd blurring as the huge mouth shut, sucking in a leg at the last. And then, within an instant, the white giant shrank, shifted, darkened.

And Cinder, smiling triumphantly, strode toward the stargate, toward the Virtual Net.

A shriek rang through the cavern, and Kelly, rage marring her face, flew at Cinder, knocking the muse back, right back toward opening into the dreamworld. Cinder collided with the old lady, who fell into the grave, leaving clawlike grooves behind.

Emerson leapt right through the fire, nabbing hold of Kelly's shirt before she went over the threshold.

"Get out!" He spun her away, placing himself before the gate. Just then, something from the other side pushed against him, misty white and bloodred, fighting to slip past, fighting to get back inside.

With a lunge, Urban snatched Kelly out of harm's way and heaved her back out into the Solid State bar. Alex saw her tumble to the floor, and then, almost instantly, start to scramble up.

"There's nothing more you can do!" he shouted at her, a panic in his heart as he looked at the shattered rocks before that opening. He had to close up this gate to real time, and fast.

He stared at the rock slivers that littered the cave, licked his lips, and willed them back. They shifted and shivered.

Damn it! He thought, throwing all his will into repairing what he had broken. The slivers sprung up on jagged ends, and then flew into place, piecing themselves together puzzle-wise. In an instant, the wall was back, hairline fractures mapping it like a dried mud plane.

And now there were only two doors again, one leading out into a machine, the other guarded by one fragile, bespectacled poet. Alex could hear the sound of a storm crashing in the distance.

"I can't hold this!" Emerson cried out. He was leaning into the doorway, hands against a cloudy white and red form. Wind was tearing at his hair and clothing. "Get out! Close the interface, then cut my throat!"

"No—"

"If you don't, she'll try again!"

Have to close the dream gate, Alex thought, *but that's the one opening I didn't create!*

"Urban!" Alex grabbed at the robot, who spun obediently. "Can you alter Emerson's brain chemistry through the cricket he's wearing?"

The oval head tilted, firefly sparks dashing across the black blindfold of an eye. "Alter it how, Sander?"

"He's schizophrenic—cure him!"

The robot only took barely a split second to think that over, but it seemed forever. Alex saw Emerson's knees begin to tremble; the white mist was seeping past him.

"I can't cure him, but I can ease—"

"Do it!"

His words echoed through the cave. And then, quite suddenly, there was a slam, a wall coming down so hard and final that Alexander cried out.

And then all was darkness and silence.

The mythic gate was gone, a dead rocky wall was in its place; upon that wall was sketched a primitive painting, outlined in ocher, of a ghostly white biped with red eyes; at its middle were a pair of red hand-prints that seemed to be permanently holding it in place.

Emerson, palms scraped raw and bloody, lay in a collapsed heap before it.

Alexander released a breath; he felt himself shaking from the adrenaline rush. And for a moment, he was unable to look away from those painted ocher eyes.

"Come on—" Alexander said, gripping Urban by the arm. It was an arm of smooth, cool plastic, but that did not matter. It was still Urban, Sander knew that.

He took them through the star blaze. When they were back in real time, and the cricket was removed from Emerson's head, then they would know if the Jabberjaw was all right.

Or if they'd destroyed him forever.

Chapter 29

The laser was back in her hand, though she remembered quite clearly dropping it. The bar quiet and guarded only by its statue. And the robot was still a robot, only now it was moving again, shifting in tiny, incremental fits and starts.

Even as she watched, a misty shape hazed out from the machine's white and chrome skin, shrouding it. Faint shifts in hue, and the robot once again wore Urban's form and face.

He looked distraught.

Kelly swallowed in a dry throat, and listened for a moment to the racing of her heart. She no longer had any inclination to fire on Urban.

"Was that real?" she finally whispered.

"Not in the sense you mean it," Alexander's voice answered. Kelly whipped around to find the Web, wide-awake, and worn-looking. He was staring at Filo's bleeding body. "Shit"—he winced—"Urban, see if you can stop the bleeding, then pick him up."

"It either happened or it didn't," Kelly ventured, her voice grating. "And you shouldn't move him."

The young man shook his head. "We've got no choice. And it isn't that simple. I'm a techno-telepath. Urban was in trouble, I reached out to help him, and I got you instead."

"Telepathically? Into . . . the net?"

"In a way." He shrugged. It was an evasion and she knew it, but she didn't dare inquire further. She could feel a twitching beginning to start in her legs and hands. Delayed shock. She fought against it.

Damn it! she thought, *look at me! See me!*

And then, he did just that, turning to meet her eyes with a face young and pale and hard. And Kelly thought that the photo had not done him justice. Far from it. There was a crazed dazzle to his eyes that hurt her, as if she were staring at the sun.

"We have to get Filo to a Holist," Alexander said. "Did you come by helicopter?"

"We're not going anywhere." Kelly took a step back so that her aim encompassed them both. "I'm going to contact the King players to—"

"They won't come," Alexander said confidently. "I can interfere or cancel any order you issue."

Her knees were shaking now, no stopping them. "I don't believe you."

"Of course you do, Kelly. You know what I am, and you have a very good idea of what I can do. At this moment, I am in complete command and control of the Virtual Net. Anything Hawthorne could do, so can I, and more! And there is no one who can stop me."

Instinctively, she tightened her grip on her weapon, only to find it now pointed at Urban. The robot had moved to stand before Alexander.

"I can even," the young man boasted, "erase the net."

Kelly's arm dropped. *The net? Erase the net!* All the knowledge, all the secrets, all the wonders that existed in the world before she was born? Her stomach twisted up inside her.

"What do you want?" she asked at last.

"I want to save Filo if I can. And I want to be taken to Hawthorne's headquarters."

"All right."

"Let's go, then." He made for the door, Urban, scooping up Filo, fell in behind. And it was then that it occurred to Kelly that Alexander's request was a mere courtesy. He didn't need her; he could have her killed, take the heliocopter, go and do what he liked. Anyone who could command the net and the robot that was Urban Myth could do what they liked.

She could agree, or she could die. For one heartbeat she thought of Hawthorne. She didn't bother to ask Alexander if her Executive was truly gone. There was no point.

"The helo's this way," she said, carefully putting the laser away.

At least in being Urban, he had learned how to argue and argue well, Urban observed of himself.

At the moment, he was very glad of that.

"This is a waste!" he said as they crossed over rippling black floors to one of the vast archways, the one with its brass doors swung open wide and as inviting as the maw of a dragon.

"Nothing necessary is a waste," Alexander pointed out, easily striding ahead. Urban following, noted with sour interest that, unlike the last time, Alexander no longer had his limp here in the net. "And this is necessary."

"It's pointless! You're handing over the most complex mechanism, the most sophisticated AI on the planet, to a computer program!"

"You've a high opinion of yourself," he said as they

crossed the threshold of one program and into another.

"Facts, not opinion," Urban insisted. "I don't have opinions, just as I don't have original thoughts. Which is why, if you'd take a moment to think about it, you'd see why this is so ridiculous! What's Joycelyn going to do with me?"

"I don't know, and I don't care. If I don't keep my promise, Joycelyn will come after me—biological son or no."

"Sander—" he pleaded, reluctantly following Alexander up the rickety stairs, but the Web wasn't listening. The indifference scared Urban. Fear and frustration, along with need and satisfaction, were among the emotions he suspected he did, indeed, experience. Not that he could ever really know if what he took to be emotions matched the chemical alterations of flesh and blood.

He did not want to lose his Urban persona; that's what he most feared. And that was an odd fear. Tinkerbell stretched out in time and Virtual space, Tinkerbell looked down on the Earth and out across the solar system and saw galaxies in gradations of light that no human could see. Tinkerbell was, at any given moment, peering into homes, listening in on conversations, watching the progress of the universe from space, and simultaneously, traveling through every program, every record ever uploaded into a computer.

But Urban, limited as humans were to such a narrow range of sight and understanding, was what he really wanted to be. The infinity within that narrow range, the interior of the human mind that had created a machine as complex and fantastic as Tinkerbell. He wanted that; he wanted to know how to think like that. Nothing else was of any value.

Joycelyn had no need of Urban. Like Hawthorne, she'd likely taken over the satellite and uploaded her persona into his robot body. And there would be the end of his exploration, his growth and his being.

They'd reached the top of the stairs, and with a push Alexander stepped up and through the attic door into the apocrypha. Urban, after the briefest of hesitations, entered the program after him.

"I half thought you'd fuck me over, *son*." Joycelyn was waiting for them. Her attic home looked slightly out of focus; with Hawthorne dead, the program was starting to alter. It no longer needed to maintain itself as before.

Joycelyn, however, was as crisp and real as ever, bangs falling into her hazel eyes, black sweater, black skirt.

"I wouldn't dream of it, *Mother*," Alexander retorted, and waved a hand back. "Tinkerbell, Urban, the robot, and everything else you invented, they're all yours."

Urban shrunk into himself; Alexander was really going to do it, then, hand him over like a thing, which, he had to admit, he was. Just a thing.

Strangely, his only "feeling" was one of regret. He wished he'd had more time to figure out the variables that still puzzled him.

"Mine?" Joycelyn looked both taken aback and suspicious. "What's the catch?"

"No catch," Alexander assured her. "You gave him to me on loan. Now I'm giving him back. Like everything else, he's yours."

"Mine!" Joycelyn said with wonder, and drew herself up. For a moment, she looked upon her robot with joy, tears of relief sparkling in her eyes.

And then, quite suddenly, everything vanished; the apocrypha, Joycelyn, even the city surrounding and protecting that inner program. Everything except Urban and Alex, who stood now upon the white noise of a dead area.

Though he knew he had none, Urban still caught his breath. "What the—*what happened???*"

"For the most complex AI on Earth, you can be terrifically dense, Urban," Alexander snidely remarked. "You ought to know that when a program finishes its task, it can be shut down."

"Finishes—" The realization dawned on him. The Joycelyn program's central task had been to retrieve the creations that, in her estimation, had been stolen from her. In giving him to her, Alexander had done just that, helped Joycelyn complete her primary purpose.

"You son of a bitch!" Urban cried.

"Yes, she was a bit of a bitch," Sander lobbed back, "wasn't she."

"You could have warned me!"

"What would have been the fun in that? Come on, Kelly's waiting."

She'd had her chance back at the bar, Kelly kept reminding herself. But when she thought about it, really thought about it, she knew that she could not have done different. In the last twenty-four hours she'd learned just how much Alexander knew, about her, about the city, and about the workings of the net. Like a Virtual. There was no escaping that comparison. And not just any Virt; Alex acted like a *Per My Executive.*

She had known it from the moment she had looked at his photograph. And had probably known too that she could not kill him.

"How much longer are they going to be?" Filo asked. They'd wheeled the CM into her office: hospital bed, tubes and all. His orders; bullet or no, loss of blood or no, so long as he was awake and conscious, he was going to be there. He brought with him an antiseptic smell that reminded Kelly nervously and uncomfortably of weakness and death.

"Do you need anything?" she asked him faintly.

"Candy," he said, "saltwater taffy." He sighed and lay back. He looked small and thin against the white sheets, this man who had covertly helped nine Mainframers escape from the Orange Kingdom. She'd recently learned about that, too. Kelly shifted her gaze.

On the other side of the desk sat Alexander and the robot. The two were sitting frozen and quiet, as if dreaming. Just before they'd gone under, the robot's imaginary face had thrown her as fretful a look as any she'd ever seen, and then smiled ruefully before going still. Not that he had to. She knew well enough by now that the thing could be in several places at once. She suspected it was a courtesy to Alexander, or maybe a way to lull her into a false sense of security.

That brought back the image. The nightmare. Something white and red, and Hawthorne with a startled look on his face. And then he was gone, and she was screaming and throwing herself at the monster who'd killed him.

All that rage, that terrible, vicious rage over the murder of a man who'd been dead for such a long time.

Strangely, she felt no anger over that deception. Hawthorne had been a lie, but he had led her out of the maze where her mother had left her all those years ago.

"There." Alexander was back, and stretching. Urban, beside him, looked pensive. "Filo, you really shouldn't be here. You look terrible."

The Virtual ignored that. "Did you find Emerson?"

"He's not in the net. Not anywhere."

"We've gone over every video a dozen times," Kelly told him tersely, guiltily. "Not one of them shows him leaving the building, though he must have. One minute he's there, the next, he's gone."

"Damn."

Kelly pinched her wrists nervously. Would Alexander blame Emerson's disappearance on her? She felt somehow responsible, even though she hadn't had anything to do with it. "Should we put out an APB to the Kings?"

Alexander thought about that for a moment. "No. Let it be."

"Sander?" the robot questioned, his first words since they got back.

"Leave it," Alexander insisted with something akin to anger. "He's done his part. Let him be."

The silence that followed was a long one, and deep.

"You knew what was going to happen," Kelly heard herself say. It was something she'd been wanting to ask for a while now. "Didn't you?"

"With Emerson? No. I had no idea."

"No, I mean, did you know what was going to happen between Cinder and Hawthorne?"

"Oh, that. Yes, I did. And I knew what you'd do, too," he said without a flicker of conscience. "I was counting on it."

"Bastard," she breathed.

He shrugged. "By the way, I put an end to certain programs while Urban and I were on the net, in particular those involving the *Isle* . . . the unpleasant parts."

Filo inched himself up a little, an effort that left him panting and gray. "But not all of it?"

Another shrug. "There is no point in taking away from most of the younger Virts the only reality they've ever known."

"Shut it down!" he snapped. "Erase it, obliterate it—"

"No!" Kelly pushed to her feet. There was panic in her heart. "You *can't*—"

"Virtual rule is collapsing," Filo insisted fiercely. "Hawthorne killed off the old guard and corrupted their heirs. There are no Virtuals, not as you know them. There are only those who live either in the library or on the *Isle,* contemplating their navels. Which is why," he looked to Alexander, "you have to wipe it all out! Put an end to the leeches and Lotus Eaters! You'd be doing us all a favor."

"I have already finished doing what I went into the net to do," Sander said softly, simply. "There is nothing left here for me to accomplish."

"The hell you say!"

Alexander glanced away at that, and then he suddenly stood and began to pace. "I'm leaving," he announced.

"Leaving? Leaving where? Leaving when?"

"Now. I'm not going to lock myself away in another prison, Filo. And I have no desire to take over where Hawthorne left off nor help you to do the same. I've ordered a motorcycle and sidecar for myself and Urban. As soon as it's brought around, we'll be on our way."

"Just like that?"

"Just like that."

Filo collapsed back upon his mattress, eyes bleak with pain. "So what do we do?"

"Whatever you like. Urban?" Alex said, and the robot obediently got to his feet.

"The Mainframers," Kelly said abruptly, her heart sinking.

Alex frowned at her. "What about them?"

"They create programs for the net. That's all they know how to do! If the Virtuals are no more, if the net is no more, what will happen to the Mainframers?"

"The Orange Kingdom," Filo said with tired disgust, "that's another abomination we'd be well rid of."

"No!" They were her Mainframers, she was responsible for them. Some would be happy enough to leave, but others—

"Perhaps," Alexander said with a knowing look, "you might ask the Brainiacs to lead the Mainframers out, teach them how to make do in this world." His tone was ironic, but also strangely sincere. "Maybe they can even help you make use of Hawthorne's radio towers."

Filo shifted, his eyelids were low, his breathing quiet and sleepy. "Maybe," he reluctantly agreed.

Alex smirked, but his eyes were still on Kelly. Abruptly, he reached out and clasped her wrist. She had to fight her instinct to break free and strike. His touch was cold and a little clammy, but his face bore that expression again, hard and bright, as if he saw vistas she'd never be able to imagine.

"You dream of a world that's safe for children," he said, simple as a fortune-teller, "Always of children. Seems we have more in common than I thought."

He released her wrist. "Filo is not the only one who wields power. Now is your time and your chance."

The robot, moving faster than she'd anticipated, was already at the door, opening it for Alexander. Urban nodded to her before following the Web out, a look that spoke of respect and regard. And then the door shut behind them.

Kelly stood behind her desk, listening as Filo's breathing became soft snores. Perhaps it *was* time for her to make her own direction, set her own goals. She hadn't told Alexander, but early this morning, when she'd snatched an hour's sleep, she'd had a dream. In it she'd stood among them: the ten venerable old men and women from Emerson's cave. They'd been sleeping, but now they were wide-awake and staring at her, even the one with the turtle on his head.

After a moment, they lifted their red-stained hands and touched her.

Glancing down, she saw that her skin was painted red. When she glanced back up, she was at Actor's Carnival, in one of the gondolas of the Ferris wheel. She was rushing upward with intoxicating speed. As her seat reached the highest point, it stopped.

The gondola swung in the wind, there atop the Ferris wheel, and in the sudden silence, Kelly could hear the crowd far below. The city was spread out before her, and she felt that she was seeing the whole of the world, what it might have been . . . what it still could be.

With her red hands, she reached out and started to paint the sky.

Kelly opened her eyes; surprised to find that she'd shut them. She looked at the chair where Alex had been sitting; then she reached across the desk and pushed the button that would ring up the Orange Kingdom. It was time to change the world.

Chapter 30

Alexander settled into the sidecar, feeling secure for the first time since he'd gone flying over a cliff. It was a larger sidecar than the one he'd ridden in with Cinder, the seat luxuriously shaped for comfort and support. It was paired to an equally splendid motorcycle, all chrome and black, almost brand-new. But Urban had yet to get on it. The robot was standing a few feet away, arms stubbornly crossed.

"Well?" Sander adjusted his bad leg so that it was nestled in comfortably. "You're driving!"

"The fuck I am," the Sierra retorted. "Not until we get a few things settled."

"Still trying to set boundaries, Urban?"

"It's what I'm programmed to do," he sneered.

"You really thought I was going to give you back, didn't you?"

"Kiss my plastic ass, Sander."

Sander looked away, and tugged at his sleeves. His mask was still in his jacket pocket, but he felt no inclination to put in on, even though his face felt strangely naked without it. "Are you going to go your own way, then?" he forced himself to ask.

Urban snorted. "With you holding my password?"

So, Sander caught his breath. *This was it, the final nightmare, the final door.*

"No," he admitted, "I-I canceled it out."

Urban blinked at him with disbelief. Then he went still and vacant for a moment, and Alexander knew the robot was confirming the information.

Animation returned to the comforting and familiar Sierra face, along with a look of pure astonishment.

"Rats and alligators! You canceled it! That was stupid of you!"

"Reckless," Sander agreed; his hands were trembling.

"What's the catch?"

Sander laughed a little. "That's just what Joycelyn said. You get the same answer: No catch."

Urban eyed him skeptically. "When you said that to Joycelyn, she disappeared."

"I don't want you to disappear," Sander said thickly.

"What? You want me to stick around? A lie, an illusion, a myth?"

Alexander winced. "It's all lies and illusions, Urban," he said bleakly, "all shadows on the cave walls. Everything, and all of us. We pick what shadows we want."

"And you want me?"

"I want you."

"Then, why cancel the password?"

Why indeed? "I don't know if you have dreams, Urban, but I want you to be free to follow them."

That silenced the robot. He shifted from one leg to the other, an awkward, human, Urban move. From under his lowered eyelids, Alexander covertly watched his companion, fondly, miserably, and fought against every instinct in him, all the selfish ones, that wanted to re-create the password.

Take him back! Keep him! Command him! He's a machine, for Christ's sake! A part of Sander insisted. *He doesn't know what to do with free will!*

Then, I don't want him, he found himself answering back, which was a lie, but only in part.

"Well," Urban finally sighed and shrugged, "in that case, let's go." And the Sierra settled onto the motorcycle.

The rev of the motor drowned out Sander's breath of relief. He felt the stress melt out of him even as the cycle rumbled and shook, comforting as the rocking of a cradle.

He was not going to have to face his new life alone after all.

"Thank you, Urban," he said, soft as a prayer.

"Where are we going anyway?" Urban shouted over the noise.

"Your choice!" Alexander shouted back.

And with that, they shoved off, the Sierra robot and the Virtual Prince, speeding down the streets of the city toward the curving highways and empty roads.

The observatory afforded a fantastic view of the city, especially if viewed through the twenty-five-cent telescopes. They worked if the magnetic fields were fluxed, which Ethelred could do.

And so Emerson easily examined the freeways that crossed and wove and tangled their way among the mirrored towers like lines of poetry upon a page.

"You won't ever try to send me away, will you?" the creature at his side asked timidly.

Emerson, pushing up his glasses, shook his head. "Send you away? Where the devil would I send you to?"

"Pacoima?"

"I've no intention of ever sending you away," he assured the beast, who let out a whiff of air. "That's good, 'cause I'm locked out, you know. You left me behind when you shoved the madness out of your head."

Emerson felt a twinge of guilt about that. "Do you miss Cinder very much?" He hated speaking the name, but his conscience was bothering him.

"Some . . . but not that much. Do you?"

"Some," the Jabberjaw admitted, and experienced a twinge of fear. It wasn't bad, the fear, not like before when it consumed him. But it was there. Fear that Cinder would break through the barrier, fear of being trapped again in his head.

Fear of the future.

You could have gone with Alex and Urban, he reminded himself. But no, that had not been a true option. They had their lives, such as they were. And he . . . he needed his. And for once, he was going to have it. A life all his own.

"Have you decided what to do?" Ethelred asked.

"About the observatory?" Emerson glanced over at the structure with its trio of scooped domes. "Well, one side's going to be a coffeehouse where only bad poetry can be recited and only real coffee served!"

"Will it have living sculptures like the ones in Jack's gallery?"

"What a fantastic idea! Yes, it'll have living sculptures! As for the other side . . . I thought I'd make that a Brainiac bar—provided the Brainiacs agree. Problem is, I don't know what to do with the middle."

"Mud wrestling?"

"I don't think so."

"No, wait!" the creature huffed excitedly. "How about an ice-skating rink? Or better yet, an ice-skating rink and—"

"Opera?" Emerson finished.

"Yes!" The creature thumped its hind leg with delight. "Yes! Precisely! With Verdi—"

Emerson nodded. "Have to play Verdi."

"But not Wagner."

"No, you're quite right. Wagner wouldn't be any fun to skate to."

Ethelred shifted a little, as if suddenly shy. "I like you Emerson. You've got real imagination!"

"Thank you, Ethelred." The poet smiled and leaned against the balcony.

"Can I tell you a secret?"

"What?"

The creature hesitated for a moment, then said, whispery quick as if afraid, "I think my ears are starting to go back up!"

Skeptically, the Jabberjaw examined his companion. The long downy gray ears, he noted, were not hanging as low as usual, the velvety tips brushing the ground instead of lying on it. "I do believe you're right, Ethelred," he said with a certain wonder, "they are going back up."

The creature puffed up proudly onto his haunches. "With my ears up," he said, "we can do anything!"

And the poet, placing one friendly arm around the beast from his imagination, smiled in agreement.

THIS SIDE OF JUDGMENT

by

J. R. DUNN

"An impressively told story."—*Science Fiction Chronicle*

The woman was found nude in the snow, in plain sight, as if she was meant to be discovered. At the same time, a computer intrusion occured at the local bank. It was a sloppy job, as if the invader didn't care if he were detected. There's no link, at least as far as the Montana police can see. However, in Washington, Ross Bohlen, an agent for the Computer Subversion Strike Force (COSSF), finds a connection that leads all the way back to a Chiphead—a cybernetically enhanced person. But there's a problem: the Chipheads are all supposed to be dead—either murdered, or as hopelessly insane suicide victims. In a dark, new twist on the Frankenstein theme, three men—a madman drunk on power, a hunter weary of bloodshed, and a protector who can no longer protect—come together in a debut novel that is part sci-fi thriller, part high tech, and part page-turning madness.

(454863—$5.99)

"I read it in California and didn't even notice the earthquakes!"
—Geoffrey A. Landis, Hugo and Nebula award-winning author

*Prices slightly higher in Canada.